Whisper

Paulina Banardi

AuthorHouse™
1663 Liberty Drive, Suite 200
Bloomington, IN 47403
www.authorhouse.com
Phone: 1-800-839-8640

© *2008 Paulina Banardi. All rights reserved.*

No part of this book may be reproduced, stored in a retrieval system, or transmitted by any means without the written permission of the author.

First published by AuthorHouse 3/4/2008

ISBN: 978-1-4343-5249-1 (sc)

Printed in the United States of America
Bloomington, Indiana

This book is printed on acid-free paper.

This story is for the families and people who suffer from this illness. It has no certain face, no certain race. It hits every walk of life. Please, if you know anyone with this illness, please seek early help for them. God Bless you all.

Paulina Banardi

Chapter 1

Looking out the window, I see the snow falling softly on the ground. What a beautiful sight to see. The world seems at peace today. I wish peace would come to me like this, but peace isn't free for me. Peace comes with a price for me: lots of pills, shots, and of course lots of good old therapy. Just what the good old doctor ordered; this all combined keeps the demons at bay. Then when I decide that I have had enough and go off my medicine, they start to rear their ugly heads again.

I look down at my shaking hands; God, they are bruised, and my veins look as if they could pop right out of my skin. The texture of my hair has changed, and I feel tired all the time. What has happened to me I am paying for dearly. If someone had listened to me when all this began, I wouldn't be in this damn place. I am so angry at the world: what a cruel place we live. In this world we are expected to be perfect, and God knows, if you are among the unfortunate, you're an outcast. Today I get to tell my story. Someone from the newspaper is coming to talk with me. For the first time in fifteen years, someone will listen to what I have to say.

I hear the doorbell buzzing, so I better comb my hair. That's right; I don't have a comb. I will run my fingers through my hair; Lord knows, I can't be trusted with a comb. Well it's showtime, and I guess I look OK for warmed-over death. A young man is walking this way. He sighs as if he is out of breath. "Are you all right?" I ask.

"Yes," he replies still breathing heavy. "Excuse me!"

I laugh and reply, "I have all the men around here breathing heavy!"

He just smiles and says, "I am Joe, from the newspaper."

I respond quickly, "I gathered that."

"You must be Isabella?" he asks.

"That's me!" I reply. Joe says he thinks I have a beautiful name. I say quickly, "Do not let the name fool you; it's the real person behind that name you need to know before you talk about beauty."

He looks at me as if I had two heads. "I got you going, didn't I?" I laugh.

Joe smiles and says, "Yes, you sure did!"

I ask him to sit down and I say, "Come on, Joe, let's get this over with."

Joe begins to speak. "First I would like to thank you, Isabella, for talking with me today. I know this must be hard on you."

I reply fast, "Yes, it is, but I really want the world to know the truth about me. I am labeled as this awful person with no heart, and that just isn't true. The only thing that worries me about my story is I wonder if the world is ready to hear the truth as it really is," I say cautiously.

"Well, Isabella," Joe says, "Let's rock their world and get the real story out there about you. Who cares if they are ready? Let's tell them!" Joe says very eagerly.

"OK," I agree, "then let us begin our journey." I begin telling Joe my story, through my eyes.

I grew up in South Georgia. I was a real Southern peach; as of matter of fact, all my friends called me that. It was fun back then. My father was a real Southern lawyer, and my mother, bless her heart, was such a social bug. She was so proper, and the smallest thing would upset her. If you didn't keep good grades, you were sent to see your father. MY father expected you to be as smart as he was, period; no exceptions. This was the way it was. My mother, she always had to keep up with the neighbors. Sky, my brother, and I grew up in an extremely strict home. Mom and Dad loved us, but we were expected to be perfect in every way. My father was a little less hard on us than Mother. My poor mother had a deep, dark secret, and she didn't want Sky and me to ever know.

My mother had a twin sister named Jessie, and we met her once when we were about ten years old, I guess. I never saw or heard from her again. My brother and I really liked her and often asked about where our aunt was. Mother always replied that she moved out of the country and wouldn't be back. She insisted we stop bothering her about Aunt Jessie. So, as children often do, we forgot. Out of sight, out of mind. I never really thought anymore about her until years later. That is a whole other story! Back on me, I was thirteen when this thing happened to me. I was in class one day, and I thought I heard someone say something to me. I looked around at the class, and everyone was looking at the board. I looked at Patty, a friend from school, and asked if she said something to me. She said no, with a puzzled look on her face. I said OK and turned back around. When I got home, Sky was outside working on his bike. I sat down beside him and asked what he was doing. He said, "What does it look like, Sis? What is bugging you anyway? When are you ever interested in what I am doing?" Sky asked me. I asked him if he had ever thought someone was talking to him, and then they aren't. He answered, "No, Isabella, I haven't." He told me to stop watching horror movies, that they were getting to me. OK, I got mad and popped him on the head. He laughed. I ran straight upstairs and flopped on my bed and began to cry; maybe I am watching too much TV, I thought.

After that I was fine for about two years.

Then one day Sky and I were at the lake swimming. I wanted to go out to the deep part, and he wanted to stay closer in. I yelled out that he was a chicken, and I swam out to the deepest part. "Isabella!" he yelled. "Come back in, that is too far!" I just laughed at him and was having a blast. Then suddenly it hit me; I felt the strength being pulled out of me. I felt like I was going to drown for the first time in my life.

Then a deep voice said, "Die, you bitch. You are a loser." Then it started to laugh so loud it scared the hell out of me.

I screamed, "Sky, help me!"

He yelled back making fun, "HELLP!" Sky laughed. "Stop clowning around, Isabella! You are just trying to get me out there, and I am nowhere near the swimmer you are."

I gasped for my breath. I yelled out, "I am not kidding, Sky, I am drowning! Please help me!" I kept screaming out.

Sky looked and me and said, "I am coming, hold on!" Finally he got to me and pulled me out of the water. Shaking all over and still in a state of shock, I could hear him say ask, "You OK, Sis?"

Finally I could breathe again and I responded. "Yes, I am OK now. Thank you, Sky," I said. I put my arms around his neck and began to cry.

"It's OK, Sis," he said. "You'll be fine; let's get you home and into some dry clothes," he said, comforting me.

On the way home he asked me what went wrong, because I was such a good swimmer. "I don't know," I tried to explain. "I guess I got cramps." I was thinking to myself, should I dare tell him what really happen? He wouldn't believe me anyway. What would be the use?

My mother talked with me after she heard what had happened. "Did you get sick in the water? What went wrong, dear?" Mother asked. So I decided I would tell her; after all, she was my mother.

"Mom, it began when I was in the water. I heard a voice, a scary voice that told me to die and then it started to laugh," I told her.

"That is the most stupid thing I have ever heard. Really, Isabella, you can really come up with some stories!" Mom laughed.

"Mother!" I said loudly. "This is no joke; this is really what happened. To me, not you." I explained more. "I am old enough to know right from wrong and what is real and what is not," I yelled. Good old mother; this wasn't what she wanted to hear, and so to her it didn't happen, end of conversation.

The next few days she acted like she hated me. "Mother," I asked her, "are you still mad at me?"

She said, "Yes, I am. What if you tell someone, this and they think our whole family is crazy?" Mom yelled.

I tried to explain more. "What can I do? Take it back?" Mom yelled at me.

She screamed at me, shaking me hard, "OK, it didn't happen," I said.

"Good," Mother said. "Let's not speak of this matter again, not to anyone. I mean it, Isabella! Do I have your word?" she asked.

"Yes, Mother you do," I said.

I was so emotionally disturbed over this. My own mother doesn't believe me, I thought; what am I going to do? Maybe I am crazy, I thought. I was sitting on the bed that night looking out the window and I saw the silhouette of myself. I wrote down this poem; I still remember it as if it were yesterday.

Looking at the silhouette of me; is this outline really I, or do I know what is real and unreal. Do I dare even try to say? Is this person I am me? Or does my mind belong to someone else you see. The voice, which speaks to me at times is it, my voice or someone else who is really unkind.

I just cried and prayed for God to take this thing away. Please, I really can't live this way, I prayed.

Again, a few years passed, but I found the voice within. I knew I had no one to talk to about it. One day in school I was in the bathroom, and the lights got real dim. The voice came again, laughing at me. "You stupid bitch," it said.

"Go away!" I screamed. I had a paper clip on my book, so I took it and the louder the voice got, the deeper I stuck that clip in my arm. "Go away!" I screamed, and it laughed louder this time.

Jill came running to me. "Isabella, what are you doing? Stop it now!" she cried out. She took the clip away from me. She sat in the floor and cried. "Isabella, you are my best friend, but why are you doing this terrible thing to yourself?" Jill asked. She hugged me, and I cried and told her about the voice and what my mother had said.

"Isabella!" Jill said. "I don't care what your mother says, you need to tell someone about this."

"Do you think I am going crazy?" I asked her.

"No, sweetie I don't," she replied. "I don't know what it is, but we need to find out, so we can make it go away," Jill explained.

For the first time, I felt relieved that someone believed what I was telling them. I covered up my arm until the cut from the paper clip went away. I acted at home how my mother wanted me to act. I smiled when I felt like crying. Doing anything to make Mom happy. I was so disgusted that I had to do whatever she wanted me to do. I had to have a lot of self-control in order to carry on; times were very hard for me. I began to think everyone was watching me. One night at the dinner table, I thought Sky was watching me eat. "What!" I yelled at him. "What are you watching me eat for?"

Sky looked puzzled. "Gee Isabella," he said, "what is wrong with you? I don't care to watch you eat."

Mother looked at me if she could eat me alive. "Isabella!" she screamed. "We will have no more."

My father looked at both of us and asked, "Is there something going on between you two that I don't know about?"

I answered quickly. "No dad!" I replied. "Not a thing. Mom is just being Mom." Then Sky changed the subject like he always did when Mom and I were into our disagreements.

Every year as I got older, I felt worse: not sleeping well, sometimes eating a lot, and other times being unable to eat. I was in the ninth grade and I went out for cheerleading, and to my surprise, I made it. I was so happy and so was my mother, for she thought this was good for her social club to tell everyone that her daughter was a cheerleader. I was just happy to do something with my friends and get out of the house. The voice seemed to go away for a while. I was actually happy for a change and was having a good time. I met a real cute guy named Matt, and he was just the thing I needed in my life. One night he took me out to eat. We were having a really good time; Jill and her boyfriend came with us. I suddenly started to laugh out hysterically, and Jill called me down. "Isabella!" she said. "What are you laughing about?" I just stopped real fast and changed the subject.

I would be walking down the street or in class, and I would feel so strange, like people were watching me. The voice would whisper to me, "Isabella, I know you hear me." I would run, trying to outrun this, but it had me. Face it, I thought, I am possessed by a demon. I need to talk to a priest, I thought, so I went to confession to talk to Father Anthony.

"What is it my child; what do you confess today?"

I talked with him about the voice. "Father," I asked, "am I an evil child?"

Father Anthony asked, "Do you believe that you are evil, my child?"

"I don't think so," I replied.

"God will remove this demon if you pray, child. Put the rosary under your pillow at night, child."

I asked him, "Father, pray for me that I may be without this demon that is in me."

He replied, "I will, my child." We prayed the rosary prayer together.

I finished high school living with this demon; some days were better than others. I had really long, blonde hair, and Matt loved it that way. We were sitting on the porch one day talking of college or what job we wanted and our hopes and dreams. Then some kids came walking down the street; their mother came and yelled for them to come back. She looked at me, and I got paranoid, and I thought she said my hair looked awful. I blacked out, and the next thing I knew, I was in the bathroom with a pair of scissors and had cut pieces of my hair off. Matt came in and said to me, "Isabella, what have you done to your hair?" I just looked in the mirror and couldn't believe what I had done. I was inflicting harm on myself without even being aware of it. I guess when I blacked out, things happened without me knowing what was going on. My world just kept getting crazier by the minute.

Of course when Mother came home she screamed at me and said, "What have you done to your beautiful hair?"

"Mother, I don't remember!" I replied.

"Of course you remember; you are not stupid!" she said. We started to argue and she threw a glass of water in my face. "Maybe this will wake you up and help you remember; you and your sleepwalking!" Mother yelled. I got so mad. I was soaking wet, and now I really felt like a fool. My mother kept screaming at me. "I just can't believe you, Isabella, you are trying to drive me crazy," Mother yelled again.

"No, mother," I replied, "crazy is what I am."

Weeks went by, and mother and I didn't speak. Then one day my father was sitting in the den reading. I walked over to him and asked, "Dad, why does Mother hate me so?"

He grabbed me by the hand and said, "Sit down, Isabella; your mother doesn't hate you. She just has high hopes for you. She loves you dearly; you have to admit, Isabella, you have been doing some strange things lately," he explained.

"Dad, I know, and I really don't understand what is going on with me," I told him.

"Have you told your mother?" Dad asked.

"Yes! I have, and she said for me to never speak of it again." I tried to explain. Dad said he would talk with her. "Thank you, Dad!" I said. I went out with my friends that night.

My mother got me an appointment with the family doctor; she had instructed him to find out what was wrong with me. "What exactly do you think you are suffering from?" the doctor asked me.

I looked at him and said, "How should I know? You are the doctor, not me."

The doctor asked, "Well then, just how do you feel? Is it a sick feeling?"

I said, "No, I am picture perfect. Didn't mother tell you?"

The doctor asked again, "Are you physically all right?"

"Yes, I am!" I replied. "I have blackouts and do things when I have blacked out," I explained.

"You don't remember what you are doing?" he asked.

"No, I sure don't," I replied.

"What else happens to you?" The doctor looked puzzled.

I announced, "Well the good news is I feel OK, but the bad news is I hear voices."

"Voices, you say?" he asked.

"Yes, voices." I said.

"What kind of voices?" he asked me. By this time I was really getting tired of the bullshit. "Listen, dear," the doctor said. "I just want to find out what to treat you for. Have you ever had a condition of this type before?" I said no. He told me to get dressed. "I am going to have a little talk with your mother," he said.

"My mother could give a rat's ass about what is really wrong with me," I yelled out at the doctor. He looked at me and shook his head and walked away.

I got dressed and went back into the waiting room. The doctor and my mother were in his office talking. My mother came out and said, "Let's go dear."

I asked, "Well what did the fine doctor find wrong with me?" Mother said he didn't know at this point. "What point is that?"

Mother said, "Isabella, I told you I don't feel like talking about this right now." That's it: not what she wanted to hear, so she shuts it out. I could be dying and she would say, "Oh, the world is bright, and Isabella isn't dying." On the drive home, she never spoke another word. I just sat there, and I knew I was alone on this trip. Whatever this thing I had was, my mother would never face it and never be able to help me. Time went by, and mother never wanted to take me back to the doctor; whatever he had told her scared her enough that she didn't want any more answers. I think she got the answer of what was wrong with me that day and never wanted to face it or have to deal with it every again. It seemed that my life was getting worse. I really wasn't getting any better. I was afraid to talk to people for fear that everyone would say I was crazy. The days were hard for me, but I was determined to make it in this world somehow. I was working in the bank and trying to stay busy. My mother and I had really lost any feeling we had for each other; she didn't tell me the truth, and I didn't trust her. I really hated that we felt this way about each other. Dad and Sky were always telling me how much Mother loved me, but that she was just so stubborn and wouldn't admit how very much she loved me. "Isabella," Dad would say, "your mother came from a very poor family, and when she and I married, she wanted to never admit she was poor or anything was wrong with our family."

"Dad, you do know there is something really wrong with me?"

Dad answered, "Isabella, there are times when there is something wrong with anyone."

So you see no one took me seriously; they all thought I was putting on an act. Sky would always say, "Sis, you really should have been an actress. You really act out some good stuff." Attention seeker, he would call me. I would get so mad at him; he would only make matters worse.

Jill called me one day and told me about this clinic she had heard about through someone at work. She said I should go in and talk to someone about my problems and that they aren't allowed to tell anyone without your permission. She thought maybe I might benefit from the clinic in some way, "just at least to have someone to listen to your problems," she said. I asked her where it was at and said I would think about, "Please go!" Jill pleaded with me.

"I told you I would think about it," I told Jill. The next day I got the nerve to drive by it. It was a small place. I decided I would go in and look around. People were waiting all in the room. The lady at the desk asked if she could help me. I said, "I would like some information on your services."

Really sharply she said, "Take a number and sit down." I sat there about thirty minutes. People were coming and going, and my number still hadn't been called. All right, I thought, I would ask her if my number was coming up soon. I walked over to the desk and she snapped at me, "Sit down until your number is called!" I tried to tell her I had been sitting there for thirty minutes already. She replied, "Well then, dear, you just have to wait your turn until you are called."

I threw the number down. "No! I won't take your number and let someone else sit here for an hour and be talked to like a dog!" I snapped back at her. Then I just walked out and looked at the others and said, "Good luck, have a good day!"

The next day Jill called me, and I told her about what had happened. "That is awful!" she said. "You need to report that rude lady!" Jill suggested.

"No!" I said. "It's not worth the trouble, but thank you so much for trying to help me. I love you, Jill, for being a good friend," I sobbed.

"You will always be my best friend," Jill said. I really wanted to get my own apartment, but I had to save up some money for it. I was working at the bank, and I got a second job babysitting my dad's friend's son. They were paying me quite an amount to watch him on the weekends they wanted to go away together. I had been doing this for about four months without any problems. Then, oh my God, one day I was sitting with him, and the voice started again. The baby was crying and the voices were talking. I pulled at my head screaming, "Stop it, stop it now!" Then suddenly I looked down at the baby, and he was covered with ants; I tried to get them off of him, but the baby just kept crying. I ran into the kitchen and got a can of ant spray. I sprayed it on the baby, and the ants still wouldn't get off the baby.

I called my mother and told her that ants were on the baby. She said, "I will be right there." My mother and father came in and saw what I had done. I really didn't want to hurt that child, but to me at that time I saw those ants, and those ants were real to me. My mother slapped me across the face and screamed, "What have you done, Isabella?" My parents took the baby to the hospital. They called the parents, and I had to face them on what I had done. The baby's eyes were hurt pretty badly, and the doctor said he might have to wear glasses all his life when he is older. My parents were so mad at me. The only way the parents wouldn't press charges was if my parents got me some help. Now my folks and my dad's friends thought I was a real basket case. My mother came screaming at me. "Isabella, you have really done it this time! You are to go see those head doctors, whatever they are called," Mother continued. "You have really destroyed my life!" she yelled.

"What!" I said, putting my hands on my hips. "Let me get this straight; I have destroyed your life? Haven't I told you time and time again I hear voices, and that I see things, Mother, but no, you just have to act like there is nothing wrong with me. Mom!" I yelled, "I have begged you to help me, and you throw water in my face, and you slap me, and tell me to be quiet?" I yelled again, "Do you know who is to blame for this, Mom? It is you!"

Mother screamed, "Don't you dare blame this thing on me, Isabella!"

I continued to vent. "Mother, you take the cake! Mother of the Year Award!" I yelled.

Then my dad interrupted us. "Stop it! You two! This doesn't help matters for you to argue like this. Let's go to bed and call it a night and thank God the baby wasn't hurt any more than he was," my dad suggested, and everyone agreed.

For the next weeks my parents researched doctors in the field in which I needed help. My mother wanted my father just to send me out of state to some hospital there. She said she was really worried about me; truthfully, she was more worried about what her friends would say. I think my dad really cared and still does, but he is helpless because even after all these years, the poor man still doesn't understand my illness. He loves me, I know he does, and Sky loves me, but my mother, she hates me for the shame I have put upon her family.

I was finally admitted to a hospital nearby. My parents were told they had the best of the best there. I was put in a room, and the nurse came in and took blood, I think about every hour. The doctor, Dr. Smith I think his name was, talked with me. "I need your help, Isabella," he said. "I can't help you unless you tell me the truth, and don't be afraid to tell me anything. I really want to help you and get your life back." Dr Smith spoke sincerely. I started to cry. "Now dear, it will be all right," he assured me.

"I really hope so," I said.

The next morning he came in to talk to me again. "What do you think is wrong with you, Isabella?" Dr Smith asked.

"The truth?" I asked.

"Yes!" he replied.

"The truth, I think I am possessed by a demon," I said.

He laughed and said, "No, you are not! If I had a dime for everyone who comes in here and tells me the same thing," the doctor replied.

"Why?" I asked.

"My dear, you don't understand the medical term for what is wrong. The things you see and the things you hear are part of your mental illness," Dr Smith explained.

"So I am crazy after all!" I asked.

"To have a mental illness doesn't make you crazy. It makes you feel that way if you don't take the right medicine. Isabella, with the right medicine you can have just as good quality life as the next person," he explained more.

"What kind of medicine?" I asked.

"This is enough questions and answers for today. We will talk more tomorrow." The doctor exited quietly.

The next day, I had another appointment with the good doctor. He walked in and asked me to sit down. "Here, Isabella," he said, "let's sit." Dr Smith patted the seat next to him. "I really need you to tell me more about the voices. Are you afraid of this voice when it speaks to you?" he asked me.

I looked at him and replied, "Of course I am! They frighten me."

"Are you sure you don't remember the things you do?" the doctor questioned.

"Listen!" I said. "I am getting real tired of telling the same story, and no one believes me," I said harshly. I got up and yelled out at him: "Either you believe what I am telling you or not! I am out of here if you don't believe me!"

With that statement, the doctor grabbed my arm. "Yes," he said, "I do believe every word you are telling me. Now I need to give you some medicine to help you. Isabella, you have to know that I will do everything in my power to help you. Do you believe in me, Isabella?" Dr Smith asked.

I looked at him and replied, "At this point in my life, I have no other choice."

The doctor gave me some scripts and told me to take as directed. "This medicine will help the voice to go away and help you feel much better," the doctor explained. My mother had the prescription filled, and I started to take it. At first it made me really sick to my stomach. I felt like I was going to throw up all the time. I was so sick for the first few days, but the doctor was right; the voice was gone. I stayed thirsty and felt like I could drink a gallon of water. Then suddenly I started to gain weight. I put on ten pounds in a month. I couldn't stand that, so I started to cheek my medication. My mother would always say, "Did you take your medicine?"

"Yes, Mother, I did!" I would show her how I had taken it. I was rather good at this game. Mother never knew I wasn't taking my medicine until later on.

My passion for life and wanting it to be as normal as it could kept me hanging on. At that time I was young, and I never realized how not taking my medicine was going to affect me and everyone around me. I was working and going out with Matt and was feeling really well. Matt was attending school for his degree in accounting, and I was just happy working in the bank. One thing at a time was really all I could handle at this time in my life. Matt and I were starting to get quite serious, and he took me to a nice dinner with candles and the whole works. I sat down and was ordering when he asked me how I would like to be his wife. That was a big surprise for me because I never saw it coming, at least not this soon. Of course, I answered yes; Matt gave me a beautiful ring. I was thrilled and showed it off to Jill. She was delighted for me.

Matt and I decided to go together for at least a year before we were married. He knew I had some emotional problems and wanted me to try to work through all of this before we gave a date to be married. I was working at the bank one day when I had another attack. The voice came to me again. There was a lady at my desk and I could see her mouth move, but I just couldn't hear what she was saying over the voice. "You bitch, you better wait on me! Right now!" the voice said. Then her eyes got red, and her mouth was just saying things I couldn't understand. I got up, grabbed my bag, and ran out of the bank into the street. The manager came running behind me.

"Isabella, what is wrong?" she yelled, but I just kept running and running until I couldn't run any longer. I sat down on the grass trying to catch my breath.

"God, I thought, what is this?" I wondered. I ran straight for the church. I opened the confession window. "Father," I prayed, "I have a demon within me." I paused. "It makes me see awful things and hear awful things. Father, I pray that you help me in some way. Father," I pleaded, "tell me what to do."

The priest in the window said to me, "Child, cleanse your soul and repent to our father."

"I have before, Father, but this thing comes back, no matter what I do," I tried to explain. We prayed for a while, and I bent in front of the candles and prayed a silent prayer. I walked back to my car and drove home. My mother was there when I opened the door.

"Isabella!" she said loudly, "the manager, Mrs. Brown, at the bank called and wanted to know if you were all right. She told me what you did at the bank."

"Isabella," Mother said, "I think it sort of meant you are going to lose your job if you keep this nonsense up. I thought the medicine was helping with all that crazy stuff you do."

I said, "Mother, what about the crazy stuff you do? Is there even a medicine for that?"

"That's about enough from you, and I am your mother!" she said and walked away. Maybe I shouldn't have said that to her, but honestly I think my mother makes me worse because she is so mean to me at times. If I ever have children, I will really be good to them, I thought to myself.

I went back to work the next day, and I explained to Mrs. Brown that I had gotten really sick and was suffering from a panic attack, and it felt like I couldn't breathe, and I had to run out or I thought I might pass out. "You poor dear," she said, "please go to the doctor and see about this." Mrs. Brown was so understanding and sweet. She continued, "I know there is something he could do for you." People would come in and I would see strange faces, but I just looked away and didn't look at them in the face. This worked for a while.

The voice would whisper softly at night. "Isabella," it would say, "I know you hear me. Give in and hear what I have to say," it pleaded eerily. I would jump straight up and turn the music up so loud I couldn't hear it for the rest of the night.

I decided to take my medicine again and see if it really would help this voice. So I took it, and I just stayed like I was a walking dead person. I was really starting to get angry at this situation. I can't function if I take the medicine, and I hear that voice if I don't. "Which is worse?" I wondered.

I was starting to get really depressed, and my hostility toward everyone around me was building up. My mother was on my case all the time about my behavior. She thought I was just putting on; she had no compassion for me whatsoever. Deep down inside my mother knew what was really wrong with me, but she was ashamed of me and the condition I suffered. Which was still a mystery to me, because she wouldn't tell me the truth.

One day I was getting dressed to go out with Matt, and I was looking into a long mirror to see how my dress looked. I looked down and then up again; right there before me was a woman in a long dress with her hair pulled up. She smiled at me and asked, "Do you like the way we look?" I trembled in shock and looked back, and the image was gone.

I tried to talk to Matt about certain things that I saw and heard and he would just laugh and say, "Isabella, you are so cute."

"You are just overworked and stressed out," he would say. He continued to advise me to take my medication. So back to the drawing board for me once again.

"What is wrong with me?" I wondered continually. I was working and really trying to keep it together; my thoughts were that I had a demon in me. My mother and father, I guess, just thought I was simply crazy. I guess we were both right, so I decided to move in with Matt. I thought maybe being away from my apartment would help me change for the better. I loved being out of the house and with Matt. This seemed to release a lot of stress. I loved fresh flowers, and I put them out every week. We got along so well, and he was the perfect guy for me.

Mother would always tell him, "Watch out for Isabella, you never know what she's up to."

Matt would laugh and say, "I think I can handle her." Weeks went on, and he and I were so happy. Then he went on a business trip, and I still to day don't know if this made me have a relapse or not. I think him leaving me threw me in a panic. Anyway, while he was gone I fell into a trace again. It was snowing, and Matt said when he got home, I was outside naked and dancing in the snow.

He said when he asked me what I was doing, I said "feeling closer to God. For you are brought into this world naked and to be naked in the beauty was to be close to God." Now, I really never had any memory of this event, although Matt said I did it, so I must have some memory of it. I know he would have no reason to lie about anything. He loved me so much at that time.

I asked Matt not to mention it to my parents. "Isabella," Matt said, "if you do anything else without remembering it, I will have to take you to see a doctor. I have heard of people sleepwalking, which can be very dangerous," he said, concerned. I agreed that if anything happened again, I would go see a doctor. Months went by and I had heard no voices, and really I was doing quite well; at least, I thought I was at this time. You see this voice really played tricks on my mind. Sometimes it would make me think I was really doing well and then just when I thought this nightmare was over, here the voice would come again. I kept this thing or demon voice or whatever the hell it was deep inside of me for so long. I lived a terrible life. God, why couldn't I just be normal? I wondered, because it just wasn't fair. All I ever wanted was a life with a good husband and someday, a family. I didn't use drugs or drink or any crazy stuff. Unfortunately, I was just crazy .... I really tried to keep my life together; I would often ask people that I trusted if they believed in demons. Some said yes they did, and some said they didn't; I just knew something was terribly wrong with me.

I began having these terrible headaches all the time. Of course, I always acted as if nothing was wrong. I would run into the bathroom and hold my head between my legs until that would ease off; then I would get dizzy and feel like I was going to pass out. I just couldn't put my finger on what was wrong with me. I felt trapped, like a wild animal with nowhere to go. I just wished I could figure out all this craziness going on with me.

Matt wanted me to marry him and I was so excited about marrying him, but I was so afraid of him finding out how crazy

I really was. One day we were talking about getting married and joking I said, "You really don't want to marry me. I am crazy."

He laughed and said, "Honey, I am crazy too. About you, I mean!" Then he grabbed me and kissed me. God what a great man he was, and I loved him dearly, but I felt that I would be doing him an injustice to marry him. Lord knows, he didn't deserve this thing or this demon that was overtaking my soul and head. Matt always told me how beautiful he thought I was. Even in my worst moments, he would tell me how lovely I was. He made me feel beautiful, and most of all, normal.

We told our parents we were going to get married. His family was so pleased and happy for us. On the other hand, my family acted really strange about it. I remember once my mother and I were doing the dishes and she said to me right out of the blue, "Do yourself a favor, Isabella, don't have any children."

I looked at her with surprise, "Why?" I asked. "Why, Mother, would you say such a thing?" I asked.

She replied, "I have my reasons," and added, "really, I am very tired, and I need to go to bed." Then she kissed me on my cheek and said good night and that she loved me.

I told Matt what she said to me and he said, "Well, mothers don't want to let their little girls go."

I just smiled and said, "Yes, I guess that is it." But I knew Mother too well; she was hiding something from me. She would have never said that without a reason. Just what I needed: more suspicions in my life to deal with. The next few weeks Matt and I were planning our wedding. One night about one o'clock in the morning, I woke up feeling like bugs were biting me on my head. I got up and turned on the bathroom light. Matt was still sleeping and I called out to him. "Honey!" I said, "Wake up, something is in my hair."

He ran into the bathroom, ran his fingers through my hair, and said, "You just had a bad dream. There is nothing in your hair, Isabella."

"Are you sure?" I asked, still looking in the mirror, pulling my roots apart. I went back to bed, but I tell you I felt bugs biting my head all night. The next morning I made breakfast, still feeling those bites to my head. After Matt left for work, I went upstairs to get ready for work. I looked in the mirror again. There they were: little black bugs running all through my hair. I ran my head under hot water, and they were still there. Finally I got Matt's razor and my scissors and cut and shaved every bit of my hair off. Then for some reason I shaved off my eyebrows too. Then I sat down in the bathroom floor and cried. "God, why is this happening to me?" I asked myself.

I must have passed out after that because the next thing I saw was Jill standing over me, calling out my name. "Isabella!" she said. "Who did this to you?" she asked.

"Did what?" I said, looking up with blurred vision.

"Your hair, Isabella, is gone. Even your eyebrows are gone," Jill said.

"Oh, that," I said. "I had to, Jill, those damn bugs wouldn't leave me alone," I told her. Jill went downstairs and brought me a glass of water.

"Really, Isabella, I think this has gone far enough. You are having some kind of breakdown," Jill said.

"No, I am not!" I said.

"Yes, you are!" she replied.

I screamed at her to get the hell out of my house. "I am tired of people thinking that I am crazy!" I screamed out at her. Then I got up and looked into the mirror, Lord, what have I done to myself now? Matt is going to be so mad at me, I thought. I put on a hat and ran to the mall, and I went into a wig store. I found a nice wig that looked a lot like my natural hair. This would have to do, I thought. That night Matt came home, and I could tell something was wrong.

"How did work go?" he asked.

"Well, I didn't make it to work today," I explained.

"Why?" he asked, looking at me strangely.

"I just felt a little sick to my stomach; maybe I have the flu or something," I said.

"Maybe," he replied and walked off and poured himself a drink.

"You know, Isabella, you really are full of surprises," he said.

"What do you mean by that?" I asked.

"Just take, for instance, why didn't you call your job and tell them you were sick?" he said. I tried to say something and he said, "Wait a minute now, let me talk. Your job called me worried about you, then Jill had quite an interesting story to tell me," he explained. Then he stood up and walked over to me. "Look at you, Isabella, a beautiful young woman, but you are a terrible liar. Is that a wig you have on?" I looked away, feeling like such a fool. "Tell me the truth, so I can help you," Matt said.

"You hate me now, so go away and I will lose you forever," I screamed out.

"You know what I will do and how I will react," he said. "Isabella, I love you. No matter what is wrong, I am here for you. The bugs you were talking about last night: that is why you did this to your hair, isn't it?" he asked.

"Yes!" I said, crying.

He grabbed me and pulled me into his arms. "It's going to be OK, honey, we will find someone to help you," Matt said.

I cried and said, "I look so awful this way!"

"No, honey, even without hair or eyebrows, you still are so beautiful; I don't know any other woman on this earth that can pull that off but you." Matt laughed. I just cried and cried. At least with all the things happening to me, God blessed me with a wonderful man.

The next day I called into work and told them I needed a week off because I was really sick and needed to see a doctor to find out what was wrong. The bank manager was really nice and told me to take off all the time I needed. So the rest was up to Matt. He told me he was going to find someone to help me feel good again and take away all the pain I was going through away. Poor Matt. He really thought at that time he would find someone to make me normal again. I wished he could have, but again there was no getting back to normal for me. Hell, I didn't even know what normal was.

It was about a week later when Matt came home so happy. "Isabella," he called out, "honey, come here. I have found someone to see you, and I talked with him on the phone today. He told me he thought you were suffering from some kind of depression or anxiety.

He will see you tomorrow at ten in the morning. Isn't this great news, baby? You will get better and we can get married," Matt said. He was so happy. Tears still come to my eyes when I think of that day.

The next morning I went to see this doctor. As I walked into his office, I began to feel so guilty to be putting Matt through this. I sat down and looked all around. Finally they called my name, and I walked into a small office to see the doctor. He was very soft-spoken and kind of an older man but had class. We began to talk. "Well now, Isabella, I talked with your husband-to-be." He lifted his eyebrow and smiled. "Nice guy, I take it," he said.

I smiled and thought to myself, "yes he is." I replied.

"He tells me you are seeing things that aren't there," the doctor continued.

I looked at the floor and then answered. "At times I do," I said.

"What kind of things do you see?" he asked.

"All kind of things at times, but I really block out this voice," I said.

"Really?" the doctor asked. "Matt didn't mention the voice."

"I know," I replied, "because he doesn't know about the voice. I am afraid to tell him. My mother already thinks I am demon possessed."

"Does she know? Does your mother know about the voice?" he asked.

"Yes, she knows everything, and she doesn't give a shit about me. Really!" I said. "I am not kidding. She hates me for all the things I am going though," I yelled out.

"Slow down, Isabella!" he said. "Let's back up. When is the last time you heard a voice? Is it one voice or more than one?" the doctor asked.

"Really, doctor," I said, "at times it's just one real scary voice. There have been times when I hear a lot of whispers, and there is more than one voice," I explained.

"Isabella," the doctor said, "you need to be put on some medication for this."

I answered quickly. "No!" I said, "been there done that; just doesn't help. All is does it make me fat… I would rather be dead than to go through all this," I cried.

"Have you ever thought of suicide, Isabella?" he asked.

"I have." He looked worried. "Oh, come now! I am to chicken to pull that off." I laughed.

"For now you are, my dear, but if your condition gets worse, I am worried about you, chicken or not," he said.

"Dr. Belmont is it?" I asked.

"Yes," he said, "that is my name."

I spoke. "You worry too much," I said.

He said, "That is my job, to worry about my patients. Please trust me, Isabella," the doctor said. "Please just try this medicine, and if you don't feel it's helping, call me, and we will work together to get you well." He spoke softly and gently.

I smiled and agreed. "Just for Matt," I said, "because I love him so."

"Good girl," the doctor said and patted me on the back.

The doctor put me on Haledon 15 milligrams at night and then some Celia 40 milligrams at night. The new medicine started to make me feel really tired, and my head felt fuzzy and really lightheaded at times. I didn't see things or hear the voice on this medicine. I had another appointment the next week, and Dr. Belmont wanted to see Matt with me. He was going to explain to us what was really wrong with me; after all these years, I would know. It was our next appointment, and Matt and I went in to see the good doctor. I sat down and Matt sat next to me, holding my hand. The doctor started off telling me I had a mental disorder called schizophrenia. Matt spoke up and said, "Exactly what is that? I don't understand. I thought she had depression."

The doctor looked over his glasses and replied, "Yes, depression is a part of this mental disorder, but it also comes with hallucinations, which Isabella has been experiencing for some time now. Also, the voices are a great part of this illness. They are real to her, and in her mind she sees things and hears voices that only she can hear or see. A very sad illness, I might add," the doctor said.

Matt looked like he was going to cry. "Will she get better or get over it?" he asked.

"Yes and no," Dr. Belmont replied. "Yes, she can get better, but on the other hand she will never be over it, I'm afraid to tell you." Dr Belmont continued. "Let me explain to you both: Schizophrenia usually begins when you are very young. Symptoms usually start at childhood, but some come later on in life. About one in every one hundred people around the world have this disorder. Believe me, you are not alone with this illness," he explained.

"I was about ten when I first thought I heard a voice," I told the doctor.

"That is about when most people who get this illness start having symptoms," the doctor told me.

"I didn't know you had this that early, Isabella," Matt said.

The doctor looked at me and asked, "Did you tell your parents, dear?"

I paused and said, "I told my mother over and over about the voice, but she would usually throw water in my face or slap me. She told me to not to say anything to anybody. She didn't want the neighbors to think we were crazy," I continued. "My father didn't believe my brother Sky and me. He thought I was just acting out," I cried.

"What a shame," the doctor said and just shook his head.

"Why?" I asked.

"My dear, you would have gotten better a lot earlier instead of going through all this alone," the doctor explained.

"So, I am not demon possessed?" I asked.

Dr. Belmont smiled at me and said, "No, dear, not a real demon, just your mind playing tricks on you. Just continue to take your medicine for now. Let me review your case, and I will call with a new appointment," Doctor Belmont continued. "Isabella, it is very important to take your medicine, OK?" he said.

I answered, "I will, doctor, whatever you say is best for me."

On the way home, Matt and I talked; I told him my life story. I told him the truth about everything for what is was; it definitely was not a pretty picture. After I finished, he was so quiet, I finally asked, "Are you OK with all this?"

Matt answered harshly. "I am mad!" he replied. "I am damn mad."

"At me?" I asked.

Looking at me, he said, "No, honey, not at you. Your damn mother knew this all along and refused to help you. What kind of mother is that?"

"Not a good one," I said. "She is still my mother."

"I will never like her again," Matt said.

One night Matt and I went over to my parents' house for dinner, and Mother started on me. She laughed and said, "I heard about your bugs, Isabella. That was a stupid thing you did, cutting off your hair!"

My heart just skipped a beat. "How did you know about that?" I asked.

"Your friend Jill called me because she was worried about you." She kept laughing.

I spoke up. "Mother, I went to the doctor. I am fine now; that's been a while. I feel much better now."

Mother said, "Went to the doctor, did you? What did he say was wrong with you?" And before I could answer, she said, "I would have told you what was wrong without charging you. You are an attention seeker, always have been since you were five, and I guess you will always be one."

"Mother," I pleaded, "please don't do this."

Then Matt spoke up and said, "Really Mrs. Garren, with all due respect, I think all of us have heard enough from you."

"Really?" my mother said, standing up from the table. "This is my house, and I will decide when it has been enough!" Mother yelled back. My father told my mother to sit down and be quiet. By this time Matt was boiling mad.

"Let's go, Isabella," he said. I told my father good night, and he apologized for my mother's behavior.

"I am sorry, Isabella," Matt said. "Your mother was out of place talking to you like that."

I said, "I know she hates me because I am not normal."

"There is more to this, Isabella," Matt said. "I can just feel it in my bones. You know what I mean?" he asked.

"Yes," I said, "I do." We went home, and both of us talked until three in the morning. I was so lucky to have Matt. I just hoped I wasn't too much for him to handle with my illness. I went back to work the next week. Everyone wanted to know what was wrong with me. I told everyone that the doctor said that I was suffering from major depression. I really didn't want everyone to know my business. I stayed on the medicine, but it started to affect my work. I could hardly keep my eyes open. I started to make mistakes, and the head teller was starting to get on my case. I was beginning to become outraged. No matter what I did, a problem would appear. If I didn't take my medicine, the voice would reappear, and if I did take the medicine, I gained weight. I would get so tired and was in danger of losing my job. I slowly started to taper off my medicine. I took half the dose I was supposed to. It worked for a while, and then one day it happened: the voice came back again.

I was driving home from work when I heard the voice again.

"Bitch!" I shook my head, and it said it again. I pulled into the driveway and ran to find my medicine. Looking through the drawers, I was shaking all over. "You bitch, you." It started to laugh. I felt dizzy, and my head started to hurt. I swallowed my pills. And sat down and began to cry. The next thing I knew, blood was all over the floor. I had a razor in my hand. I looked down and on my upper thigh I had carved the word bitch into it.

"God," I cried out, "what have I done?" It was really bleeding badly. I wrapped a towel around it and called Matt. I sat in the floor crying, waiting on him. Finally I heard him come home.

"Where are you, Isabella?" he yelled.

"In here," I cried.

"Honey, are you OK?" Matt looked worried.

"No, I am not!" I cried, "Look! Just look at what I have done now."

"Why did you do that to yourself?" he asked.

"I don't remember!" I told him. He took me to the hospital. While we were there, they called Dr. Belmont. They cleaned the cuts and put bandages on me. I thought I was going home when the doctor came in and said I had to be in the hospital awhile for my own good. "Please, Matt, take me home," I begged.

He looked at me with tears in his eyes and said, "Not this time, honey, you need to stay, just for a day or two."

"No!" I said. "I am going home."

The doctor looked at me and said, "No, Matt signed papers for you to be here for a while." I got mad at him, and I really didn't understand what was going on.

That night as I sat on the bed, I began to write how I felt the voices within are. They are evil; they tell me what to say. They make me hurt myself without me knowing it. Is there no hope in sight? This demon in me, this voice as it is? Mental illness is what everyone says it is. Please, God, heal my very soul. Then I began to cry for myself and for Matt.

Matt went to my mother's house to talk to her about me. "I need to know," Matt told her, "did you know something was wrong with Isabella when she was a child?"

"I always thought Isabella was just an imaginative child. She had a friend she always talked to, but children often do those things, you know," she said. "Isabella would often talk to herself and talk to someone who wasn't there. Matt, Isabella just wants your attention; that's it! That is how she works. She almost drove her father and me crazy with her stories," she said.

"Mrs. Garden, your daughter is sick. She isn't pretending; this is real. I will be back later to talk to your husband," Matt told her. He came home and told me what had happened between my mother and him. "Honestly, honey," he said, "there is something wrong here."

I said, "No, that is just the way my mother is."

Matt tried to assure me. "We are still going to get married, Isabella," he said, "just as soon as you get better."

I looked at him with tears in my eyes. "What if I don't get better?" I asked.

"You will, Isabella." He hugged me and walked upstairs. I know this was hard on Matt, but he loved me. I never questioned his love for one minute. I just hated that he was going through all this.

For the next few days, I questioned myself on what to do. I didn't want to see Matt go through all this pain. So I called Dr. Belmont, and I asked him if he would put me back into the hospital. "You signed yourself out last time." Dr. Belmont said.

"I know this," I replied. "I am really tired of being sick. Please put in the hospital for a few weeks to see if this helps," I begged. When Matt came home from work, I told him I had decided to go into the hospital for a while.

"Are you sure about this?" he asked.

I looked at him, thinking of how this is affecting him, and replied, "Yes, I am sure." The next day I checked myself in the hospital. I had to take responsibility for my own life. I had a roommate named Nancy. She seemed to be nice. She told me she was suffering from bipolar disease.

"What do you have, dear?" she asked me.

"I don't know," I replied. As if I was going to tell my life story to some stranger in a mental ward. The nurse brought in some consent papers to be treated. I signed them and my treatment was on its way.

The next morning the doctor came in to see me. He said he was going to start me on a shot, which had been very effective in the past. I told him I had no choice but to do whatever he wanted, as long as it made me feel better. That evening Matt came to see me. He was so sweet; he brought me lovely flowers that smelled so sweet. We talked until visiting hours were over. I lay in the bed and tried to sleep, but I tossed and turned. They gave me the shot in my hip, and it was really sore. "God, can't I get a break here; I am in the damn hospital to feel better, and I don't feel any better," I said out loud.

Nancy said, "Give it time, Isabella; soon you'll feel better."

I just looked at her and said good night and looked at the ceiling; as I lay there, the voice started with me again. "Hey you!" it said, "you piece of shit!"

I turned the light on and Nancy asked me, "What are you doing?"

"I thought I heard something," I explained.

"Cut the light out, Isabella, and go to sleep," Nancy said, covering her head with her pillow. Shit, I thought, I can't live this way. I will take every pill they will give me. The next morning the nurse came in with our medicine, and I swallowed every one of them. Gladly, I thought, I would take all the pills to get feeling better and go home to Matt.

My mother and father came to see me. I wasn't happy to find out my mother knew I was in the hospital. They came in, and my father walked over and kissed me, and my mother patted me on my back. "Hope you are feeling well, my dear?" Mother asked.

"Yes," I replied, "I am feeling much better, thank you, Mother. Let's you and me bury the hatchet," I said.

She smiled in the way only Mother could do. "What is there to bury, dear? I love you and I will always love. You are my daughter," Mother said.

I smiled back and said, "OK." I felt like she was saying that because she was in front of dad. "Where is Sky?" I asked.

"Oh, off with his college buddies, I guess," Mother said.

"Well tell him I said hello and that I love and miss him, will you?" I asked. After they were gone, I went to the group session. I listened and began to learn a lot of ways to deal with the problems I was having.

Just as I was in the shower getting ready for bed, the voice started again, saying to me, "You worthless bitch, you. Do you really think I will go away with just a few little pills?" it asked me. I sat down in the shower with the water running all over me, crying. When I went back into my room, Nancy said I looked like I had seen a ghost. She asked me if I had seen one.

"No," I said. "I have not seen or heard from an old ghost." I sat on my bed writing in my journal. I wrote down this poem, and this is so true; anyone that has mental illness will agree.

Chapter 2

Mental illness has no certain form or no certain face it doesn't affect a certain race.

It has no sympathy to those who mourn,
It runs a face to a killing throne. That no one normal could ever condone.

Mental illness what a joke for those who lives is at stake. For no one normal could under the pain for people like us have to take. –

Nancy said, "What a poem. You are a really deep person, aren't you?"

"Yes, I guess you can call me that," I answered.

I stayed in the hospital for ten days and was released. Matt was happy I was home. I had missed my home and I was glad to be home, but I needed something to do. I began to gain weight again and looked like Porky the pig. I started to cook, but the only problem was I ate so much. I weighed in at the doctor's office, and I weighed 207. My God, I couldn't believe that I weighed that much. My friend Jill wanted me to go to a gym with her. I looked so bad, you just wouldn't believe it. I said OK, but I knew I had to stop the medicine. I talked to Dr. Belmont, and he advised not to do that. I did and I started eating hardly anything. Then one night at the dinner table, I started seeing bugs again. They were climbing all over the wall. I got up and said, "Look at that bug."

Matt asked, "Where? Sit down," Matt said, and then I looked down and there was a huge bug digging its way into the palm of my hand.

"My God, get it out!" I screamed.

"Get what out?" Matt cried. I went to the sink and grabbed a carving knife and stuck it straight into the palm of my hand, trying to cut the bug out.

Blood flew everywhere, and Matt was screaming at me to "put the knife down now, Isabella!" He grabbed the knife and threw it to the floor. "God!" he said, as he grabbed my hand and wrapped it in a hand towel. "Come on, sit down, let's see how bad it is," Matt said.

"Is the bug out?" I screamed.

"Yes, honey, you cut it out. Isabella, you are going to need stitches. I am going to bring the car around and let's get you some help," Matt said. I sat in the kitchen chair waiting on him to come get me. Matt came and helped me to the car. On the way to the hospital, my hand began to bleed and really hurt. "Isabella," Matt asked, "why do you keep hurting yourself?"

"Matt!" I cried, "I saw a bug digging into my hand. It's real. Look in the sink and you will see where I cut the damn thing out," I yelled. "Oh!" I said. "I get it; you don't believe me, do you?"

Matt yelled back, "It isn't I don't believe, Isabella, it's just I don't see the things that you see."

"Damn it!" I screamed, "I wouldn't hurt myself for no reason." I began to just cry and then I screamed, "Let me out of the car." I tried to get out of the car.

"Isabella, what the hell are you doing? You are bleeding badly!" He grabbed me and pulled me back in. "Calm down," he said. Breathing heavily, he said, "just sit still and calm down. I believe that you really do see and hear the things you say," Matt said.

"You aren't just saying that, are you Matt?" I asked.

"No, honey, I really do believe you," he said.

I went back into the emergency room, and the doctor stitched up my hand. I was in a lot of pain. They gave me a shot, and it must have knocked me out. The next morning I woke up, and I was in this hospital I had never seen before. I was in a room by myself, and when I tried to open the door, it was locked. I found the call bell and began to ring it. A nurse came on and said, "What is it you need?"

"Need?" I screamed, "I need to know where I am at, and where is my boyfriend?"

"Calm down," she said. "I will be right there." Finally this fat, old lady called a nurse came in. God, she was dirty and crude as could be. "You are here because you are a danger to yourself," she said.

"Really?" I replied, "and who in the hell has made this decision for me?"

"Your parents, my dear, have requested you stay here for a while." Then she walked out and slammed the door, and I could hear her lock the door beside her.

I began to scream, "Let me out of here." I screamed and screamed until I hardly had a voice left. The next morning, two nurses came in and gave me three shots. I screamed and fought as hard against them as I could. I got dizzy and passed out. This is where I had no control over my body anymore. More pills, more shot for weeks and weeks. This was a nutty, dirty hospital and to top it all, I never even knew where I was. No one came to see about me. I would ask to make a phone call, and they refused. One day they let me out for a day program, and I acted like I was interested and started to follow someone else out the door. They grabbed me, and I bit one of the nurses. The next thing I knew, I was in a straitjacket. Damn, I thought, what in the world is going on, where is Matt? They put me in a chair and finally let me out of the jacket. By this time, I was so doped up, I couldn't move a muscle in my body. One lady sitting at the lunch table had her head in her food. She had slobber running down her mouth. The nurse came by and grabbed her hair and lifted her up and then just shoved her face right into the food. "Gee!" I said, "help that lady. Food is in her hair, and she is so medicated that she can't even eat," I yelled. Women were walking around with shit on their pants, half dressed, and those damn nurses just walked right by them without helping. The next morning, I was taken into a dim office. As I walked into the room, I saw an old, gray-haired man sitting behind a large desk. It smelled old and dirty to me.

"I am Dr. Orr," the man said. I just sat down in the chair in front of him. "I hear that you are giving our staff some trouble, young lady," he said.

"I don't know what you mean." I replied.

"I think you do; trouble isn't something we put up with around here. If you want to go home, you need to follow the program. Do you understand?" he asked.

"Yes," I said. "By the way, when can I go home?" I asked.

"Soon," he said, "if you follow up with your treatment."

"I will," I said. He told me thank you and good luck. Time went on, and I still didn't get to go home. I don't know what they were giving me because I began to get physically sick. I lost weight and was beginning to look like a skeleton. My eyes hurt really badly, and when I looked into the mirror, they were red. I began to feel more paranoid. I thought they were trying to poison me. All this puzzled me. What kind of hospital is this place? A place from hell. I got to where I couldn't get out of bed.

One day finally, after months and months of being in this hospital, Matt came to see me. I saw a figure in the doorway, but I could barely make out the image of who it was. Finally, I called out, "Matt is that you?" I cried.

"Yes," he said.

I sat up straight up in the bed crying. "My God, it is you. Where have you been?"

He walked over to the bed and sat down and put his arms around me. "My God, honey, what has happened to you? You are bruised all over, and you are so thin, and you look like you are so sick," Matt said.

"I am sick," I replied with a weak voice. "Why haven't you come to see me?" I asked.

"Your mother fixed it so that you couldn't have any visitors."

"Why?" I asked.

"I don't know, honey. I had to get an attorney to get to see you," Matt said.

"Can you take me home?"

"Yes, I can. That is why I hired an attorney, to override your mother. We are going to get married soon, so your mother can never do this thing to you again." Matt smiled.

Matt helped me get my things together and signed me out. "So this is what a mental hospital is about?" Matt asked. "I wouldn't put my dog in this damn place."

I replied, "This is the crudest place I have even been. The way they treat people is inhumane." We checked out and Matt took me home.

One of the nurses said, "I wouldn't advise you to take her home this early."

"Five months is early?" Matt asked. The nurse just unlocked the door and let us out.

On the way home, Matt explained to me that he had no control over the situation at the hospital that night. "I was worried and called your parents. I had no idea your mother was going to send you to that terrible place," Matt explained.

"It's OK," I told Matt. "I just thank God I am out of that crazy place."

Soon my parents heard that Matt had gotten me out of that hospital. My father and Sky came to see me. My mother refused to come. She said I was still sick and she was afraid of me. In a nutshell she just was mad that Matt got me out. They left to go home, and Matt sat down to talk to me. "Isabella, let's face it. You do have something wrong with you, and we need to find someone who knows what they are doing to treat you. I know you can have some kind of quality of life even with this illness you have. People every day have this, but honey, you have to take whatever medicine they give you. Now I don't want you overdosed, but at least so you won't see things or hear that voice. OK?" he asked. "Will you please do this for me, for us?"

I told Matt that I would if I could return to see Dr. Belmont. "He makes me feel safe, and I think he really cares for his patients," I said. Matt agreed that was fine as long as I agreed to see someone.

The following week, I went to see Dr Belmont. I asked him questions about the hospital I was in. "Child," he said, "you shouldn't have been sent there, but a lot of folks like yourself are sent there." We talked about my treatment and how I could get my life back. I trusted him, and believe me, I didn't trust a lot of people. He gave me scripts to fill, and I promised him I would take them. I was to see him every two weeks for a while. For the first time in a very long time, I had hopes and thought just maybe I could make it with my doctor's help.

Weeks went by and I took my medicine and went to the doctor. I even got a part-time job at a department store, selling cosmetics. I loved my job, and I could actually be around people again without fear of them staring at me. I was beginning to reach a quality of life that I had dreamed of since I was a child. Matt was so proud of me, and we started to plan our wedding. Matt bought us a new house, and he let me decorate it. I loved fresh flowers, and he let me do each room with flower prints. We planned to marry in the spring of the year if my health was still improving.

Finally the spring came, and Matt and I were to be married. I picked out this beautiful grown, and the bridesmaids were to be in pink. Pink was my favorite color. The day came, and it was warm and such a nice day; we were getting married outdoors. My parents came, but mother and I still had bad feelings toward each other. What a beautiful wedding we had. We said our vows and we were so in love. After that, we went away to the beach for a week. We were going to move straight into our new house when we returned. The voice had gone away, and I didn't see things anymore. The medicine was working, and I was so happy. After a week, we came home, and Matt had to go back to work. I took another week off to get the house in order.

One day when I was home alone fixing up the house, the doorbell rang. I ran to the door thinking Matt was playing a trick on me, and lo and behold, it was my mother. I just stood there in shock. "Well, Isabella," she said, "aren't you going to invite your mother in?"

I stepped back and said, "Yes, come on in." She walked over to the couch and made herself at home. "Well, Mother, can I get you some iced tea?" I asked politely.

"No!" she said sharply. "Come here, I have something important to tell you. Isabella, do you remember your aunt Jessie?" she asked. I thought for minute, but I hadn't heard her name in years.

"Yes, I do," I replied. "Why, Mother? Why are you bringing her name up after all these years?" I questioned her.

"Well, Isabella," Mother began, "Jessie is in a hospital up north somewhere. I lost contact with her years ago. I just can't bear to accept this illness she has."

"What illness is that, Mother?" I asked.

"Dear, the psychiatrist said she suffers from the same illness you do. She heard those voices and saw things just like you do, Isabella," Mother continued.

"Why now, Mother, are you telling me this after you let me suffer all these years? You knew what was wrong with me?" I screamed.

"I was afraid to tell you because I never even told your father about Jessie being sick," she said.

"Why are you so ashamed of this, Mother? Someone can have cancer or any health issue illness, and everyone feels sorry for them, but someone with a mental illness is looked down on and labeled just plain out crazy," I yelled.

Mother put her hands over her face and began to cry. "I should have told, Isabella," Mother admitted.

"Yes!" I yelled at her. "You certainly should have. Mother, you really have no idea how I have suffered all these years," I told her. She just sat there and cried like a baby. "Mother," I said, "it's OK."

"No, Isabella, it's not OK. You are married now," Mother said.

I asked her, "What in the world does me being married have to do with this?"

"Because you may have a child, and Isabella, your child may have the same thing you do," she said.

"No, Mother, I will never have any children and take a chance on them having this awful disease," I said firmly. Mother left that day, and she was sad from then on. I think finally she accepted what I had and blamed herself for it because it was from her side of the family. My mother was never the same after we had that talk.

Matt and I had been married for two years now, and I was still in good shape. Then one day I got some really bad news. I had gone to see Dr. Belmont, and he told me he was leaving; he wanted to move closer to his children. I was so sad. "Don't worry, dear, the new doctor is really good and will take really good care of all my patients."

"Dr. Belmont," I said, "I trust you and I depend on your knowledge. You have made me normal again."

"No, Isabella," he said, "you have made yourself normal. I was just there to show you the way." My best friend, my doctor, someone I loved in a very special way was leaving me. I knew it was right to wish him the best, but God how I would miss him. I just hoped the new doctor was as good as Dr. Belmont said he was. ....
....

The next week I went in to see the new doctor; he was quite different from my old doctor. I listened to him and really tried to trust him. My heart was hurting for the man that helped me when no one else could. Matt kept telling me to give him a chance. So I did, and I was still doing good, and my mother still stayed away from me. She would call me from time to time. I could hear the sadness in her voice.

Matt started to work late at night, and I was getting lonely. I would call Jill and ask her to come over. Sometimes she would call me and ask why Matt was working late all the time. "Well," I replied, "we have two car payments and a house payment, and I really don't work that much." She would get me thinking: what if Matt has a girlfriend? And then I would think no, he loves me, he has stuck with me all this time, he has to love me. I would say something to him, what Jill said, and he would laugh.

"Jill hasn't anything else to do but try to cause trouble. Really, Isabella, you need to pick a new friend," Matt would answer and laugh off my questions.

One day at work I started to get headaches again, and they hurt so bad. My brain felt like it was going to jump right out of my skull. I was taking my medicine, and I didn't understand why these headaches were coming back. I went back to the doctor, and he said I might be under a lot of stress, which was causing headaches. Maybe

Dr. Belmont leaving might have stressed me out. He gave me some new medicine for my headaches. I took it and it seemed to help, but I felt myself slipping back somehow.

I tried to pretend everything was OK, but I could feel myself getting sick again. When I was around people, I felt like they could read my mind. Even sometimes when I was watching TV. I would feel like it was controlling my thoughts, and I was causing things to go wrong in the world. I felt tense and afraid, and I didn't want to put Matt through anymore than I already had. He was working later and later all the time. Honestly, I would think he was trying to stay away from me. Maybe really he just couldn't stand the pressure.

One night we were sitting eating dinner and Matt asked if I was feeling OK. I told him I was just tired. I got up and cleared the table. I walked slowly into the kitchen as if I was in a daze. I started to wash the dishes, and taking the dishcloth I was cleaning every dish. I picked up a knife out of the water, and before I knew it, I cut both my wrists. It was as if I couldn't feel the blade go through my skin. I just kept washing the dishes, blood filling up in the dishwater. I started to sing a little song, and I was in no pain at all. Matt came over behind me and put his arms around me, kissing on my neck. He must have looked down and seen the blood in the sink. "Isabella, is that blood all in the sink?" Then he pulled my hands out of the water and saw I had cut my wrists. He screamed at me, "God, what have you done to yourself, Isabella?" I was bleeding so bad that he had to call 911. He wrapped my wrists and put pressure on my cuts. We waited for the ambulance to come to take me to hospital. Matt followed the ambulance to the hospital. I was tired and was in a different world. This time the voice didn't tell me to harm myself. I just did it without any reason.

Finally, we got to the hospital, and they took me back, taking my blood pressure and temperature. The doctor walked back and looked at my cuts and said to me, "This is a pretty deep cut. Were you trying to kill yourself?"

I laughed and said, "No, of course not. If I wanted to kill myself, I would have. I really don't know why I did it, and it really doesn't even hurt," I said.

"Isabella, this has to hurt," he said.

"No, doctor, it doesn't," I replied.

He looked at me strangely and said, "Let's get you stitched up."

I really didn't feel any pain that night. It was the next day before I felt any pain, and I didn't remember doing it. I went back to see Dr. Belmont's replacement, and he talked with me about what happened to me. "Are you taking all of your medication?" he asked me.

"Well," I replied, "at times I do, and then sometimes I just hate swallowing those damn pills."

"Isabella, if you want to get better, you are going to have to take your medication, or you will live in pain and probably someday have to live in a hospital," the doctor said. That really scared me, so I promised I would take all my medicine. This illness was starting to affect the way I looked and acted, so I decided it was enough. Fat or not, that was better than people labeling you crazy.

I got up every morning and took my medicine, and every night I was beginning to feel a lot better. However, Matt was changing. He began becoming distant and stayed at work a lot. Then he got a nurse to stay with me, and he started to take business trips. I hated this and pleaded with him to stay home. "I can't, Isabella," he would say, "we have all these medical bills, and your medicine is so expensive." I felt so guilty that he was working so hard because of me. So for me it was a pill a day to keep the demons away, whatever it took. Hell, I just wanted to live a life like all my friends and get my husband back home again. One morning I was looking at myself in the mirror, and God, what a mess I was. I had done so much to myself over the years. The self-mutilation had left scars everywhere; it's a wonder Matt wanted to stay with me. My mother would say, "My poor daughter, I can hardly recognize her." I always thought she was being mean, but I guess she was right. I did look really bad, and I just didn't realize it at the time. For the next few months I took my medicine and did everything the doctor told me to do. I still felt dizzy and just not the way I had felt the weeks before. The doctor ordered blood tests on me. His office called me one day and asked me to come in for appointment. When I got there, the doctor came in and looked at me really seriously.

"Isabella," he said, "I thought you told me you were taking your medicine." The doctor looked annoyed.

"I am," I said loudly.

Looking at me suspiciously, the doctor said, "Your medicine isn't in the blood work."

"That can't be," I replied. "I have been taking my medicine. I know I am not that crazy," I said. The doctor said he would do blood work in two weeks and see how I was then. "OK," I agreed, still puzzled about the medicine. I got home and went upstairs to the medicine cabinet and looked at my medicine. I know I am taking this, why isn't it in my bloodstream, I thought. I was trying to figure out all this craziness, so I called my friend Jill and told her about it.

"Well," she said to me on the phone, "you know sometimes, sweetie, you don't remember things. Just maybe you just thought you were taking your medicine." After I hung up, I thought yes, I guess that could be possible. I have done things in the past like that. So after that, I just tried to make sure that I took all my medicine.

The next week I got worse. I started to hear the voice again and see things. I would be talking to myself, and Matt would hear me and ask, "Did you say something, honey?"

"No," I said and walked off so he wouldn't hear me argue with someone who wasn't there. One night I woke up and I was pinching myself till I was bruised really badly. I wore long sleeves for a week until the bruising went away. I just kept getting worse, and then when I went to the doctor, to my surprise the blood work showed no medicine in my system again. Lord, I thought, I am going crazy again. The nurse Matt ordered to stay with me now was ordered to give me my medicine.

That was so strange; when the nurse gave it to me, I got better. I know I was taking the same dose that she gave me. Jill would come over, and she and I would go out shopping. She often would say, "When is Matt coming home? He stays away a lot. Doesn't that bother you, Isabella?"

I would always reply, "Matt does what he has to do for us. I trust him, if that is what you mean, Jill."

"Oh, no, now I didn't mean to imply anything like that, Isabella." Jill said. We continued to shop to get all the good buys we could. I thought at that time Jill was my best friend ever. We went through school together, and I thought I could tell her anything in the world. She knew about my illness and stuck with me through the years.

The doctor was thrilled with my improvement. "You did it, Isabella, you are doing great!" the doctor said happily. I was so excited I called my father and told him the good news.

"Oh that's great, honey," he said. "Do you want to tell your mother?"

"No dad," I said. "You tell her and Sky for me."

When Matt got home, he was so happy he picked me up and swung me around and around. "I love you," he said, "that's my girl." Matt laughed.

The next few weeks I started to exercise and starting taking care of myself. I went and got a tattoo to cover some scars on my legs. I let my hair grow out and covered some of my scars with makeup. I was starting to look not as good as before this happened but better than I did a few months ago. Jill often would tell me the tattoo looked tacky or make me second-guess myself. But I did what I had to do for me. She started to tell me things other people were saying about me. I would cry, and she would say, "Oh well, who cares what they say." I would get hurt so easily. I was ashamed of this illness and things I had done.

One morning I started to get sick and thought I was going to die. Then I realized I had skipped my period. I went to the doctor and found out I was going to have a baby. At first I was so happy; then I realized that my child could have the same illness that I have. I told Matt about the baby, and he was thrilled. "Matt," I said, "what if this child has all this crazy stuff I do?"

"Isabella, it's our child, no matter what. If God didn't want us to have a child, you would not have gotten pregnant." Matt sounded sincere. I decided Matt was right; we just couldn't worry about this at this time. I was worried about a lot of things, so I started to read up on everything I could get my hands on.

I told Jill about this, and she seemed to be happy for me. Now my parents were a different story. They said that it was a bad idea, but what was done was done and to make sure I see a doctor for everything physical and mental. But I know my dad deep down inside was happy. Sky always loved me and said he just wanted me to be happy; whatever it took, he was there for me. Matt and I talked about our plans for our child. I explained to him how my mother never believed me when I told her about the voices and seeing things. I told him if the doctor had known, he could have helped me before my illness got out of hand. I asked him to please promise if our child acts sick in any way to watch for it and believe him or her if she tells you something strange. Matt told me he would, but he thought I was just worried over nothing. Time went by, and I made sure I took all my medicine. And I was fine. I felt a little tired, but I did better than I expected. I got really fat and gained a lot of weight. The doctor said the baby was fine, and I started a nursery for our child. Those were some of the best memories I have of us back then. Matt and I were so in love, and we were so happy over having our own child. My mother actually started to call me and come see me.

She was very hard on me as a child, but I understand she was afraid to face the truth. Truth for me is the only thing that keeps me sane. Matt's mother was so good to me. She was forever bringing me food and clothes for the baby. Matt still had to work lots of hours and take lots of trips. I pleaded with him after the baby was born to please let the nurse go and trust me. I would never hurt my own child, I told him. "I know you wouldn't," he would say. "It's just what if you forget to take your medication and start to get sick again?"

"For heaven's sake," I told him, "I wouldn't do that with my child in the house."

He kissed me and said, "We will see; I'll think about."

"OK," I said and started up the stairs. "I am going to go read baby books," I said.

"Well, good night, Isabella. I will be up when I finish my business calls," Matt said. I fell asleep waiting on him. The next day, he left for another trip, and I was left with a nurse in the house I really didn't need. Jill called me the next day and asked me if I wanted to go for lunch. I told her that would be fine.

"You know, Isabella," Jill told me, "people in this town are talking about you having this illness and now you are going to pass it to your child." I looked at her. Why would she tell me this, knowing that I think people are talking about me as it is?

"Wait just a minute," I said to her. "The doctor told Matt and I our baby has a good chance of not having this illness."

Jill smirked and said, "Well, I guess you will see."

"I am leaving," I said and threw twenty dollars on the table, grabbed my purse, and left.

On the way home, I started to cry. Why are people so cruel and try to hurt people? What if this had happened to them; then they might not be so quick to judge? No one knows you hurt inside for being different and feel like you are so evil for this illness. God, I said, what the hell is wrong with Jill. I thought she was my friend. I guess I really don't have any friends in this world except my husband. I felt so bad for days, but I thought no, I will not let anyone ruin this for Matt and me. I have been through so much and put Matt through so much; we deserve this child. I don't care what anyone has to say.

One afternoon I called Jill to talk to her. After we had the fight, maybe I was too hard on her, I thought. When I called her, Jack told me she had gone out town with a friend. "Oh really," I said, "when will she be back?"

"Friday, I think," Jack said. I hung up the phone, thinking whom does she know to go out of town with. Then walking up the stairs, I thought, Friday, that is when Matt would be back too. That's strange, I thought. Oh well, I was being silly, and I trusted him. Later on that night, I called Jack back. "Jack," I said, "I hate to bother you, but who did Jill goes out of town with?"

"Kristy. You know Kristy, Isabella, the cheerleader you and her were friends with."

I laughed softly and said, "Oh, yes, I remember. I didn't think Kristy and her kept in touch anymore."

"To tell you the truth, Isabella," Jack said, "that woman drives me crazy. I could really use a break from her time to time," he said laughing.

"Well I'll let you go, Jack."

"It was nice talking to you," he said. "Oh, by the way, congratulations on your baby." We said good-bye and I hung up.

Well, I thought, I guess I am just overreacting. After all, I just look like the Goodyear blimp. I really enjoyed being pregnant, even though I was sick. I loved the idea of a baby being around the house: something special that Matt and I brought into the world together. I often worried about my baby having my illness, but I couldn't stand to think of it. I just prayed that God would spare my child from this illness. I started to decorate the nursery and loved every minute of it.

One day I was going shopping for things for the crib, and I asked Jill to come with me. She apologized and said she had other plans. So I just decided to go anyway. I was a big girl; I didn't need anyone around to shop. I would have just liked the company. When I was passing by a little coffee shop, I gazed in the window. I thought I saw Matt sitting there with Jill. My heart started to race, and I could feel the blood run through my veins. I walked in past the group, and there sat Matt by himself. "Hey there," I said, out of breath.

Matt looked at me with surprise in his eyes. "Hey honey," he said, getting up and kissing me on the check. "What are you doing here?"

"Well," I said. "I could ask you the same question."

He laughed and said, "Coffee. A coffee shop is where one gets coffee."

"I know that," I said, "but this isn't your lunch break."

"Isabella, what is the big deal here?" Matt asked.

I paused and took a deep breath. "I thought I saw Jill sitting here with you."

"Jill for heaven's sake? Isabella, are you getting delusions again?" he asked.

"No," I said madly. "I could have sworn I saw her right here sitting with you."

"Well now, honey, you can certainly see I am by myself, can't you? Just relax, and I will order you something."

"No," I said, "that's all right. I really don't want anything, just dropped in to say hello and that I love you."

"I love you too, dear, with all my heart," he said, kissing me goodbye. I still was puzzled. I walked out of the coffee shop thinking I hope I really didn't see them together. If they were, where did Jill go so fast? My mind may have been playing tricks on me again.

The next Monday was my appointment with Dr. Orr about my medicine for my illness. I had to be careful with taking the right thing because of the baby. I mentioned to the doctor about my husband and best friend and questioned whether or not I was getting sick again. We talked for about thirty minutes, and he told me, "Isabella, you seem fine, and I haven't seen any sign of partied thoughts today. Maybe you saw someone else that reminded you of your husband and friend."

I thought about it for a minute and said, "Yes, that's probably it." I said, "Well, 'bye." After making another appointment, I left. I still couldn't shake the feeling of something bad happening. No one wants to believe their husband and their best friend would be together. I have been so sick for so long. God, please, I thought, don't let me slide back. No one in this world understands the strange things I have experienced, even as a young child. The voice that haunted me night and day. The damn thing seemed like a demon to me. The things I saw and the way I acted, the way I hurt myself time and time again, not realizing it until it was over. The way people looked at me and acted toward me. I just can't bear anymore, and to start seeing things that aren't there is just too much for me at this time in my life. I wanted to live my life, what was left of it, with my husband and baby in peace. I was excited about this child, and I was going to have a normal life and give it a good mother. I never wanted much in life but to be happy, and I always loved life and loved my parents and my brother, Sky. I was a good kid until all these crazy things started to happen around me. What is mental illness? Isn't it almost the same as being possessed by a demon? I really could debate whether mental illness is a brain disorder or demon worse of the two you tell me.

All I know is your life is taken from you, and you are put in a state of mind that it is so hard to return to reality. I hope I can stay sane for my child's sake. I want to be there for my baby. I know I always thought my mother was against me, and I always felt like she was ashamed of me because of this craziness I put her and my dad through.

Well, I just have to stay positive in every way I can, I thought. I have a beautiful girl or boy coming soon. Thank God for that, and this thought kept me going. My mother came over to see the nursery one afternoon, and she and I started to talk about the baby. She said to me, "Isabella, I do love you so, but I just didn't want to face that you had the same illness Jessie did. I wanted you to be normal, and I thought if I just pretended it was going to be OK, it would. But life just isn't fair," she said. "When you were born, Isabella, that was the happiest day of my life. I always wanted a girl. One reason was I had four brothers, and I was the only girl. I hated being the only girl in the family. I used to comb your long, blonde hair, and everywhere we would go, there wasn't anyone that wouldn't stop and tell me how beautiful you were." I began to cry because all these years I thought my mother hated me. And to tell you the truth, I loved her but really had some hard feelings toward her. Now after all these years, the truth comes out: My mother was haunted by these demons as much as I was. She just didn't know how to handle things.

We talked a lot that day, and for the first time in years, I got to know my mother. I still wanted to be close to my child and never have the lost time that my mother and I had. Some days for me were better than others. Some days I would get so depressed, especially when Matt would have to go on business trips. God, I hated that, being alone in that great big old house by myself. I would try to do things to keep my mind off him. Being pregnant was bad enough, and trying to stay sane was even harder for me. My brother, Sky, would come over sometimes, and we would go out to eat or go to the movies. Bless his heart, he had his own life and was trying to babysit his baby sister.

Whisper

One night when Matt came home, I asked him if he would quit traveling and stay home with me. He got really mad at me and yelled out, "What am I to do, Isabella? We have doctor bills coming out our ass and medicine that costs hundreds of dollars. How are we going to make it: car payment, house payment, and you want me to quit my job?" he yelled.

I started to shake, and my lips trembled. "No, not quite, just stay home, work here," I said.

"Isabella," he said. "I've told you over and over the company pays me more to travel and fix other companies' accounts."

"What about the baby?" I cried out.

Throwing his hands in the air, Matt said, "What do you want me to do, Isabella? You aren't able to work, and I have to pay the mortgage on the house. I really want to be here with you more. Baby, my heart is with you, always has been, since the day we met. I would love not to travel. I don't like leaving you alone; God, baby, I don't," he said, hanging his head down. Right then he made me feel so selfish. What really did I expect? Matt really did have all the bills on him. I hugged him and told him I was sorry. He kissed me on the neck and said, "That's OK, baby, I know it's hard; it's really hard on both of us."

The next few weeks I started to feel funny again, just like I had no feeling in my body; I felt limp and had no energy again. I went to have a checkup for the baby. I mentioned to the doctor that I had no energy and I felt dumb. "What do you mean by that?" he asked. "Give me an example of how you feel."

"Well," I said, "it's like when I get into the bathtub, I don't feel whether the water is hot. I will get out and then feel the burning sensation. I can cut myself shaving my legs, and it doesn't hurt. I will see where I have cut myself, and yet it's like I can't feel pain."

The doctor pulled on his beard. "Well, that is interesting. We will run some tests and try to find out what is going on. The baby, Isabella, is fine and growing like it should be, and everything else checks out. Come in tomorrow, and we will run some tests, but really I don't think it's anything to worry about right now," the doctor told me.

The next day I went in, and they ran tests on me all day. I was poked and tested until I was so tired. I went home and had to wait on whatever it might be. Finally the following Friday, the doctor called me. He told me that all my tests were normal, and there wasn't anything wrong. "Well," I said, "thank you." I hung the phone up and thought, I wonder what this can be. I told Matt about it, and he told me I was just worrying too much. That I needed to relax and try not to borrow problems, that we had enough without any extra ones.

The next few months, I could see Matt changing right before my eyes. He became more hateful and short with me. He had no patience at all anymore. He would complain about what I cooked; it was too done or not enough. It needed more salt, less pepper. God, he was getting awful. I got mad one night. He was complaining there were no vegetables, so I said, "You want vegetables? Here they are," and threw a bag of frozen peas on the table.

"Look," he said, "Isabella, I have had enough of this behavior," and he shook me.

I cried and said, "Let me go. You are hurting me." Then he called me a stupid bitch. I turned around and said, "What did you say to me?"

"Nothing," he said, turning his back to me.

"Listen," I said, "Matt, be a man. If you are going to call me a name, at least admit it." He just went to the wet bar and poured himself a drink. I got so mad I went upstairs and started to cry. The only person that has stuck with me through everything is now turning his back on me, I thought. I cried myself to sleep that night.

The next morning I woke up and looked around, and Matt hadn't even come to bed. I went downstairs looking for him. He was nowhere to be found, and his briefcase was gone, so I assume he just left without saying good-bye or that he was sorry. I was beside myself; I didn't know what to do. I tried his cell phone, but he wouldn't answer, so I left him a message. I called my friend Jill and talked to her. "What are you doing?" I asked.

"Oh, just cleaning up after Jack," she said. "He had some of his drinking buddies over, and they trashed the place."

"That's too bad," I said.

"Well," she said, "I am used to it. All Jack does is drink. I wish I had never married him."

"Jill, it can't be that bad."

"Listen, Isabella, you just don't know. You are married to someone with class who buys you anything you want. You don't work, you drive a very nice car. For heaven's sake, Isabella, you have a beautiful house, and your husband is sweet, good-looking, shall I go on?" she said. "I live like a poor church mouse and work nights to make ends meet, and Jack drinks up his check."

"Really," I said, "I had no idea you had all these problems."

"Yes, Isabella, and you think you have problems," she said. "Isabella," she said after a pause, "I am sorry. I didn't mean to unload on you."

"That's all right," I said. "Everyone needs someone to talk to now and then."

"Well, anyway, what did you call about, Isabella?"

"Oh," I said, "I just wanted to see if you wanted to go out and get some lunch today. My treat," I said.

"Well, I guess I could do that," she said.

"Where do you want to go?" I asked.

"Oh, anywhere is fine with me. You pick since you are paying," she said.

"How about the coffeehouse on Main?" I said. They have great tuna sandwiches."

"OK," she said, "I will met you there." I got ready to go for lunch still feeling bad about the fight Matt and I had. I was going to talk to Jill about it, but after what she told me, I didn't want to worry her with my problems.

I got to the coffeehouse, and there sat Jill at a booth. "Is this all right?" she said.

"Sure," I said and sat down. "Wait a minute," I said. "We need a nonsmoking area.

"All right," she said as if that made her mad. "Really, Isabella, you can be a pain sometimes."

"Jill, you know I don't smoke, and it's not good for the baby," I said.

"The baby isn't here yet, Isabella," she said.

I just smiled and said, "Let's get the waitress's attention. Wave to her, Jill." Jill waved to the waitress and she came over. "We would like to order now," I said. "We know what we want."

The waitress looked at Jill as if she knew her. "Do you want you and your boyfriend usually order when you guys come in?" she asked.

Jill looked at her real mean and said, "Really, I don't know what you are talking about. You must have me mixed up with someone else."

The waitress just looked starrier and said, "Well, I am very sorry, it's just you look like the woman who always comes in on Tuesdays with her boyfriend or husband. I never asked if they were married."

"Listen," Jill said getting really mad, "you have me mixed up, so please just take our order. Now would be nice," Jill said. The waitress took our order and left.

"What was all that about?" I asked.

"God, Isabella, are you deaf? Didn't you hear me tell her she was mistaken?" asked Jill.

"Yes," I replied, "but she sure thought it was you."

"Well," Jill said drinking some of her drink, "they say we all have a twin. Maybe she saw my twin." We sat and talked about the colors for the nursery and about a baby shower. Jill told me she was going to help my mother with it. I told her that was sweet of her. Jill finally mentioned Matt. "How is he doing these days?" she asked.

"He's fine," I said, and then I changed the subject and we finished our lunch. I got the bill and laid down three dollars. Jill reached down on the table and put the three dollars on anther table. I grabbed her arm and said, "What are you doing? That was for our waitress."

"Well, Isabella, our waitress, as you call her, is a bitch."

I was so embarrassed and walked out of the coffee shop. Jill came out and said, "See you later, Isabella. Call me tomorrow, and we will talk about the baby shower," she said.

I drove home thinking how strange Jill was acting lately. I really hated to hear about Jack having a drinking problem; I never even knew he drank.

I went home and lay on the coach. I dozed off, drifting in and of sleep. When I woke up, it was dark in the house. Must be close to five, I thought. I got up and started to turn the lights on when I heard the door open. "Is that you, Matt?" I called out.

"Yes," he said, "It's me, Isabella." He came over to the coach and told me he was sorry for talking to me that way, and he was in the wrong.

"I am sorry too," I said.

We hugged each other; then Matt said, "Get dressed, and I will take you out for dinner."

"Don't like my cooking?" I said, joking.

"Yes, baby, I love your cooking. I just want to do something special for you to make up for being such an ass."

I smiled and said, "OK, I will be right back."

When I came back downstairs, I could hear Matt talking softly on the phone. I heard him say, "Now isn't the time. I will call you later."

I poked my head in the kitchen and said, "Is that your girlfriend?" kidding with him.

"No, baby," he said. "I have only one girlfriend, and believe me, she is more than I can handle." We went out to a really nice restaurant, and Matt was so sweet to me. We talked a lot about the baby on the way home. We were so happy at this time in our lives. When we got home, Matt said he had some work to do and he would be up later. I went up and took my bath and got ready for bed. I finished and went downstairs to tell Matt good night. We didn't make love anymore because I was so big and felt so bad, but I still wanted my kiss at night. Matt was very understanding and said he would wait for me. As I went downstairs, I saw Matt with his head bent over his desk.

"Honey, are you all right?" I asked.

Lifting his head, he answered, "Yes, honey, I am. I was just resting for a minute."

I walked over to him and hugged him, and then I asked him, "Matt, do you know Jack has a drinking problem?"

"What?" Matt said. "Jack Jones?"

"Yes," I said. "Jill and I had lunch the other day, and she mentioned Jack was drinking a lot."

"No, I don't believe that," Matt said.

"Why would Jill say he did then?"

"Just stay out of their business," Matt said.

"I am going on to bed," I said.

"Good night, Isabella," Matt said.

Matt left again the next weekend, and I was so unhappy and felt so lonely. I knew that I couldn't do anything about it, because we did have a lot of bills. I knew poor Matt was doing all he could. It was getting closer and closer to me giving birth to our child. Matt called me every night to check up on me, and he had the nurse to come stay with me while he was gone. One day I came home from a walk and going upstairs, I could smell smoke. I sniffed as I walked into my bedroom. "Mrs. Smith," I called out, "come here."

The nurse walked upstairs into my bedroom. "What is it?" she asked.

"Do you smell that?" I asked.

"Smell what?" she asked.

"Smoke," I said loudly.

She sniffed and said, "Yes, I do."

"Who has been smoking up here?"

"I don't know," she said. "No one has been here, so I just don't know." I looked, and my book I had on my bed was missing.

"Now look," I said. "I know I am not crazy. My book is missing, and smoke is in the bedroom."

The nurse looked at me and said, "I swear to you, not a soul has entered this house. If they did, it was when I was cooking in the kitchen, and they would have had to have a key." I told her I believed her and not to worry about it but just keep an eye on the house.

Whisper

The next week strange things began to happen. The doorbell would ring, and I would go to the door, and no one was there. I would call Jill, and she would tell me I was hearing things and I was just tired. God, I hated that. Since I have this illness, whenever something happens, everyone thinks I am hearing things and seeing things. But honest, I was better. The whole time I carried my baby I was in the best frame of mind that I had been since I came down with my illness. Still in the back of my mind, I felt that Matt wasn't happy with me anymore. He talked sweet and was treating me better than before, yet something was missing. I only hoped when the baby was born, things would return to normal for us.

Finally the night of my baby shower came. My sister-in-law Tammy came to pick me up. I was thrilled. I knew soon my baby would be here. I guess over fifty people came, family and friends. My mother had everything done up so pretty, and the cake was just beautiful; it had pink and blue icing. She laughed and said it was for girl or boy, and I just loved it. Most everyone there was so nice to me. Some of my family I hadn't seen for a while were nosy. I guess that was to be expected. I walked into the kitchen, and Jill was on the phone. She said real fast, "Got to go, love ya."

"Don't hang up because of me," I said.

"I was hanging up anyway," Jill said.

"You and Jack getting alone better now?" I asked.

"Who?" Jill said.

"Jack," I replied, "your husband."

"Oh yes," Jill replied, "yes, we are getting along great nowadays." I threw away some paper, and Jill said, "Come on down, you are the guest of honor, no work for you. Come sit down." I went back and sat down and talked to all the guests.

Finally the party was over. I thanked everyone and was so tired. My mother kept asking, "You OK, dear?"

"Yes, I am fine, just tired," I said.

Tammy said, "Come on, Isabella, let's get you home to rest. You look like you could have that baby anytime.

I said to Tammy, "I think you are right. I feel like I could have the baby anytime."

The next few weeks were hard. I had to roll myself out of the bed and roll myself in the bed. I felt like I couldn't go on this way much longer. My skin looked like it was paper-thin, and all the veins in my stomach were dark blue. I was ready to have this child. I was going to strangle that doctor if I didn't go into labor soon. I waddled around the house for weeks. I ate everything that wasn't nailed down, and when Jill came to see me, she would say, "You need to slow down, Isabella, you are going to have a hard labor."

"Mind your own business," I would tell her.

She would laugh and say, "OK, you will be sorry." I thought at that time she had my best interests in mind. Whenever Matt came home, he would say I looked beautiful and not to worry, it would be all over soon.

Matt went with me to my psychiatrist one day and sat in on our session. He wanted to make sure everything was OK as far as my mental state with what I was going through. Dr. Orr assured him I was fine. "You must remember," Matt said, "Isabella hurt a child when she was younger, thinking bugs were on it."

"Yes," the doctor said, "but Isabella wasn't on medication at that time."

Matt said, "What if she gets, you know,..." he paused looking at me, "sick again?" he asked.

The doctor said, "Listen, I can't tell you Isabella will never get sick again, only she has a better chance if she makes sure she takes her medicine."

"Just one more question," Matt said. "Is the baby going to have this illness?"

Again the doctor replied, "I don't know, maybe not, just have to wait and see. But even if it did, there is medicine that works really good."

Matt got upset and said, "Medicine that works really well, you say? Well, medicine that works really good sure did fail my wife."

"Please," the doctor said, "mental illness is a guessing game. Just make sure Isabella takes her medicine. That way you can be sure your wife will maintain a quality of life." I thanked the doctor and asked him to overlook my husband. He patted my hand and said, "It's OK,

I understand. See you next time, Isabella, and good luck with your baby." I thanked him again and walked out.

Matt had walked out and left me. I got to the car and opened the door. "Thanks, honey, that was really sweet of you to leave me. I can barely walk, and you leave alone and talk to my doctor like you thought I was a real nutcase. Do you really think I would hurt my own child? Matt, you are a fucking asshole to even think I would do something like that."

"Well, Isabella, you hurt a child in the past," he said.

"Yes, I did in the past, and I have never forgotten about it and still to this day feel bad. Matt, why are you bringing all this up now? I am two week away from having our child." Then I started to breathe hard and started to shake. I was really mad at him this time. I don't know if I will ever forgive him, I thought. Asshole, I thought, he was supposed to love me, and now he's digging in my past. As we drove home, I didn't say anything, and neither did he.

I got out of car and slammed the door and went upstairs and locked myself in the bedroom. I could hear Matt walk up the stairs. The door knob twisted. "Come on down, Isabella, let me in."

"No," I said. "Go away."

"I am sorry," he said. "I really was out of line. I just worry about the baby."

"So do I, Matt," I replied.

"Isabella," he said, "let me in. Please don't be mad at me."

"Matt, give me some time to calm down, and then we can talk."

"OK, honey, come down and let's talk when you feel better. I will be downstairs working on some paperwork." I lay on the bed crying and thinking of all the things I had done in the past, but that was the past. Why would Matt of all people keep doing things to hurt me? I cried until I fell asleep. Finally I heard Matt knocking on the door. "Isabella," he said, "let me in." I slowly got off the bed and walked over and unlocked the door. There Matt was with a red rose, smiling at me, sorry.

I just shook my head and said, "It's OK, let's just forget about it." We had a quiet dinner, and I tried not to have hard feelings for him.

I thought if he keeps treating me like this, when I do have the baby, I will take it and go to my mother's the next day. I needed someone to talk to, so I called Jill. "Hey," I said, "could you come over? I don't feel good and need someone to talk to."

"I'll be over in a few minutes," she said. Jill came over, and I got us some iced tea, and we sat down in the kitchen to talk. "What's going on?" she said.

"Jill, Matt is acting so strange. I don't think he trusts me with the baby."

"What makes you think that?" she asked.

"Because he asked the doctor pretty much if he thought it would be safe for me to be alone with our child."

"Isabelle," she said, "not taking up for Matt, but you got to admit over the years you have done a lot of dangerous things to yourself and that one incident with the little boy you babysat."

"I know that," I said, getting mad. "That was a long time ago. Jill, we are talking bout this baby I am carrying. I would never hurt my child."

"Isabella," she said, "calm down. I know you would never hurt your baby. Come get your coat, and let's go walking through the park." I smiled, thinking what a good friend, and we went walking on a fall day. I can remember that day as if it were yesterday. The wind was blowing slightly, and the air was so fresh, and I loved the fall. Walking always helped me when I was stressed out.

While we were walking in the park, I told Jill I loved Matt, but if he keeps on at me when the baby is born, I would take it and live with my parents. "Hell, he wouldn't miss us. He is never home anyway."

Jill just listened and said, "Isabella, I really think you are overreacting. After all, you are just about to give birth."

Jill left, and I went home. I was really tired and emotionally stressed. I really hoped that Matt and I would start getting along better. I talked to my parents, and I asked them if they thought I would be a good mom. They both said they thought I would be. I told my parents if I ever thought I was getting sick, I would leave and go away and leave the baby with them. "What about Matt?" they asked.

"Matt?" I said with anger. "He would never be home enough to take care of a baby."

At home that night I thought a lot about my illness. Would the baby be safe with me? I just knew I loved it now even before he or she was born. Was I really such a bad person or a person born with a terrible illness that I had to keep paying for my entire lifetime?

Matt called me one afternoon and said for me to be home; he needed to talk to me. He was really short with me and sounded mad, so I thought what have I done now? When he came home, he said to me, "Come sit down, Isabella, I would like to talk to you. I don't want to upset you, so I am going to tell you this in the calmest way I know how. Don't you ever think that you will be able to take my child away from me." I just didn't know what to say. "Isabella, I know you can't help what you have done in the past, but your past will certainly keep you from taking our child from me. So don't you ever think you can win over me. Now, honey, do we understand each other?"

I was choking up inside. "Yes," I said, "I do. Now," I said to Matt, "who told you that I was going to take the baby away?"

"Nothing, Isabella, and I do mean nothing, gets past me. I know what you are doing and where you are at even if I am out of town," Matt said. "Just remember this," he said, patting me lightly on my face.

Now I really didn't understand what was going on. Someone had told him what I said when I was mad. I called my parents, and they said that they hadn't talked to Matt in a while now. So that just left Jill. Would she tell Matt something like that? So I gave her a call. "Jill," I asked, "have you talked to Matt lately?"

"No," she said quietly, "sure haven't, hon. Why?" she asked.

"Just wondering," I said.

"Good guy, your Matt," she said. "You should consider yourself lucky."

"Yes, lucky, that's me," I said. "See you, Jill."

"Sure thing," she said and we hung up. No matter. What with all this stress, I could be getting myself sick. The next morning I got up and was brushing my teeth. I leaned down to rinse my mouth out, and when I rose up and looked into the mirror, I saw an old woman with bright, red eyes. I threw my toothbrush down and sat in the corner of the bathroom floor. Scared out of my mind, I curled in a ball like I had done ever since I began having these delusions. This isn't happening, I kept saying to myself, not real, not real. I heard Matt walking up the stairs.

"Honey, are you up?" he said. God, I thought, that's all I need is to let him see me like this. I got up and glanced at the mirror; the image was gone now. I tried to get my senses about me.

Swallowing hard, I yelled out, "I am up, Matt."

He walked into the room and began rubbing my stomach. "I just can't wait to see our little girl or boy," he said.

I smiled, trying to hold back my tears. "Won't be long now," I said.

"Come on down," Matt said. "Breakfast is ready."

"You go on," I replied and said I would be right down. Matt left the room, and I sat back down on the bed. I was frightened. Is this starting again? I thought. I am taking my medication and doing everything that is supposed to keep me well. What is going on? I just can't let Matt know, but I've got to get in touch with Dr. Orr without him finding out. With everything he has been saying, I don't trust him. He will try to take the baby away from me. There has to be an answer. It just isn't right. I had to go eat and act like everything was OK. This was one time when I had to make sure Matt didn't notice anything different about me. I knew now he didn't trust me, and if he thought for one minute I was getting sick, I was really afraid of what he might do.

I noticed my things in my room were being moved around, and my purse would have changed around from where I had laid it. I was getting so mad, but I knew if I said anything, he would swear I was getting sick. I even questioned myself if I was. I just knew I was taking my medicine, and this kind of stuff shouldn't be happening to me. Matt came in one afternoon and said, "Honey, let's go for a ride." We were out in the country; it was a warm day, and the smell of freshness was in the air. While we were out, I started to have labor pains. I grabbed my stomach and told Matt I thought this was it. I was hurting so bad that tears came to my eyes, Matt took me to the hospital, and they called my doctor. I was put in the labor room. I was so happy while hurting so bad I couldn't stand it. I was so afraid. My poor heart was pounding so hard I thought I was going to have a heart attack. Matt came back in the room with me and held my hand. He tried to assure me it was going to be fine, and it would be over real soon. The doctor came in and excised me and told me I had a few hours to go. Those were the longest and hardest hours I had gone through in my life. Finally the hour came, and Matt and I had a beautiful eight-pound baby girl. She was so pretty, blue eyes and a little round face and a cute little nose. Matt was so proud, and he leaned over and kissed me and said, "You did great, baby." They took the baby away for all the tests and to put her in the nursery. I fell asleep and when I woke up, I was in a private room. I looked around the room with the sun shining in and thanked God for my little girl. There on the table beside me were a dozen red roses with a card that read, "I love you, Isabella. Always have, always will. Matt." I kissed the card and held it in my hand, thinking how much I loved him too. I put the card on the table and lay down and went back to sleep.

Soon the nurse came in and brought me the baby. I took her and held her close to me. I could feel her breathe so softly, and she was so sweet. Even the way she smelled was so sweet. The nurse came in to take the baby back and asked, "What are you going to name her?"

I looked at her and said, "I really don't know. I guess when Matt comes, we will decide on a name together."

"That's a good idea," the nurse replied. "You know how men are if you leave them out."

I smiled and nodded, "Yes, I do." Matt came in later that afternoon, and we talked over what we wanted to name our child. Finally we agreed on Summer because she made us thing of happy times, and summer was our happiest times together. Summer Lee was to be her name. That night my parents and Matt's parents came to see Summer, and everyone was so proud of her. Then Jill and Jack came and brought more flowers. Everyone had an opinion on who she looked like, and I just laughed because to me she just was a sweet, little angel.

Jill hugged me and said, "Good job, girl, you did good." Then she walked over to Matt and hugged him. He pushed her away a little, and just then, something just didn't seem right to me.

Jack smiled and said, "What a beautiful baby girl." I told him thank you and we all said good night. Matt stayed with me until visiting hours were over. The next morning, the nurse brought Summer in and handed her to me, and then she sat down in the chair next to me. I looked at her strangely and told her she could go now.

"Oh, that's all right," she said. "I will just sit here and talk to you for a while." I told her I really would like to spend some time with my daughter alone. "Well," she replied slowly, "your husband has had the doctor to order for a nurse to stay with you when you are taking care of your baby."

I really got mad. "Oh, did he now?" I said. I picked up the phone and called Matt, "Why did you order the nurse to stay with me when I was taking care of Summer."

"Isabella," Matt said, "calm down, honey. It's just you are weak from having the baby, and I didn't want the stress of all this to make you sick again. Isabella, you will have all this on you soon enough. Enjoy the help while you have it."

I said, "OK, honey, whatever you say." I didn't want to make a scene in front of the nurse. I thought to myself, he just doesn't trust me with Summer, that is all there is to it.

The next day the doctor released me and Summer to go home. I was so excited to have the baby home with me. Matt tried to get the nurse to stay with me, but I said, "No, I want to take care of Summer myself." Matt still acted strange about it. He had my mother and his mother coming over to check on me every day. Summer was such a good little girl, and I loved her so. Matt stayed on my back about taking my medicine, and I would always say, "I know to take it. Honey, please, I know." Time passed and Summer grew so fast. One afternoon I invited Jill over for a small lunch and just to talk to someone besides Matt and the baby. She came over and she held

Summer and talked about how she loved children, but Jack always said they couldn't afford them.

"You are so lucky," Jill said. "You have the whole world. You have a beautiful baby girl, nice house, good husband. What should anyone long for?"

I smiled and said, "I know I am lucky, but I have my problems the same as you do, Jill. Matt works a lot, travels all the time. I get lonely in this big house and feel sad a lot, even with Summer. I worry about whether I will be a good mother to her. There are lots of things I don't have that you do have."

Jill started to light up a cigarette, and I asked her to go on the patio to smoke. "I'm sorry," she said. "I forgot you and Matt don't smoke," and then she walked outside. I watched Jill from the sliding-glass door, how she smoked and how she acted. Sometimes I loved her to death, and other times she just acted so strange to me. Stop it, I said to myself, don't think like that. Jill has been your friend since high school. She came back in, and I started to cough. "For heaven's sake, Isabella, it can't be that bad," she said. I told her I was sorry, but smoke really bothers me. She said, "Well, bye" and for me to call her later. I got out the spray and got the smoke smell out of the house. I was tired, so I took a nap when Summer did.

It was about six when Matt got home, and he was tired, and we sat and played with the baby for a while. I was walking up the stairs when I heard Matt's phone ringing. I heard him say, "I told you not to call me, that I would call you," and then he hung up.

I yelled down the stairs, "Who was that, honey?"

"No one important," Matt said. That night when he came to bed, he was undressing, and I thought I smelled smoke on his jacket.

"I smell smoke," I said to him.

"Don't be ridiculous," he said. "You know I don't smoke."

"I know that, Matt, but I know smoke when I smell it."

"Here we go, Isabella," Matt said, "starting your bullshit again."

I got mad and said, "Really, Matt, since I have been sick you use that against me every time I say something you don't agree with.

I would give anything in this world not to have a mental illness. I would rather be blind or in a wheelchair."

"Isabella," Matt said sharply, "don't say that."

"Well, it's true. Everyone accepts other illnesses, but everyone thinks once you act crazy, you will always be."

"Isabella, I am saying," Matt said, "there is no smoke on my damn clothes. Stop with all the asking who are you on the phone with. I am beginning to feel like you don't trust me. I love you, Isabella." And before he could speak another word, I said, "Always have, always will."

"That was really crud," Matt said and went into the bathroom and slammed the door.

I just went to bed and didn't say another word to him. I knew in my heart something was going on, and I was going to get to the bottom of it. Damn it, I thought, I know I smelled smoke, but then again I thought, he does travel and a lot of people travel. He could have been sitting next to someone who was smoking.

One afternoon I lay down with Summer and fell asleep with her. The next thing I knew Matt was standing over me screaming, "Isabella, wake up."

I rubbed my eyes, and looking at him said, "What on earth is the matter?"

"I just can't believe you," he said. "If Jill hadn't dropped by, something could have happened to Summer."

"What are you talking about?" I said.

"You have been sleeping since I left this morning," he said.

"No, I have not," I said, sitting straight up in the bed. "I laid down about one this afternoon."

"Isabella," Matt screamed, "it is eight in the evening.

"It can't be," I said, looking at the clock, but he was right, it was eight. "Where is summer?" I yelled, afraid for her.

"Jill called me, and I came over and took her to my parent's house. We have been trying to get you awake since then."

"Nonsense," I said. "I don't know why you are saying this."

"Isabella, I found the bottle of pills in the bedroom floor."

"What pills?" I asked.

"Your sleeping pills. You took too many of them," Matt said. "How do you expect me to trust you with Summer after this?"

"Matt, the only pill I took was the pill the doctor told me to take at lunchtime. I promise you, Matt."

"Then how in the world can you explain to me what has happened now?" he yelled at me.

I looked at him and sat down on the bed. "I can't I honestly say."

This was the beginning of my downfall. I just started to slowly seem to be getting worse again. Matt had his mother come stay with us for a while. She did all the cooking and watched over us, especially when I was taking care of Summer. She would ask me if I was feeling OK and watched every move I made. I was getting so upset having our family thinking I would hurt my child in any way. I tried to deal with Matt's mother and my mother coming over all the time.

I talked to Matt about it and he just said, "Isabella, we just can't take any chances right now. Summer is so young." I agreed for now. I went to all my doctor's appointments. I even attended classes that explained in detail what this illness was that I had. I learned to look for the signs of me getting sick again. I wish Dr. Belmont had never left. I did the best I ever did when he was here. I have heard from the groups I attend that everyone he saw did better when he was here. He had such a way about him; he treated you like a person not a nutcase. I know I felt he cared about my well-being. I don't think any doctor anywhere could take his place, but he has to be happy too. I will have to get used to the new doctor I guess, I thought, but he is a strange little man. I just need to stay as stable as I can be for Summer's sake. I knew in my heart Matt would take her from me if I didn't anything that was wrong.

One afternoon Matt came in and told me that he was sending me to his parents for the weekend. He said that he had to go away for a week and needed to make sure Summer and I were going to be safe. I pleaded with him to let me stay home. He wasn't going to have that at all. So I had to pack and go to his parents for a while. I just hated to have to do this. I felt like I was being watched all the time. One afternoon Matt's mother was watching Summer, and I asked her if she cared if I ran to my house just to get a few more things. "No," she replied. "Go right ahead, dear. We will be just fine."

As I drove to the house, I noticed the bedroom light on. I thought I had turned it off when I left. I turned the key, and I heard someone run out the back door. "Who is there?" I yelled out, but no one answered. I walked through the house. I grabbed my cell in case I needed to call the police, and there was a big, old flashlight lying on the end table. I picked it up and looked in every room. I didn't see anyone or find anything out of order, but I know I heard someone in the house. I got the things I came for, still thinking that someone was in the house. I locked all the doors and went back to Matt's mother's house. When I returned to his mother's house, I told her that I thought someone might have been in the house. "I know I turned all the lights off when I left," I said.

"Oh, dear," she said, "probably just your imagination, and you just thought you turned the lights off." Later that night Matt called, and I heard her tell him she thought maybe I was starting to hear things again. And then when she saw me, she said, "Oh, here she is. Here, Isabella," she said. "Matt would like to talk to you, dear."

"Hey there," Matt said, "are you OK, honey?"

I replied, "Yes, I am fine."

"Mother was telling me that you thought someone was in the house."

"Listen," I said, "I know for sure that I turned all the lights off, and then when I drove up, the lights were on. You tell me how that happens?" I asked him.

"Honey," he said, "someone who gets delusion when you are frightens. Are you taking your medicine, honey?" he asked.

"Yes, I am getting mad. I get so tired of no one believing anything I say anymore." Then I just slammed the phone down and turned to walk away.

My mother-in-law said, "That wasn't nice, Isabella. Matt is only worried about you."

"Leave me alone," I said, giving her a dirty look. I went back in the room with the baby and picked her up. "Summer," I said to her, looking into that sweet, little face of hers, "your mama isn't that crazy. You don't think she is, do you?" Then she just gave me a sweet, little smile. I hugged her and thought, what a sweet child I have. Of all the bad things that have happened to me in my life, God gave me a gift of love. I just can't tell anyone how much I love my daughter, and for anyone to think I would hurt her. I would kill myself before I would hurt her.

Matt came home the next week, and things were better for me. I really loved being home. I just wished Matt would quit traveling so much. One night it was storming really bad, the lighting was striking everywhere. You could hear it crackle left and right. The power blinked on and off. I was lying in the bed, and I smelled smoke again, like someone was smoking right next to me. I looked up and Matt was beside me sleeping, and I could smell it, but I didn't see anything. Then suddenly I heard a lighter click, and I saw a small flame from across the room. "Who is there?" I yelled out.

Matt said, "What is going on?"

I turned on the bedside lamp and sat up and looked around. "There was someone there with a lighter," I said.

"What are you talking about, Isabella?" Matt asked.

"I smell smoke, don't you?" I asked him.

"No, I don't," he said angrily. "What in the hell is wrong with you, Isabella? I have to get up in the morning and go to work while your ass lays in the bed."

I stood up and said, "My ass gets up, cooks and cleans, and takes care of our daughter." With that I left and went into the guest room. I cried myself to sleep that night, and I felt like I was started to get sick again. If Matt didn't smell the smoke, maybe there was no smoke; it was all in my head again.

The next few months, I watched Summer grow. She was such a beautiful little girl. I enjoyed her so much, and Matt loved her, but then again he certainly was gone a lot. I would go to all the group meetings and see the doctor and do everything I thought that would help me stay sane. Then one afternoon I started to get phone calls. Someone would call and then hang up. I would be taking care of Summer, and the phone would ring. I would race to get it, thinking it might be Matt. Then when I would say hello, they would hang up on me. I would get so tired of this happening, and then here we go again, if I tell Matt, he will think I am a nutcase again. So for the next few weeks, I just had to deal with this problem by myself. Then this caller went from hanging up on me to calling me a whore. Every time the person called me, the voice on the phone would call me a whore. I would really get mad and slam the phone down and sit down on the couch and cry. Finally I had enough; I was going to tell Matt about this. When he came home, the calls would stop. It was like whoever it was knew when he was at home or gone. This was getting stranger every day. But what was worse for me is it made me look like I was getting delusional again, and that wasn't good for me. I was caught up in a web of deceit, and someone was trying to hurt me for some reason.

The next week Matt told me he wanted to go to the doctor with me. When we walked in, Matt started to fuss at the doctor. "My wife," he began, "is getting sick, and we have a child now. I can't take a chance on her really getting sick again."

"Wait just one minute," the doctor said, waving at the chair for him to sit down. "What is all this about?" he asked. And before I had a chance to answer, Matt spoke up and told him about the phone calls, the smoke in the house.

"Well," Dr. Orr said, "Isabella has been just fine every time I have seen her. She is stable, no voices and says she has no delusions."

"Well," Matt stated, "she has been lying to you."

The doctor stood up and walked over to me and asked me, "Isabella, is this true?"

"I have not been seeing things or hearing things that are not there," I said. Then I paused and said, "Listen, this is really the truth, I think someone is setting me up to fail. I just can't believe this is happening to me."

"Isabella," the doctor asked, "why would someone want to set you up or hurt you?"

I just shook my head and said, "I really don't know, but I know I am not crazy."

"Now, Isabella," the doctor said, "your illness is a sickness, you know that."

"Yes," I screamed at him, "but damn it, you know, it makes you crazy." The doctor started to write down something in my file. "That's quite a large file you have on me," I said.

The doctor just looked at me and said, "I want to try you on some new medications."

"No," I said, "my medicine is just fine."

The doctor just kept writing, and then Matt spoke up and said, "You will do what the doctor says, Isabella, for Summer's sake."

I looked at him and thought, you aren't the one having to take the damn shit. I just put on my little happy face and smiled and said to Matt, "Whatever you say, dear."

The doctor wrote out some new medicine for me and said, "Isabella, I am starting you on haldol five milligrams at bedtime. And I also want you to come in the office once a week and get a halo injection."

"What?" I said. "I will take the medicine, but I will not take any shots."

"Well, now, do you want to get better?" the doctor asked.

"Of course, I do," I replied, "but no shots."

"Isabella," the doctor said, "you have schizophrenia, and this medicine will really help you with the delusions you are having."

"No," I said again. "I will take the medicine but no shots." I grabbed my purse and ran out of his office. I waited in the car for Matt. "That's just great," I said to Matt. "You got everyone thinking I am sick again. I saw the lighter in the dark. I smelled the smoke. The phone calls were real. Why won't you believe me?" I screamed at Matt.

"Right there," he said, "the way you are acting now like you have lost your mind."

"God," I said, pulling my hair, "you want me to act crazy, I will," and stomped my feet on the floor of the car and started to cry. He just turned up the radio in the car and ignored me until we got home.

When we got home and I walked up the stairs that day, I knew I would lose my daughter some day and my life was going to change for the worse. I didn't know when or where, I just knew it was a storm waiting in the air, but it would come and take my life away.

The sad part is for some reason I thought my husband was behind this, and that was what really hurt the most. The next day I started on the new medicine. It really made me sick to my stomach. The doctor said just to make sure you eat something before you take it. I was really getting to where I didn't trust anyone, especially anyone in my family. I called Jill and asked her to come over and keep me and Summer company.

"Sure," she said, "I'll be there in a few," so I started some tea and waited for her. I really needed to talk to someone who would listen to me. Finally she came, and I let her in. Jill said to me, "You looked stressed. What is wrong?"

"God, I am very stressed. You just wouldn't believe all the bullshit I have been through this week."

"Really," she said, "like what, may I ask?"

"Things have been happening around here, phone calls, just crazy things. I just don't how to explain," I said.

"Just try, honey. I have all the time to listen to you." She hugged me and said, "After all, what are friends for?"

I smiled and said, "Yes, Jill, you are my only true friend."

So I began to tell her everything that went on, and she said to me, "I believe, Isabella, someone is trying to upset you."

"Who," I asked, "would do such a thing?"

She took a drink of tea and said, "Maybe it is Matt."

I looked at her with surprise. "Matt? Are you kidding?" I asked.

"No," she said. "Just listen to me for one minute before you say anything. One day I heard Matt talking to his mother on the phone. He was saying that he would never let you hurt or take his child away from him, no matter what he had to do."

"When was this?" I asked.

"It was when you first came home with Summer. Remember, Jack and I dropped by?"

"Um, I really can't remember," I said. "I was quite tired after she was born, and you may have, I just don't remember."

"We were sitting on the couch talking when Matt's mother called. He walked into the kitchen, but we still could hear what he was saying," Jill told me. "So I think he has had someone to do the things just to get you sick again and put you back into the hospital."

"I just can't believe that he would go that far. Matt loves me, whether I am sick or not. God, Jill, we were high school sweethearts."

"I know that," Jill said, "but people change, and the baby is real important to him."

"Sure," I said. "She is important to me too."

"Well," Jill said, "just study what I have told you and watch his actions and see where all this leaves you." We then started to talk about other things and then Jill said she had to go home. She hugged me and told me if I needed her, to let her know, and then she left.

That night when I was settled down for the evening, I started to think of what Jill had said. It made some sense to me by the way Matt had been treating me. I know I have had problems in the past, I thought, but even the doctor said I was better. When Matt got home, he came up and opened the door, peeking his head in. "Hey there, baby, what are you doing?"

"Oh, just resting," I replied.

"How are my two favorite girls in the world?" he asked.

I smiled, having to force the muscles in my face. "We are just fine, honey," I said.

"Great," he said. He sat down on the bed touching me, and I thought I was going to throw up. God, he made me sick. This was the first time in my relationship with Matt that I felt this way.

I said to him softly, "Not tonight. I really am not feeling up to it."

"Um," he said, "you never feel up to it, Isabella." He got mad and walked out. I could hear him call someone, but I couldn't make out what he was saying. I got up and crept down the staircase to try to hear who he was talking to. Just as I came down the last step, he came around the corner. "What are you doing?" he asked.

"Just coming to get something to drink," I told him, and then he told whoever it was he had to go.

"Call you later," he said to whoever he was talking to. "Go back to bed," he yelled. "I thought your ass was sick."

"I am going right now," I replied. Gee, I thought, he sure is hateful lately. I turned and went up the stairs and back to bed my ass went.

Matt was changing. He sure wasn't the same sweet guy I had meet in high school. He used to be so understanding and accepted me the way I was. That was one of the reasons I fell in love with him. Now all of a sudden he acts so different about me, I thought. Time went by, and I still was starting to hear that whisper I used to hear. I would think when I was driving that someone would be in the back seat. I would get so frightened I would pull the car over and take a flashlight and look in the floor of the back seat. And even after I had looked good, I would glance in the mirror and see a man sitting in the back seat. I would tell myself over and over, "This is not real, Isabella." After this began happening, I got to where I wouldn't drive at night.

One week it would seem I was fine, and then some weeks I just really didn't understand. Matt was trusted me less and less. Matt traveled more and more, and our relationship seemed to be falling apart. At home things just kept getting stranger: things missing and phone calls when Matt was gone. I quit telling anyone about the things happening, but my nerves were getting worse by the hour. I called Jill one afternoon to come go out with me. I really needed to get out of the house. We went running in the park. It was such a sunny day, and the flowers were in full bloom. I was telling Jill all my problems, and when we sat under a tree and took a break, I told her, "Jill, I hate to unload on you like this."

"That's OK," she said. "You need someone to talk to. I am here for you. By the way, my marriage is falling apart if it's any relief to you that you are not the only one having problems."

"I'm sorry to hear that," I told her. "What has happened, Jill?" I asked.

"Jack is cheating on me," she said.

"No way," I said.

"Yes," said Jill, "with a waitress somewhere."

"How do you know?" I asked.

"I caught him kissing her in his car outside the diner. I tell you, Isabella, I took a bat out of my car and smashed the hell out of Jack's car, and then I dragged that little bitch out and slapped her around a few times. When she got loose, she ran away as fast as she could."

"Gee, Jill," I said, "that's awful. Who would have imagined Jack doing something like that?"

"Well, Isabella," Jill said, "I am going to take his ass to the cleaner. He won't have a pot to piss in when I get through with him. The thought of him cheating on me with a cheap little waitress."

"That a little haze, isn't it?" I said.

"Well, Isabella, I get what I want, and Jack will regret the day he met me." I looked at her strange. Now that was a side of Jill I had never seen before. "So see, Isabella, we both have men problems. Why don't we go to a bar tonight and have a few drinks and have a girl's night out?"

"I don't know about that," I said. "I take medication, and I am not supposed to drink with it."

"Oh, what will one little drink hurt?" Jill asked. Pulling me up from the grass, she said, "Come, just one, and then we will leave."

"I still don't know," I said. "Matt will really get mad."

"So what?" she said. "Let him get mad. Really, Isabella, do you know what he does when he is on his little trips?"

"I trust Matt," I replied.

"I trusted Jack too, and just look where that got me. Come on now, let's have some fun for a change."

I went home and told Matt's mother I was going out with Jill for a while this evening. She said, "OK, dear, it may do you some good to get out of the house." Jill called me and said for me to met her at Bratty Bar and Grill.

"I thought you were coming to get me," I said.

"Just meet me, there," she said, then hung up. I got into my car and drove there. I hated to drive at night, and Jill knew that. I promised her, so I will go for a little while, I thought. I walked in, and it was so dark and smoky and smelled of beer. Jill yelled at me from across the room, "Over here, Isabella." She was sitting with two guys.

I didn't know what to do. I walked over puzzled and asked, "Jill, what is going on? I thought it was me and you and girls night out," I said, looking at the guys.

"It is, honey, chill out. Let's just have one drink with the guys and we'll leave." I was so uncomfortable that night, but I had one beer and then another. With my medication, I got drunk really fast. My vision was blurry and I felt sick. I looked for Jill, but I couldn't find her. I needed her to drive me home. I stumbled around in the bar. Finally I found my way outside and to my car. By this time, I was really drunk. I got into the car and started to drive home. My vision was really bad at this time, and I was swinging all over the road. Wouldn't you know it, I got blue lighted and pulled over. I pulled to the side, and the police officer asked me to get out of the car. He wanted to see my license.

He said, "You have been drinking and driving. I am taking you to jail."

I started to cry and say, "What about my car?"

"Your car will be towed and someone will pick it up for you."

I was so frightened. Never had anything like this happened to me. I called my father, and he came and got me. "Really, Isabella, what is wrong with you? Why on earth would you be out drinking?"

"I went with Jill, and then she left me there," I told him.

"Isabella," my dad said, "I told you about that girl years ago. She is not your friend. Friends don't let other friends drink and drive."

"Dad, she is the only friend I have," I said to him.

"Well, Isabella, your definition of a friend is different from mine, I guess." My father took me home and told Matt's mother what had happened.

She said, "Leave Summer alone tonight, Isabella. Don't let her see you this way."

"I wouldn't do that," I replied, giving her a dirty look. I was so ashamed of myself, and I was so sick. I had the bed spins, and it was a very long night. I had never been a drinker, and I will never do that again, I thought.

The next weekend Matt came home, and I had to tell him what I did. He hit the ceiling. "What on earth possessed you to do such a thing?" he said. "I forbid you to leave this house again without your mother or mine. You are to stay at home at all times when I am gone. Do you understand me, Isabella?"

I said, "Yes, just stop screaming at me."

"I am calling Jill and telling her she better not ever take you to a place like that again."

"Please don't do that, Matt," I said. "It's not all her fault. I agreed to go."

He called her anyway. He came back and said to me, "Why didn't you leave when she asked you to? She told me, Isabella, that some guy was buying you a drink, and she tried to get you to leave with her, and you wouldn't."

I couldn't believe my ears. I said, "She did not, it was the other way around."

"Sure, Isabella, I would believe Jill over you after everything you have done lately."

God, I thought, why would she do something like that to me. I was so mad at her, and believe me, I would tell her about this the first chance I got. My life was like a yo-yo, up and down, and the people in my life that I loved were treating me really badly. The next day I called Jill and asked her why she lied to Matt like that. "I didn't lie, Isabella," she said. "I did try to get you to leave, and I went to the bathroom and when I came out, you were gone."

"What about the guy you said I was with, Jill?" I asked.

"I told Matt I was with a friend, that was all. He was trying to trick you, honey. I told you he is out to get you." I hung up the phone and started to think how badly he was treating me lately. I was so upset about my life, and it seemed it was getting worse with every day that came. I went to my parents' house one afternoon and talked to my mother. She told me that I was stressed out from the birth of my daughter. My mother was really upset about not getting me help when I was younger, and I really tried to understand her reasoning.

I went home one night and asked Matt if we could talk. He just looked at me and said, "About what, Isabella? Really," he said, "all the things you have done lately are becoming trying. And I am going to tell you right now, if you keep this bullshit up, I am going to put you back into the hospital."

"Oh, I see," I said, "if I don't act the way you think I should or do the things you want, you have the nerve to put me in a mental hospital. That's not fair," I screamed.

"I tell you, Isabella, what is not fair is that little girl upstairs with a mother who don't give a damn about her."

"I do love Summer. How can you say that about me?" I screamed. "Crazy?" I said. "If I am going to be put into the hospital for being crazy, then I will show you crazy." I picked up a flower vase and smashed it on the wall. I started to scream and pull my hair and run through the house breaking things.

Matt's mother came out and said, "What is going on here, Matt? Make her stop this," she screamed.

Matt grabbed me and threw me on the couch. "Sit your ass down now, Isabella," he yelled. I started to cry. I knew he would put me back into the hospital. So be it, I thought. It's better than being treated as a prisoner in my own house. He ordered me to go to bed and be quiet or he would go commit me to the hospital.

The next morning Matt took me to Dr Orr. When we got there, I knew Matt had already spoken to him. "Come in and sit down," the doctor said, pointing to the chair next to him. "Well, Isabella," he said, "I hear you aren't doing so well.

I asked, "By whose standards? Matt's?"

"Now, Isabella," the doctor said, "talking like that isn't going to help matters." I just sat there, knowing I was getting ready to be shipped out. I think the doctor said, "Being in the hospital to stabilize your medicine might be a good idea for a while."

"Um," I said, "how long is a while?"

"That depends on you," the doctor said, and then he called the hospital for someone to come and take me to a room.

I looked at Matt and said, "Please, don't leave me in here too long."

He said, "I am only doing what I think is best for you, honey; I want my sweet wife back," and then he hugged me and kissed me and walked off.

The nurse came and said, "Come on, Isabella, let's go now," so I followed her to my room.

Chapter 3

The next few days, no one came to see me. I wasn't allowed to use the phone. I kept asking the nurse at the desk, had my husband called?

"No, he hasn't," she would tell me.

"Has anyone called for me?" I asked again.

The nurse said, "No, I will let you know if they do. Now go to your group sessions, Isabella." Really nice people in this hospital. You are just a room number to them. If you don't behave, they find a way to make you. Weeks went by, and I had no visitors or no phone calls. One day when I was seeing the doctor, I asked him why hasn't my family or husband been to see me.

"Well, Isabella," he said, "I told them it might be best for you to let you have time to get better."

I looked at him. "I am really getting tired of everyone thinking that they know best for me," I said. "No one believes anything I say anymore since I have been sick. It's like I am labeled this crazy person that hears things and sees things that aren't there."

"Isabella, it's hard for a person, I know, in your situation," he said.

I replied, "With all due respect, you really don't know. You are on the outside looking in, and I am in the inside looking out if that makes sense to you," I said.

He nodded his head and said, "Yes, I can understand that. Your family will be here soon, but your husband is still out of town."

"Go figure," I said. The days were so long in that place. I hated every minute of it. I had my problems, but some of these poor people would eat stuff off the floor. They would be so dirty and walk around like they were sleep walking. Some of them had a look like the lights were on, but there was no one home. Some of them would wet on themselves, and some of them would fight and bite and have to be put in restraints. It's so sad for people like this to have such an illness that made them be treated like animals. And I do mean they were treated like animals. Weeks went by, and finally my parents came to see me. I was so happy to see someone. We went back to my room to talk. I asked my mother how Summer was, and she said, "She is fine. You know Matt's mother takes care of her. They let your father and I see her, but we aren't allowed to take her home at any time."

"Why?" I asked. "She is your granddaughter too."

"I know, dear, but I could tell you this, and I hope it doesn't upset you too much. Matt has an attorney that is going to take all your rights away from you, and he will have total control over your life."

"Mother, he already controls me. Look where I am. Who keeps putting me in the damn hospital?" I asked.

"I know, dear, but this is different and very serious. Isabella, he can take your rights away from seeing Summer."

"No, he better not, I would kill him before I couldn't see my little girl."

"Isabella," my mother said. "Be careful what you are saying; someone might take you seriously."

"Mother, why is Matt doing all this to me?"

She hugged me and said, "I don't know, honey, and me and your father are helpless."

"I know, Mother, it's not your fault; it's mine for getting mad at the house, and he took me seriously and had the doctor to put me in here."

"Well, dear, just try to get well and don't worry."

"Are you getting better, dear?" my dad asked.

"Yes, I think so, but I tell you there is something strange going on with Matt. It's like he is trying to get me out of his life."

Dad said, "Well, we will help you, honey, in any way we can."

"I know you will, Dad, but the sad part is I really don't think anyone can help me. Matt is a very powerful man." My parents told me good-bye and they left. I went to bed that night thinking how I could get myself out of this hospital.

Finally after two months, my husband came to see me. He walked in as if he owned the place. He pulled me by the hair slightly and kissed me and said, "Well, how is my beautiful Isabella. Been behaving yourself?" he asked.

"Yes," I said, "the doctor said I might be able to go home next week."

"Really," he said, "that is wonderful, honey," and we walked down the hall into my room.

I asked him, "Matt, can I come home next week?"

"Well," he said, rubbing his chin. "I will think about it." I wanted to just slap his face, but I knew I had to act right or he wouldn't let me out. I just thought how he controlled my life because of this damn illness.

Finally the day came and I was to go home. Matt came to get me and collected all my things. He was really quiet on the ride home and would look over and smile. I just smiled and acted like everything was fine. We drove into the driveway and Matt said, "Listen, Isabella, you better not do anything at all wrong, or I will put you somewhere you will never be able to get out of." I knew in my heart he meant business. He put me in the guest room and told me for now that was where he wanted me to stay.

"What about my clothes?" I asked.

" I've already taken care of that. You will find all your clothes in order in your new room."

I looked at him real puzzled. "I have been demoted to the guest room. What is your reason for this, Matt?" I asked.

"Because," he said, "until you get better and show me you are, I really don't want to be around you that much." I had tears in my eyes, and I felt like someone had just cut me with a knife.

"Matt," I said fighting back the tears, "why don't you just kick me out? I could go to my parents."

"I know you can, but Summer needs her mother. But you will always be supervised when you are around her."

"Matt," I asked, "do you hate me?"

"No, honey," he said quizzing my face. "I love you. Remember, I vowed till death us part. I will always take care of you, and if your damn mother would have helped you, then I wouldn't be having to do all this." Matt was getting mad. He was really mad a lot. I think deep down inside he hated me for being sick. At first I think he had a lot of patience with me. But I have put that man through so much. Sometimes I really get mad at him, but if the shoe was on the other foot, I don't know how I would really react. I just knew I didn't want to lose my daughter. I was hurt and confused about everything that was going on. I would deal with it all somehow for Summer's sake. I had so many pills to take; they made me sleepy and thirsty all the time. My mouth was always dry, and I was so hungry all the time again; I put weight on and looked like hell. Jill on the other hand was thin and looked great, and she just loved rubbing it in.

"Really," she would say, "you need to do something with yourself." As if I didn't already feel bad about myself. When I was in good health and not taking all these pills, I could run circles around her. But I was too tired and too depressed to even care anymore. I just had to do what Matt said, and that was that.

One day he let me go to confession, and I talked to Father Anthony. I sat down in the confession booth and Father Anthony slid the confession door open and said, "What is it, my child?"

"Father, I need your help. I need to get well for my daughter's sake."

"My child, you must ask God to grant good health to you, my child."

"Father, someone is trying to make me think I am losing it again. Father, I don't know whom I can trust."

"My child, you can always trust in God."

"I know," I replied. "It's the ones here on earth that I do not trust."

"My child," Father Anthony asked, "why would someone want you to think you are getting sick again?"

"Father, I tell you it's some sort of plot. I just can't figure it out, but I feel it within. Father, what can I do to understand what is happening to me?"

"My child, you must trust God; he knows your heart and will guide you through your times of hardship." We prayed for a while, and then I left to go home. I walked home that day thinking of the time when Matt and I were so in love. Has my illness driven us apart, I wondered. Has this craziness been too much for him? I just don't know. I am damned by a demon, and it has destroyed my life. The wind was blowing quietly that day as I walked home. It sounded like it was speaking to me: "Isabella." It would sound like it was whispers, and then just out of the blue, I heard that voice again. "Isabella," it said, "do you really think a priest can help you?" it asked. Then it just laughed and got louder.

I covered my ears and started to scream, "Leave me alone, just leave me alone."

An old woman was walking by, and she stopped and asked me, "Are you all right?"

I just looked at her and started to run as fast as I could. My heart was pounding; I was sweating, and I felt like I was going to pass out. I got to the door of the house and I was shaking so bad, I couldn't get the key in the door. I struggled with it, and finally the key went in. I ran to the kitchen and got a paper towel and started to wipe my face. I sat down in the chair, and I pleaded with God, "No, not now, I have a daughter. I don't want to be sick. I will give up my legs. Arms or anything in trade of this demon in my head." I was still shaking when I heard Matt come in.

"Anyone home?" he yelled out.

Trying to get myself together, I answered, "I am in the kitchen, honey."

He walked in the kitchen and looked at me. As he walked over to kiss me, he said, "You don't look too good, honey. Something wrong?"

"No," I said softly, "I am fine. Just went for a walk, and it just tired me out, that's all," I said.

"Good, honey. I am glad you are OK. I do love you, Isabella, and I know at times I am hard on you, but it's just I love you so. Always have and always will," he said.

"I know, Matt, you have been saying those exact words for years, but Matt those are just words. Meaning and it and just saying it are two different things."

"Gee," Matt said, "must you go at me like this. I can't be sweet to you without you thinking I don't mean it."

"Listen," I said, "please don't get mad at me, but just try to look at this from my point of view. If you love me, then why don't you believe that I am better and some really strange things have been going on?"

Matt got up from the table and said, "Isabella, these thing seem strange to you because of your illness. I could have you locked away for the rest of your life if I didn't love you, so I suggest that you just be very careful the way you talk to me," and then he grabbed his coat and walked upstairs. I went into my bedroom and just sat on the bed thinking of what I could do. Matt had total control of my life and my daughter's life. I had to be very careful in whatever I did from here on. I knew something was really different about Matt, but what it was I had figured out yet. I went into Summer's room and was playing with her. Matt walked in and said, "Get out," and pointed his finger.

"What?" I said, not believing what I was hearing.

"You heard me," he said. "Get out until I tell you that you can come into Summer's room." I got up and walked out, not wanting to frighten Summer. I went back into my room, and he walked in behind me.

"What was all that about?" I asked him.

"Well, Isabella," he said, "if you are still thinking things are strange around here, you might think something is wrong with Summer like you did with the baby from years ago. So until I know for sure that you are well, I am taking Summer back to my mother's, and you are not to see her for a while until I have you checked out again," he said and shut the door without letting me say a word.

Damn, I thought, I've got to get a plan to stay sane for my daughter's sake. I could still hear that voice at night, and I would just cover my head. The next morning I got up and went down the stairs. The house was a little dark, and as I walked into the living room, I thought I saw a shadow on the patio. I walked over and cut the light on and it was gone. Cold chills ran up and down my spine. I went into the kitchen and poured me some orange juice. I was drinking the orange juice and I felt something in my mouth. I spit it into the sink, and out came a roach, and I ran water over it. I poured all the rest of the orange juice into the sink to see if there were any more, and there were no more in it. I thought to myself, is this real or am I having a delusion? I knew one thing, I would never tell Matt anything again. I went to the doctor that morning, and he asked me how I was feeling. "Oh, fine," I answered.

"Good," he said. "Taking all your medicine?" he asked.

"Yes, of course I am," I replied.

"Next week I want to do some more blood work on you, so don't eat or drink after midnight." I agreed and then left. I hated all those needles, and what was this all really for? I sure wasn't getting better. But I didn't trust anyone: been there, done that, if you know what I mean. The next week I went in for blood work, and then I went home and was working around the house trying to stay busy. I heard the door open, and I heard footsteps coming down the hall.

"Is that you, honey?" I asked.

"Yes, it's me," Matt said. He walked over to me, and looking me straight in the eyes, he asked me, "You really don't want to get well, do you, Isabella? I think you enjoy driving me crazy, but what about Summer? Do you not care about her either?"

"What are you talking about?" I asked. "I don't understand what you are saying."

"I am saying you have not been taking your medicine again."

"What?" I screamed at him. "Yes, I have been taking it."

"Well, Isabella, explain to me why it's not showing up in your blood work."

I threw the dusting cloth down and said to him, "I really don't know what is going on here," and started to cry. "I am telling you the truth, I want to be well. Do you really think I have enjoyed my life, Matt? The self-mutilation I did, the scars I have, the voices, all this? Right, I just love being crazy. It's fun for people to look at you different and to live a life just filled with seeing things that aren't there. That's me, Matt," I said. "Crazy Isabella. I just love being me." Then I ran upstairs and shut the door and locked it. I sat down right under the door and I cried. At this point in my life, I really didn't know what was real or unreal. I just cried and asked God, "Why? What have I done so wrong in my life to be burdened in this awful way?" I felt asleep that night right where I sat. I woke up the next morning with Matt banging on the door.

"Open the door," he yelled. I stood up and opened the door. "Are you all right?" he asked.

"Yes, I am just don't under stand about my medicine." Matt walked into the bathroom and got the medicine bottles out.

"I got an idea," he said. "Be back shortly." He was gone for about two hours. He came back and said, "Isabella, come here and sit down. I would like to talk to you. I took this medicine to the drugstore, and they said it wasn't the right medicine."

"Not the right medicine?" I asked, confused.

"No, it's not yours. Now, Isabella, what have you done with your medicine?"

"That is my medicine," I said.

Again Matt said, "It is not yours."

"God," I said putting my hands over my face, "just put me back in the hospital; I would rather be there. I want to go to the hospital," I screamed.

Matt said, "Calm down and let me call your doctor." I sat there for about an hour. My head was starting to hurt and I was getting dizzy. Finally Matt said, "Come on and let's go see the doctor."

We got to the doctor's office, and I walked in, and the doctor said, "Sit down, please. Now," he began, "Isabella, can you tell me why you are not taking your medicine?"

"I don't know," I replied. At this point I figured what was the use. No one believed anything I said.

"I want her back in the hospital," Matt yelled.

"Calm down," the doctor said. "Isabella has been in and out of the hospital, and it's not helping her. She needs someone to give her the medicine and watch her swallow and then do mouth checks on her. If you do this for a while, she will get better. Can you get someone to do that?" the doctor asked.

"I will think of something," Matt said. Matt called my mother and talked to her. She asked to speak to me.

"Isabella," she said softly, "honey, will you come and stay with Dad and I a while, just until you feel better?"

"Whatever Matt wants to do, Mom," I said. I hung the phone up and slowly walked up the stairs, hanging my head down with defeat.

The next day my mother came and got my things and took me to her house. She made me swallow, then looked into my mouth to see it was all gone. I was so sad in my life, but I was beginning to feel so much better, and my mother and I were getting closer. We made cookies together and laughed and had lots of fun. My dad would laugh and say, "Sounds like you two are having too much fun. Now cut that out." One afternoon Matt came by and told my mother he wanted her to get my things together. He was going to take me home.

"Are you sure?" my mother asked. "She is no problem to Father and me. We are enjoying her being here."

"I thank you for what you have done, but it's time for Isabella to return home."

"Who will see she gets her medicine?" my mom asked.

"Well," Matt said, "Isabella's best friend, Jill, has offered to come by twice a day and see that she takes her medicine and help her with the house. She needs extra money, and she is Isabella's best friend."

My dad heard what was being said and walked in. "Jill is no true friend. Look what happened when she took Isabella out to the bar?"

Matt interrupted him. "Now you can't put all the blame on Jill. Isabella had a part in that too."

Dad just threw his newspaper down and walked over to me and kissed me and said, "If you need anything at all, baby, call us." I thanked them both and Matt grabbed me, pulling me out the door.

The next day Jill came by, all bubbly and full of energy. "Come on, Isabella," she said. "Let's get breakfast and take your medicine."

"You certainly are happy nowadays," I said. "What's up with that? Back with Jack?" I asked.

"Oh no, honey," Jill said. "I have a new man in my life now."

"Um," I said. "What's he like?"

"Very handsome and lots of money. Everything a woman wants," she said. Then she said, "Just one little problem."

"What's that?" I asked.

"He's married."

"Married," I said. "Now that can be a problem."

Jill looked at me and said, "Well that want be a problem too long."

"Why is that?" I asked, kidding. "Are you are going to kill her?"

Jill lifted her head and just laughed. "Won't have to. She will leave him soon."

"You certainly are sure of yourself," I said.

"Come, Isabella, you know I always get what I want. Remember when I set out to get Jack, and I took him away from Marry?"

"Yes, I remember that," I said, "but Jack wasn't married either."

"I will get him," she said. "Come on now. What's new with you?" she asked. Now at this time I thought Jill was my friend, and I was going to learn real soon she was the worst enemy anyone could have.

I was starting to get paranoid again, especially about food. I thought Matt was out to poison me. I started to lose weight and get weak. I was in the bed a lot, and sometimes I thought I could hear Matt in his bedroom with another woman. I could hear him say, "You have to keep it down. She is in the next room." One night at the dinner table Matt's friend Bob was over, and I was sitting at the table, and Jill was trying to get me to eat. My legs started to shake and bump the table, making an awful noise. Matt came in and said, "Really, Jill, can't you make her stop that?"

Jill said, "It's just her nerves."

Bob walked in and asked, "Who is that?"

Jill spoke up and said, "Why it's Matt's lovely wife, Isabella."

Bob looked at Matt and said, "That is Isabella?"

Matt sharply said, "Yes it is. She has been sick."

"Sorry to hear that," Bob said. "I wouldn't believe that was Isabella." They walked out and I could still hear them whispering.

"Poor Matt," Jill said. "Isabella, I think you embarrassed him." At this point I really couldn't help anything I was doing. Time went by, weeks and weeks, and I was hearing and seeing things. I missed all my doctor's appointments, and I was getting to the point I was afraid to get out of the bed. The doctor called my mother and wanted to know why I hadn't been to any of my appointments. One afternoon my mother dropped by to see me.

"God, Isabella honey, you look awful. What is happening to you?" Jill walked into the room and spoke to my mother. "The doctor says no one will answer the phone," my mother said. "He wanted to know what is wrong that Isabella isn't coming to her appointments."

"She has been too sick to leave the house," Jill said.

"Where is Matt?" my mother asked.

"Out of town. Won't be back until next Tuesday."

"You tell him," my mother said very madly, "he is to call me right away."

"Sure thing, I will tell him as soon as I hear from him." Jill walked my mother to the door and let her out, closing the door hard; then turning away, she said, "Bitch."

I looked up and said, "What was that you said?"

"Oh nothing," Jill said and helped me upstairs. Matt came home the following week, and he wanted me to sit down and have dinner with him. He had bought some Chinese food. Jill told him, "Isabella is too weak to come down and eat. I will take hers upstairs to her."

"Nonsense," Matt said. "I will go get her myself." He came in and helped me out of bed. In his eyes that day I saw the love he had, but he just couldn't handle my illness. He combed my hair and said, "Honey," kissing me on the neck, "why can't you get well? Please, Isabella, come back to me." He helped me down the stairs and sat me down next to him.

Jill said, "Really, Matt, she is too sick to be up."

"She needs to be up," he said.

I was sitting there trying to eat, and I looked at the long noodles in that Chinese food, and to me it looked like worms. "God," I screamed, "it's worms. You are trying to feed me worms." I got up, throwing my dish in the floor, shaking all over. I took the fork and stabbed it into my throat screaming, "Get it out, please." Matt came over and took the fork away from me and cleaned up the blood on my throat. He sat down that night and hugged me and cried and yelled at Jill, "Call 911. Hurry."

"I told you," Jill said, "she is crazy."

"Shut up," Matt said crying. "She is my wife." That night I was taken back to the hospital. My parents came by and saw me. I was to be sent to a special hospital that had a very good recovery plan for people like me. Matt wanted me to get well, and the doctor agreed that for some reason I wasn't getting well, and the medicine wasn't working for some reason. Matt let me see Summer before I left. It was so strange. No matter how crazy I got, I was always better when I could see her. Sitting there holding my baby, not knowing when I would see her again, was so hard. I got tears in my eyes, and I could barely see. I hurt inside like I had never before. I was so sad that day. As Matt pulled Summer out of my arms, I felt empty inside. Seeing my baby leave that day was all I could bear, and I just didn't know when I would see her again.

The nurse came and said, "Come, Isabella, let's get you to your room." I got up and felt so weak and so broken. I felt like a shell of a person, like I was on a courtly that I would never return home. The nurse smiled at me and said, "It will be OK, honey," and held my arm, leading me down the long hall into my room. I got in the room and she said, "Here are some books, and if you need anything, let me know."

"I will," I replied, sitting on the bed, looking out the window. I got lost in a train of thoughts. How did all this begin? And then I recalled the day in class when I heard the voice whisper. It used to whisper to me, "Isabella," it would say, "I know you hear me." Then later on in years, it graduated to a loud voice that frightened me so. The pain I feel no one knows, no one understands, and I am at a loss for words to describe my life. My husband has lost hope; I can see it in his eyes, I thought. Matt has given up on me. My parents are so stressed out, and my brother, Sky, is ashamed of me. I can go on and on, but I won't. It just doesn't matter anymore, I thought. The nurse came and told me she was going to give me a shot.

"What kind of a shot?" I asked.

"It's just something to help you relax and sleep better tonight," she said.

I gutted and said, "I guess I really don't have a say in this anyway." After the shot, I got really tired and lay down. Before long I was asleep, and the dreams I had were awful. I went back in my memory of the past of everything I had done and the time all this happened. I saw the demon in my mind that was chasing me. What is this thing, and if it really is a mental illness, why doesn't medicine control it? When I woke up, I was pouring sweat. My hair was drenched with sweat, and my heart was pounding. I was shaking so bad that the bed shook. I reached out and grabbed the call button, shaking so badly I could hardly hold it. "Please come help me," I said.

"I will be right there," she replied. It seemed like it took her forever. Finally she walked in the door. "What is wrong?" she asked.

"I think I am having a reaction to the shot you gave me," I said.

"Now, Isabella," she said, "honey, you are just overreacting. It was just something to help you rest, that's all."

"Well," I said, "I got news for you, rest isn't what I got. Bad dreams, a trip into my past that almost killed me."

"What do you mean it almost killed you?" she asked.

"My heart felt like it was going to quit beating," I replied. She took my blood pressure and got a strange look on her face.

"I will be right back," she said, and then she walked out. I lay back down, just knowing I was either going to have a heart attack or a stroke. Finally the nurse came back in and said, "Here, please take this pill."

"What is it?" I asked.

"It's for your blood pressure, dear. For some reason, your blood pressure is up." I swallowed the pill and she said, "I will be back in a little while to check on you. Lay down and rest, and this should help you feel much better."

"I hope so," I replied. Finally I began to feel better. In a little while, I was able to get up and bathe and fix myself up. The doctor came in the next morning and said I could go out to the terrace and sit in the sun. I was glad. Maybe being outside would help me, I thought. I always love the outdoors. I put my clothes on and got a book and walked outside. I walked over to the bench under the tree to sit. The little squirrels were running around everywhere; the birds were singing. How pretty that day was.

A young girl walked over to me and said, "May I sit with you?"

"Sure," I said and moved over.

"What a nice spot to sit," she said.

"Yes, it certainly is," I replied.

"My name is Meg," she said.

"Nice to meet you," I said. "I am Isabella." We talked for a little while. "How old are you, Meg?" I asked.

"I am nineteen this year," she replied.

"Not being nosy," I asked, "why are you here?"

"I am sick," she answered. "Really sick," she said again. "I heard things, whispers in my ears. Like someone is always trying to tell me a secret. Sounds crazy, doesn't it?" she said. I looked at her and thought, my God, she has the very same thing I do. There are other people who hear these voices, and I am not alone in this illness. Meg looked at me and asked, "Isabella, what is wrong with you?"

I paused and then said, "Meg, I have the very same illness that you do."

"No joke?" she said as if she was happy to hear that. "Do you see things?" she asked me.

"Yes," I replied, "hear things, see things. For years I thought I was demon- possessed."

"Me too," she said. "Maybe in some way we can help each other."

"Yes, maybe we can," I replied. We sat and talked for about half an hour, and then they made everyone come back inside.

"See you tomorrow," Meg said.

"OK," I replied. I walked back into my bedroom and thought, that poor child, she has a long road ahead of her. The nurse came in and gave me my medicine and told me I had to attend a group the next morning. I woke up the next morning, and this strange woman was standing over me. She had long stringy hair and dark circles under her eyes. She had drool running down her mouth. I screamed and screamed, and she just kept standing there as if she was in a trance of some kind. Finally the nurse heard me screaming and came running in.

"What is wrong?" she yelled.

"Look," I said, "look at this woman."

"Oh now," the nurse said. "This is Jessie. She won't hurt you. She has been at this hospital for years." The nurse took her by the arm and said, "Come on now, Jessie, let's go back to your room. You must not frighten the other patients." The woman looked back at me as if she was trying to tell me something. What a strange woman, I thought. I got dressed and went into the group. I felt a little out of place when I first walked in. Everyone turned to look at Mr. Jones introduced me to the group. The group focused on trying to deal with your illness and to understand it. I guess really that is the hardest part, is really understanding how this disease can affect your life and the others in your life. As each one of the members talked, I listened so carefully and tried to understand what they were saying. Some of them were bipolar, and they were either happy or they were so sad they didn't know what to do. Some were multiple personality and thought they were more than one person. One woman actually changed into another person right before my eyes: talking in a different voice and acting like she was a different person. This was the strangest thing I had ever heard of. The group helped me understand my own illness better. Talking in the open about it and not being ashamed seemed to help me a lot. These people in this group, some of them were so young, some older, but all had the same thing in common. All of us were mentally ill and throughout our lives had been ashamed of the burden we carried. People of all races, all walks of life. This illness didn't favor anyone, it picked its victims at random. This hospital had a better program than anywhere I had been. It made more sense to me, and I finally realized that I wasn't alone on this journey; there were others who heard the whispers in their heads. For some reason I thought I was the only one in the world. One afternoon that strange woman who had come into my room one day walked over to me again. She stood right in front of me, looking me in the eyes. She looked really evil. I was frightened.

"What do you want?" I asked. She didn't answer; she just kept looking at me.

A nurse came by and said, "Now come on, Jessie, leave Isabella alone."

Then the woman suddenly jerked loose and said, "Isabella, I thought that was you. I am your aunt Jessie."

"Sure you are," the nurse said. "Now come back to your room."

"Wait a minute," I said. "I do have an aunt Jessie, and I haven't seen her in years. Maybe this is my aunt.

The nurse said, "OK, let's put you two in the lounge and let you talk."

Jessie's voice was weak, but she began to speak to me. "This thing got you too, didn't it?" she asked. I looked at her with tears in my eyes. I knew exactly what she was talking about.

"I am afraid so," I replied.

"I am so sorry, Isabella," she said with her voice seemly.

"It's OK, Aunt Jessie," I said.

"I hate this damn thing," she said. "I had hoped it would skip you. Is Sky normal?" she asked.

"Yes, thank God," I said. "At least one of us is sane."

"I tried to tell your mother years ago when you were small to have you checked out. But no, Alice couldn't bear to hear that someone else was sick in the family beside me. Once I heard you tell her when you were about six that you saw little people running around in your room and they played and kept you awake at night talking to you. Alice would say 'that's just her imagination; she is creative, that's all.' I thought that might be the beginning for you."

"How about you, Aunt Jessie? How long have you been sick?"

"Since I was sixteen. When it started for me, I tried to tell my mother that there was a ringing in my head. I would hear a whisper saying things softly to me. My mother was like Alice, just didn't want to hear it. Back when I was young, it was called the crazy disease. Nowadays they have a fancy word for what you and I have. I call it gone crazy. I have been in and out of these hospitals, Isabella, till I am sick to death, just wish the good Lord would take me on home."

"Aunt Jessie," I said. "Please don't talk like that."

"Honey," she said, "my husband left me years ago for a woman ten years younger than him. My son moved away and won't have anything to do with me, and of course there's good old Alice, your darling mother, who disowned me years ago."

"Aunt Jessie," I said, "I would have come to see about you, but Mother told me and Sky that you left the country."

Aunt Jessie leaned her head down and laughed. "I would not have expected any different from your mother, honey. I have always had her right on the money." I was so sorry for my Aunt Jessie, for the life she had to lead by herself. I truly wished I had known about this years ago. Now it all makes sense to me. I inherited this illness from my mother's side of the family. No wonder she didn't want me to know the truth. It was her side, and she really was ashamed of her own sister. How sad that was. I love my mother, but how selfish and self-centered that was. To turn your back on your own flesh and blood is wrong, and my mother will be sorry for that some day. My Aunt Jessie and I talked until we both were so sleepy we couldn't hold our heads up. Finally Aunt Jessie said, "Let's go to bed. I bet we both sleep like babies."

Whisper

 I said, "I bet so, even with medication," and we laughed and hugged each other. We knew we had found a friend that night, one who knows what the other has been through and knows what will occur again. We said good night, and back to our rooms we went. I lay in bed that night thinking how hard this has been on me. I had Matt. Poor Aunt Jessie had no one. How could my mother do this to her own sister? The only thing that frightened me now was knowing this illness ran in my family. What if Summer comes down with this illness when she is older? I worried. Aunt Jessie had assured me that it probably would skip Summer. I sure hoped so. This was a terrible life to live, and I couldn't stand to think about any longer. I prayed that night that everything would work out for me and Aunt Jessie. I was going to call my mother tomorrow and let her know that Aunt Jessie was in the same hospital I was. I started to get a headache from all the stress of the day. I rang the buzzer for the nurse. I asked her if I could get something for a headache. She was very sweet to me and got me something. Soon I was fast asleep. The next morning when I got up and started my day, I walked up to the desk and I asked to use the phone. I called my mother, and at first she was glad to hear from me. I told her Aunt Jessie was here in the same hospital that I was.

 She asked, "Are you sure it's her, Isabella?"

 "Yes," I replied, "Mother, it's your sister. You need to come see about her, Mother. She has spent years by herself in these hospitals."

 "I can't," she said sharply.

 "Why not?" I asked.

 "No, I just can't bear to see her," my mother said.

 "Mother," I said, "she needs you. She has no one."

 "I just can't help, Isabella," she said. "It's bad enough to see you the way you are. I just can't stand it," she yelled into the phone, and then she hung up on me. I just stood there with the phone in my hand. I just couldn't believe what I had just heard. I walked down the hall back into my room in shock, thinking about my poor aunt Jessie. My mother was truly ashamed of both of us having mental illness. I was so upset with her. I called back later that day, and my father answered the phone. I explained to him about Aunt Jessie and what my mother had said.

"Yes, I know," he replied. "Your mother told me about your conversation. She was really upset and went upstairs to lie down."

"Dad," I said, "can't you talk to Mother and make her understand that her sister needs her?"

"Listen, Isabella, I didn't want to ever tell you this, but since you are pushing the issue with your aunt, I will tell you."

"Tell me what?" I asked.

"Your mother is afraid of your Aunt Jessie. As a child, Jessie would chase her and throw things at her. She locked her up in a building outside their house when she was a child for two hours. Your mother's parents found her later and asked Jessie why she would do such a thing, and Jessie just kept whispering, 'the voice told me to do it.' Jessie talked to herself all the time. She would scream and yell and throw things in her room for hours at a time. Isabella, even Jessie's own parents were afraid of her. They took her to doctors, and no medicine worked, and your mother was tormented by children in school saying 'crazy Jessie,' and your mother would fight other girls over her. Jessie would sit in school in a daze and walk around talking to someone who wasn't there. Finally it got so bad Jessie's parents had to take her out of school. She got better for a while and married, and your mother and her parents thought she was going to be fine. Then when you kids were young, it happened again. This time she got stopped by a policeman for speeding. He asked her to get out of the car, and she started to cuss at him, she called him every name there was, and then started pulling her hair and talking in strange voices, kidding him. He called for backup, and she was arrested and taken to jail. Later on, the court order her to go for treatment in the hospital, and then that's the last time we heard of her."

"I understand Mother's pain, Dad, but still that is her sister. Do you want to give up on me? I am crazy as they come, you know that. I hear voices; people whisper every day in my ears and tell me I am not worth a shit. But yet I try to go on, and I don't think you and Mom have given up on me, have you?"

"No, honey, we would never give up on you. We love you too much."

"Really, Dad, I am just as crazy as Aunt Jessie."

Dad paused on the phone. "Isabella, dear," he began, "you were only hurting yourself except the one time you thought you saw bugs on the baby."

"Dad," I replied, "no matter how you candy coat it, I have the same illness as Aunt Jessie."

"Isabella," my dad said. "Don't make friends with her, and watch yourself around her. Really, sweetheart, she is a lot different than you think or even should imagine she is." I told him I had to go, and he told me my mother and he loved me. I hung up the phone, remembering everything my dad said. I just couldn't believe that little woman could be all they said she was. I went back into my room. The nurse came in and gave me my medicine, and I asked her if she knew anything about my aunt Jessie. She told me she wasn't allowed to tell me much, but she could say she was in and out of the hospital a lot. I was between my parents and my aunt: which was telling me the truth? I knew that my mother was ashamed of Aunt Jessie, but then again she was ashamed of me. The next morning my father called me and asked if I was OK. I told him I was just fine, not to worry so much over me.

"Isabella," he said, "I hate it when you and your mother don't get along."

"Dad," I said, "we will never really get along. Once in a while, she will act really caring, and I will think we have finally captured our relationship as mother and daughter. Then she will start her stuff with me again, just like she has over Aunt Jessie. Dad, you should see her how awful she looks and has no one, and I do mean no one.

"Isabella, that is her own choice. She isn't telling you all of the truth. Once when your mother was about twelve, your Aunt Jessie did something awful to her."

"What?" I asked.

"Your mother had this little poodle. It was soft and so cute, she told me. Your mother slept with it. It's name was Teddy because she said it looked like a cute, little teddy bear. Jessie hated the dog and would kick at it at times, and she and your mother would argue over the dog. Then one afternoon your mother came in from school looking for Teddy. She called him and he never came. She went to her parents and asked if they had seen Teddy, and they said no. Your mother went to her room looking under the bed and calling out for Teddy. She went into the bathroom, and in the floor lay Teddy with his heart cut out, and the dog's heart was in the bathroom sink. She screamed for her mother and her mother came running, asking 'what is wrong?' and she saw the dog and said, 'What a horrible thing to do. Who would do such a thing?'

"Your mother cried and cried, and then Jessie came into the room and started to laugh. 'That dog got just what it needed,' she said.

"Your mother screamed out, 'Did you do this to Teddy?'

"'No,' she replied, 'the voice told me that he was going to do it and for me to watch. It whispered to me everything it was doing, and it just kept whispering the dog is bad; its life must end.'"

I told my dad that was awful, and I was sorry for my mother, but Jessie was hearing voices and probably didn't mean to do such a thing. "Look at all I have done, Dad, over the years. This whisper, we hear it, like you can never get it out of your head or your ears. It's like you can never escape this thing in your head, no matter what you do. Medicine helps sometimes, and then at other times it doesn't touch the pain we go through."

"Isabella," my dad said, "just be careful around her and know she has a dark side also."

"I got to go, Dad, someone else wants to use the phone. Tell Mother I love and miss her, and please come to see me and Aunt Jessie."

"I will," my dad said. I hung up the phone and walked back down the hall thinking could this sweet, little lady be capable of doing such a thing? I don't know, I thought to myself, boy have I done some crazy stuff over the years.

Aunt Jessie walked in behind me and said, "What are you doing, girl?"

"Oh nothing," I replied. "Aunt Jessie," I asked, "if Mother comes to see you, can you and her make up and try to be sisters again."

Aunt Jessie got a real frown on her face, and her face turned red. "I don't know about that," she said.

"Come now," I said, "it's been years."

"I know how many years it is. I don't need you to tell me," Aunt Jessie said hatefully.

"OK," I said, "it was just an idea."

"A real bad idea," Aunt Jessie said. "Your mother hates me, Isabella, and always will."

"You need to make up, and all of us need to be a family again," I said.

My aunt Jessie grabbed me by my arm and said, "Leave this alone. Let it go, Isabella. I mean it."

"OK," I said, "let go of my arm. You are hurting me."

The nurse walked by and asked, "Is there a problem here?"

"No problem," Aunt Jessie said and let my arm go. "See you later," she said and walked away.

The nurse looked at me with concern and said, "You need to stay away from her. She is trouble."

I looked at her and said, "I know," and then walked back into my bedroom. The next few days I stayed away from Aunt Jessie, just thinking about all my father had told me. What a crazy family I came from. Why, just why, couldn't I have a normal family and live a normal life without this awful illness? But how in the world could I judge my aunt for anything because I am a product of my family? On Friday it was raining and thundering and lightning outside so bad you could hear it crackle. I was lying on my bed reading a book, and I saw a shadow on the wall. I turned around and it was Aunt Jessie, just staring hard at me. "What?" I yelled out. "What is it?"

"I want to say to you," she said, "this is all your mother's doing, me being in this damn hospital."

"No," I said, "it's not. My mother hasn't really done anything to you, except she doesn't understand our illness."

"Damn it," Aunt Jessie scrammed out, "quit defending her. She has known about this illness from the beginning and never told you." By this time I was starting to get angry, and I called for the nurse. She came and told Aunt Jessie to go back into her bedroom. The next day the doctor came in to see me and told me that he was going to send me to another hospital.

"Why?" I asked.

"Your parents called me. They were very concerned about you being here with your aunt. They felt that it wasn't good for you to be here in the same hospital she was in." I sighed and thought, here we go again, my parents are controlling my life all over again. My husband has completely forgotten about me, and my daughter is growing up without me. I have to get well and home again soon, I thought. I was just sick to death of this in and out of the hospital.

The nurse came in and said, "They are here to take you to the new hospital." I thought she was talking about my parents. To my surprise it was Matt and Jill. They walked in together, and my heart skipped a beat.

Matt walked over to me and kissed me on the neck and said, "Well, we'll get your things together. Jill agreed to help me, honey," he said.

"Well, this is interesting," I replied, "and would you please tell me why we need Jill to drive me thirty minutes away?"

"Honey," Matt said, "she called to see if you were all right, and she would like to come and see you. I explained to her that your parents wanted you in a different hospital, and she offered to come see you and help out."

"Really? How sweet," I said, hugging Jill but somehow knowing something just wasn't right. "What about Summer?" I asked.

"She is doing great. Mother says she is growing."

"I want to see my daughter, Matt," I said loudly.

"OK, honey, calm down, you will."

"When?" I asked.

"Soon, honey, really soon," Matt said. I looked at Jill and she was dressed like awful. She had tight jeans on and a really low top with her breasts hanging out. Lots of makeup, and she was up to something. I knew her well, and I knew that day my life was about to get worse. They drove me to the new hospital, and Matt checked me in. We got to the room, and Jill just walked right in, starting to pull drawers out and put my clothes away.

"Stop that," I said. "I am not a child. I'm very capable of putting my own things away."

"Just trying to help," she said.

"Jill," I said, "thank you for coming and helping out, but now I would like to talk to my husband alone if you don't mind."

She looked at Matt and said, "Do you want me to leave you two alone?"

I got really mad. "Of course he does. I am his wife, and we need some time here, please. Get the message, Jill?" I asked.

"OK, you don't have to yell at me like that, Isabella," she said. She walked out, looking at us like she really didn't want to go.

She finally closed the door, and I asked Matt straight out, "What is going on here?"

"What do you mean, Isabella?" Matt asked.

"Why on this earth would you bring my best friend with you here?"

"There's your answer, honey. It's your best friend, and she wanted to come see about you."

"Matt," I said, "do you not realize how this looks?"

He looked at me puzzled and said, "How what looks, honey?"

"Damn it," I yelled. "I am here in this hellhole, and you are out driving around with my best friend. Who is wearing tight jeans and a top with her breasts hanging out. While your crazy wife is put away for a while. Now do you see what I mean?" I asked.

"Now, Isabella, I have no interest in Jill. I love you, always have and always will."

"Matt," I said, "if you tell me that riddle again, I will throw up right here. Matt, please never bring her back here again and take her home right away," I demanded.

"OK, honey," Matt said, "you are making a mountain out of nothing." We started to argue and Matt said, "Isabella, you are just tired, and I will come back when you are in a better mood."

"That might be never," I replied. He kissed me and walked out. I felt so betrayed that day as I watched them walk down the hall. I threw myself on my bed and screamed and cried so hard that day; I just wanted my husband and my daughter.

I lay there on my bed that night with a plan to get to go home and take care of my daughter. My parents came to see me the next day, and they encouraged me to get well and take my medicine and get my life back. For once in my life, I really wanted to get well more than anything in my life. I had my daughter, and I had already missed out on a lot on her life. The next day I was going to see a new doctor, and I felt like he was going to be good for me. It was about ten the next morning, and the sun was shining, the birds were singing, and I felt really happy for some reason that day. The doctor came in about ten o'clock in the morning.

"My name is Doctor Barns," he said. "Come sit, Isabella." He pulled over the chair and pointed for me to sit down. "What do you want out of your life, Isabella?" he asked. I hung my head down in shame, thinking of my whole life that had passed. "Now, dear," he said, "never feel bad about your illness. You can overcome this and have a good quality of life, but you really have to want to, Isabella. Your recovery is really up to you."

I sat there and thought about what he said. "Yes, you are right," I replied.

"Now let's talk, Isabella," the doctor said. "I read in your records of all the things that have happened in your life. Do you feel safe right now?" he asked.

"Yes, I do now," I replied.

"Isabella, tell me what goes on in your mind," the doctor said.

"Well sometimes I hear things or see things, but when something happens, I start to hear a buzz first in my ears; then it becomes a whisper that tells me that I am a bitch or that I should do something to myself. All my life, Dr. Brown, I wanted to have fun and be a normal teenager. But instead I was cursed with this awful disease that torments me every day of my life. I started to hear this whisper in my ears, and then it would escalate into a loud voice. At that age it scared the hell out of me, and my mother would never listen to me. She would say I was just acting out for attention. It went on for years until I am sure you have read about the baby that I saw bugs on."

"Yes, I have," he said, "and to you, they were really there, but you were the only one that could see them. This is common with people who have your illness. They are delusions and are dangerous to you and others without the right medication."

"I am so sorry for all the things I have done in the past," I told him.

"I know, Isabella," the doctor replied, looking over his glasses. "I know," he said. "We all have skeletons in our closets."

I smiled slightly at him, but I was in pain over my life. However, I did trust this doctor and felt he was going to help me. We talked for about an hour, and he told me he was going to try to get me released back home in a week or two. That made me so very happy. I tingled inside thinking of returning home and being with Matt and Summer. For once in my life, I felt I had a second chance. I prayed that night for God to please help me get well and be with my family. I went to the group sessions every day, and I met a lot of people who were trying to get well like me. I would beat this illness, I knew I would, and be the person and the mother I had always wanted to be. Time went on, and I was on my second week being in this hospital. Finally I got to see the doctor again. I walked into his office.

"Sit down, Isabella," he said. He paused and looked over some notes he had in front of him. "I see you are making progress," he said. "That's good; I am very glad to see this."

"When can I go home?" I asked.

"Well, let's see here. I have a note here from your husband and your parents. They think a short stay would be a mistake," he said.

"What?" I asked. "Are they the doctor, or are you the doctor?"

"Now, Isabella, don't get angry. Let's see what we can do," he said. He sat there in his chair and looked through papers. "I will release you next Friday," the doctor said "and see how you do at home for a while."

"What about my husband and my parents?" I asked.

He looked over his glasses and said, "After all, I am the doctor." I smiled at him and thanked him and told him I would give it my all this time. "I know you will, Isabella," he said. I left his office so happy. I am going home on Friday. I will see my baby soon, I thought, and I had not been this happy in a very long time. The week just dragged by, and I thought the time would never pass. My father called me and told me he and my mother were going to pick me up

I said to him, "That is fine, but what about Matt? Can't he come too, and bring Summer?"

"No, honey," my father said. "Matt is going to be out of town, and Summer is still with his parents."

"Well that's OK," I said. "The main thing is I am going to get to go home. If I never see another hospital, it won't hurt my feeling at all." Finally Friday came and I was going home. I said good-bye to some of the people I had met and wished them well. My parents came to the hospital and started all the papers to check me out. I had all my discharge papers and my follow-up appointments. On the drive home we never spoke of Aunt Jessie. I didn't want to upset my parents, especially my mother. We talked about my plans on how I wanted to get my life back on track. My mother and father told me if I needed anything, that they would be there for me. We finally got to my house. I unlocked the door and opened it and turned the lights on. To my surprise, the house was extremely clean.

"Well," my dad said, "Matt certainly is a good housekeeper. He probably had a housekeeper come in and clean, knowing that Isabella was coming home."

"Yeah," I said, "I guess." I went upstairs and put my things away. Then I went into the kitchen to make Mom and Dad coffee. The whole time I was in my house, I felt like I was in someone else's home. Mom and Dad stayed for a while, and then they left to go home. I walked them to the door and told them "thanks again for everything." They hugged me and said I was welcome. I just wandered around the house looking at everything while I was waiting on Matt to call. I went into his room and looked around, thinking maybe he will let me move back in his room soon. Matt finally called around ten o'clock.

I answered and he said, "I see you made it home."

"Yes, finally," I said.

"Please be good this time, Isabella."

I paused and said, "Matt, it's not a matter of being good; it's called being well."

"That's right honey, but you know what I mean," he said.

"Matt," I asked, "when are you coming home?"

Whisper

"Tomorrow," he said.

"Thanks, great," I said. "I miss you, and I want to see Summer."

"Call Mom in the morning," Matt said, "and tell her to let you come see Summer for about an hour."

"Thank you, Matt," I said. "I miss my baby so."

"I know you do," he replied. We talked for a while and we hung up and I got ready for bed. I made sure I took all my pills. The doctor had fixed it so I knew what to take and when. I took a long bath and relaxed, and it felt so good. I finally went to bed, and it felt so good to sleep in my own bed. The next morning I got up and took my medicine and ate. I called Matt's mother and told her that Matt said I could see Summer today.

"I don't know, dear," she said.

"Listen," I said, "I need to see my daughter, and Matt said I could."

"Let me call him," she said, "and I will call you right back."

"Sure," I said, "but I would never tell you something without Matt really saying that."

"I know, dear," she said, "but I just have to check."

"Just call me back," I said. This upset me because she acted like I couldn't even see my daughter. Finally the phone rang, and it was Matt's mother.

"Come on over, Isabella," she said, "and I will get Summer ready for you to see her."

"Fine," I said. "I will take her to the park."

"Oh no, dear," Matt's mom said. "Matt said that you must stay with her at the house when you visit until he gets home." I was really upset about that, but I only wanted to see Summer at any cost. I got ready and went to the store and bought her a new baby doll. I drove to Matt's house and pulled in the driveway. My knees where knocking, I was so excited. I rang the doorbell and Matt's mom came to the door. "Come on in," she said. "Sit down for a minute and let's talk before I go get Summer."

"OK," I said, really not having a choice in the matter.

"Well, dear," she said. "You look like you have gained a little weight."

"I guess I have," I replied. "My medicine does that to me."

"You look weak eyed, dear. Not sleeping?" she asked.

"I have been sleeping fine," I said really I said even about how bad I look .Can I just please see my daughter?" I asked.

"Isabella, dear," she said, "I just want you to know a woman must keep herself up if she intends to stay married, if you know what I mean."

"Really," I said, "I don't mean to be rude, but I just came to see my daughter and not to get advice on my marriage."

"Fine," she said and turned up her nose at me, and then she went to get Summer.

Finally my little girl came in the room, running to me saying "Mommy," and jumping right into my lap.

"Oh, how I have missed you, Summer," I said.

"I missed you too, Mommy," she said. I held her in my arms and smelled of her hair and felt my little girl in my arms. I cried and tears ran down my face. Summer looked at me and said, "Don't cry, Mommy."

"These are tears of joy," I told her.

Matt's mother said, "Really, Isabella, don't upset Summer."

Finally I said, "I know Matt said I couldn't take Summer off, but can we please just have a visit without you in the room?"

Looking angry, she said, "I guess thirty minutes, and that is it," she said.

"OK," I said. "That's fine, anything just so I can visit my daughter. Summer," I said, "look Mommy got you a new baby."

She smiled and kissed me. "I just love my new baby," she said. She asked me was I going away again.

"No, honey, I hope not," I said.

"Mommy, please be good so I can come home with you."

I looked at her and said, "Honey, Mommy is OK, she just was sick for a while."

Whisper

"I know, Mommy," Summer said. "Daddy told me you were being bad and had to go away for a while. But the doctor would make you good again."

"Oh, honey," I said, "you are to young to worry about that. Summer," I told her, "no matter where I am, I love you with all my heart."

"I love you too, Mommy," she said. We played with her new baby and talked and enjoyed our visit. Soon my visit was up, and Summer had to leave. I went home that night thinking how messed up that whole situation was. I am going to talk to Matt, I thought. I want my daughter back home where she belongs.

The next evening Matt returned home. He walked in and yelled out, "I'm home, Isabella." I came out, and he hugged and kissed me. "I have missed you, baby," he said.

"Me too," I told him. "Listen, let's sit down and talk."

"Sure," Matt said, holding my hand and walking to the coach.

"Matt," I began, "I need Summer home with me. It's not right that she can't be with her mother."

Matt thought about it for a minute and then he replied: "Tell you what, Isabella, if you take your medicine and don't hear that whispering shit that you always say you do, then we will see? I just need to know that you don't frighten her with those voices and those things you think you see, honey," he said.

"Matt," I said, "I have been in and out of hospitals, taken pill after pill. I only want my baby home. Whether you like what I am, I still am Summer's mother."

"Yes, you are honey," he said, "and I really want us to be a family again. You can do it, honey, and then Summer will be here with both of us again."

"Just how long do I have to prove myself to you?" I asked.

"I guess there is no timetable, Isabelle," Matt said. "We will know when the time is right." What could I do? He was holding all the cards in this game. So I had to play his game in order to have my baby back home. The next day I thought I need a part-time job; that might help me keep busy and keep my mind clear. I had to have my baby home; I missed her so. The phone rang and changed my thoughts.

"Hello," I said.

"Hey there," the voice on the other end said.

"Jill, is that you?" I asked.

"Sure is," she replied. "Are you going to be nice to me this time, Isabella?"

"What are you talking about?" I asked.

"At the hospital, remember how rude you were to me?"

I thought for a minute. "Oh yes, that," I said. "That just didn't seem right to me, Jill," I said. "Nothing against you, just I didn't like it. You know how people talk," I told her.

"Sure do," she said. "Right after that, everyone I knew thought Matt had left you and thought he and I were going together."

I thought, I just don't trust you anymore, but I didn't say it. I just said, "I certainly hope you told them different."

She laughed and said, "I sure did, honey. Listen, can I come by and see you? I have missed you, Isabella."

"Listen, Jill, I really have a lot to do. Maybe another time," I told her.

"Sure thing," she said, "just give me a ring when you are up to it."

"OK," I said and hung up the phone. Maybe my mind was playing tricks on me again. I was beginning to think Jill was a snake in the grass. I started to look through the newspaper for a job. I really wanted some kind of part-time job. Finally I saw an opening for a part-time saleslady at a department store. I got dressed and went for an interview. To my surprise, I got the job, and I was so happy. I called my mom and dad, and they were so happy for me.

"That's wonderful," my dad said. That night I made a real nice dinner for Matt and me.

"What's the occasion?" he asked.

"Well," I began, clearing my throat. "I got a part-time job today. Is not that great?" I said.

Matt looked at me and said, "Why didn't you ask me about this?"

"Well I didn't know I needed your permission to work," I said.

"Did you happen to mention to your new employer that you have a mental illness?"

"Well, Matt," I replied, "that question wasn't on the job application, but if it was, I would have sure signed where it said 'do you have a mental illness?'"

"Listen, Isabella," he said, "you don't have to be a smart-ass about this. I am only looking out for you."

"Matt, I have to have some kind of life. Lots of people work that have sort of illness of some kind. I want to be able to feel like I am normal, and normal people work, Matt."

"I know, honey, but I worry it will be too much on you, and what about when Summer comes home? I thought you wanted to be with her," he said.

"I do, Matt, but Summer will be in day care, and I can work while she is there."

"Isabella," Matt said, "if you really want this, then try it and see how it goes. But," he said, "if it gets too much for you, please quit before it causes problems for us."

"I will, Matt, I promise," I said, and I ran over and kissed him. Then we began to talk about my visit with Summer. I told him how sweet she was, and he said he was glad I had a good visit. I told him his mother wasn't very nice to me, and he said he would have a talk with her about the way she had treated me. I was to start my new job on the following Monday. I was nervous and happy at the same time. I wore a nice dress and heels. I wore my hair up and wore light makeup, and I tried to look as nice as I could. It was hard the first day, but I knew I would get used to it in time.

One day I was helping a lady with a purse, and guess who walked over to me? It was Jill. "Well," she said, "I didn't know you were working here."

"Yes, I am, Jill, but I am busy trying to help this lady." She walked over to the other side of the room and then came back when my customer had left.

"Well," she said, "I just can't picture you here. Are you OK working and all that?"

"Of course I am," I replied. "Listen, Jill, unless you want to buy something, I have to get back to work."

"Oh by the way," she said, "I took Summer to the park this morning."

I stopped what I was doing and walked over to her and asked, "Just why would you do a thing like that? She is in day care."

"Not today. It was closed for some reason, and Matt's mother called me and asked me if I would take care of her for an hour while she went to the doctor."

"Oh, really?" I said. "Why didn't she call me? I am her mother."

Jill just looked at me and said, "I guess she must have known you were working and couldn't, so she called me."

"Listen," I said, really getting mad, "I have to get to work, so we will talk later." Holding my tongue and trying to be a lady, I said the words, "Thank you for helping with her."

"No problem," she said, smiling that smile of hers. What a bitch, I thought. How could I have ever thought she was a friend?

That evening when I got home, Matt and I were having dinner, and I asked him, "Matt, did you know Jill took Summer to the park today?"

"Yes," he replied, "Mother called me, and I told her you were working, so I told her to call Jill."

"So Jill knew I was working at the store?" I asked.

"Of course I mentioned that to her," he said.

"Matt, she came in the store today acting like it was a surprise to see me."

"Well honey," he said, "maybe she thought I didn't want her to let on she knew."

"Jill is getting really cozy with you lately, isn't she?" I asked.

"What is that supposed to mean?" Matt asked.

"I mean, Matt, she seems to pop up everywhere in my life lately."

"Isabella, don't start anything. Is this job already affecting you?"

"No," I said, clearing the table. "I don't like Jill taking care of my daughter," I said.

"Gee, Isabella," Matt said, "it was one time. Don't make a big deal of it."

"The big deal is, Matt, I can't take Summer to the park, but someone who isn't her mother can."

"Isabella, when I know you are well, you can take Summer anywhere, you know that." I just kept doing the dishes and thinking something is not right here: I am treated like shit around here, and I am about to get tired of it. A month had gone by, and I was taking all my medicine and working and doing really well. Then one afternoon my boss called me into her office.

"Isabella, sit down, dear," she said. "You have been doing really good here at the department, but yesterday I had a phone call, and someone warned me about you."

"Warned you about me? What do you mean?" I asked.

"Well, it seems you have been in and out of hospitals and have cut yourself and might attack others if you get sick on the job," she said. "I feel really bad about this, dear, but I have to let you go."

"Please," I said, "I am well now, and I am on medicine, and I would never hurt anyone."

"But you do admit you have hurt yourself in the past?"

"Yes," I replied, "in the past."

"Sorry, Isabella, I wish you luck, but company policy." I walked out that day with my spirit broken. Who would do such a thing to me? I bet Matt did this just so I would stay home, I thought. When he comes home tonight, I will let him have it for doing such a thing to me. That night when Matt came home, I met him at the door. He turned the knob of the door, and I opened it

"Hey, honey," he said, "what's wrong?"

"This evening at work the manager of the store took me into her office. It seems someone called her and told her I was a real mental case. She asked me if I had been hospitalized, and I told her the truth. Then she said she was sorry, but she had to let me go."

"That's too bad," Matt said.

"Yes, it is," I said. "Did you call, Matt? I want the truth."

He looked at me funny and shook his head. "No, I didn't. I would never do such a thing to you, Isabella," he said. I sat down on the coach and just began to cry.

"You know, Matt," I began, "when you really try and make your life be normal, it seems it always has a way to fall apart."

"Honey," he said, pulling me into his arms, "there will be other jobs."

"I know," I said, "but someone will call and tell them I am crazy and I will lose that job, so what is the use?" I asked.

"Come on now, let's go out to eat and have a nice dinner together. What do you say?" Matt asked.

I smiled and said, "That would be nice; I would like that." I went upstairs and started to get dressed, then that little whisper came to me again. "He did it, Isabella. Are you really going to fall for his story?" I shook like a leaf. I hadn't heard that whisper in a while. I am taking all my medicine, so what is going on, I thought. I will call the doctor tomorrow. I don't want this demon to take control of my life again, I thought.

Matt called for me. "Isabella, come honey, let's go so we won't be late, OK?"

I yelled back, "Coming. Just fixing my hair, be right down." I pulled myself together so Matt wouldn't notice anything different about me. Matt brought the car around and walked me to it, opening the door for me. "Thank you," I told him as I sat down in the car. I could smell smoke really bad. I looked around in it and noticed the ashtray had ashes in it. He started the car and we were driving along when I finally got the nerve up to ask him. "Matt," I began, "I smell smoke in the car, and ashes are in the ashtray. Have you started to smoke?" I asked him.

"Isabella," he said, "you just don't stop, do you?"

"Stop what?" I said.

"Your nagging, that's what. It's always something you try to start with me. Can't we just have a nice evening out without the suspicion? By the way," he said, "Guy rode to the airport with me on Monday, and he happens to smoke. Does that answer your question now?"

Whisper

"Sure," I said. "I just wondered. I have never smelled smoke in your car before, and I know you hate the smoke of smokers." So we started to talk about Summer again, and I told him that I wouldn't work if he would let her come home.

"We will see," he said, "but tonight is about you and I."

"OK," I said, "you and I, like we used to be."

"That's right, honey. Remember when we got married how close we were? I miss you, Isabella, I miss your touch. Honey, please let tonight be about you and me."

I smiled, but in the back of my mind I knew Matt; I knew he would never let anyone smoke in his car. But I had to be calm and not get angry. I had to get Summer home again.

We got to the restaurant, and Matt and I went to our table. It was a quiet little place, and it was nice to spend a quiet evening with my husband. The waitress came to take our order, and I ordered salmon and salad and a small glass of red wine. We were talking, waiting for our order, when one of Matt's fellow workers came over. "Hey there," he said, "Matt, is that you?"

Matt looked like he had seen a ghost, and he jumped up and said, "Hey, James, it's good to see you again." Then a lady came right in behind him, and Matt was acting so nervous. "Honey," he said, "This is James. I work in LA with him, and this is his wife, Lucy."

Lucy looked at me and said, "Matt, what's going on?"

"What do you mean?" he asked.

Lucy said, "Matt don't act dumb with me. You need to get your life together," and then she grabbed her husband's hand and said, "Let's go.

James said, "Sorry, man, I didn't know."

Matt said, "That is all right, no problem," and then they left.

I looked at Matt and I asked, "What was that about?"

"That," he said slowly, "James's wife doesn't like me and just tries to act funny around me when I see her."

"Seems to me, Matt, she was surprised to see you with me."

"Oh, come on, Isabella, she knows I am married."

"Maybe so," I said, "but does she know you are married to me?"

"Of course she does. Like I said, she doesn't like me for some reason and tries to make trouble for me whenever she can. Now come on, honey, let's eat and enjoy our night out together." Now I know I am not too out of it to notice something was wrong with that picture. While I was in the hospital, my dear, sweet husband has been up to something, I thought. We ate dinner, and I laughed and played the part of his sweet, little dive wife. We danced and stayed late to hear the band. I really enjoyed my night out with Matt. I kept all of my feelings hidden, and I wouldn't argue the point at this time with him. When we got home that night, the wine had made me tipsy, and I was really tired. Matt wanted to make love, and for the first time in six months, he allowed me to sleep with him in his bedroom. By this time my love for Matt was getting less with each day that passed. He was so self-centered and thought he knew everything. He held my mental illness as a trump card to control my life, and I knew the game he was playing. But tonight I would play the game of making love but not feeling it, plain out faking it the whole time. We made love for hours, and do you know after it was over, he had the nerve to tell me to go back to my room.

I looked at him and asked, "Why must I sleep in a room away from you when we just made passionate love."

"Isabella, I'd just rather it be this way for now. Baby, trust me, it won't be long before you are back in my bed for good, and Summer will be home." I went back into the guest room and took a shower and cried. How could he treat me this way? I got to where I could hardly breathe. I just couldn't believe what was happening to me. I cried myself to sleep that night. I felt used and controlled, and I knew something was wrong. But God knew I wasn't in the position to say or do anything right now. The next morning I went downstairs to make some coffee, and Matt was already up and had it made. "Good morning, my darling," he said, walking over to me and kissing me on the neck. I moved away from him, and he asked, "What is wrong?"

"Listen," I began, "I really don't like the way you treated me last night. Are you afraid I will hear a voice that tells me to kill you in your sleep?" I asked. He looked at me strangely and said no. "Matt,"

I said, "if I was going to kill you, I would much rather you be awake so you could see me kill you."

"God, Isabella, that is it. You are acting crazy again."

"That's it, Matt. You always thinking I am acting crazy. One of these days I am going to get so mad and fed up with all the damn bullshit you do to me, and I will show what crazy really is."

"Calm down, Isabella," Matt said. "You don't need to say anything that you will regret later. This kind of talk and behavior is why I can't allow you to be around Summer by yourself right now. Get your appointment with the shrink again, and I want to know when you are going. You can't start this behavior again. It gets old after a while."

"Do you know what gets old, Matt, is you treating me like this all the time like I am a criminal. I am your wife, and I would like to be treated with dignity and respect. Matt, you show me none of that, and then you kick me when I am down."

"Isabella, let's just end this right now. I am going to work. I love you, but go see your doctor, and I will call you later today." Then he put his cup in the sink and walked out like it was nothing. I was so boiling mad that he would do the shit he does. What has happened to me, I wondered. No matter how hard I tried, I just couldn't win. I thought I would just go for a run and clear my head. As I was running, my head felt funny and my ears began to ring. I felt like I did years ago when I first heard that whisper. And then damn, there it came again. It whispered, "Isabella, I know you hear me. We will be together forever," it said. I stopped, breathing heavily.

"No," I yelled, "we will never be together. I will get rid of you some way." A lady and man were walking past me, and they heard me talking to myself.

The woman stopped and asked, "Dear, are your OK?"

"Yes," I replied.

"Whom are you yelling at? Was someone here and bothering you?" she asked.

"Yes," I said to keep from embarrassing myself. They said OK and began to walk away. I have got to quit this some way before Matt puts me back into the hospital, I thought. The next day I had an appointment with my doctor, and I wanted to get some help before

I got really sick again. The doctor began to talk to me about my medicine. He wanted to know if I was taking it like I should. I told him I was and that I still had this whispering going on in my head. He then asked me if I under a lot of stress. I told him about losing my job and about how I wasn't allowed to be alone with my daughter and that my husband treated me like a real mental case.

The doctor looked over his glasses and said, "That is part of the problem. Stress can make delusions reappear. I would like to talk to your husband, Isabella, and maybe I can help him understand the danger of stressing you out."

"Thank you," I said, "that might help. But." I said, "I think maybe my husband has been cheating on me while I was in the hospital."

"Really?" the doctor said looking at me real seriously. "What makes you think that, Isabella?" he asked.

"One night last week Matt and I were at a restaurant, and the wife of one of Matt's friend's walked over, and I think she knew Matt had been with someone else. Because she told Matt he needed to get his life together."

"Well, Isabella," he said, "she might have been referring to something else. Just relax and slow down and try not to worry over everything," he told me. "Isabella, you will get your life back, but schizophrenia is certainly a hard illness, and you will have it hanging over your head." I left the doctor's office and went to the mall to shop for something for Summer. I was looking at the little girls clothes when I noticed a woman who looked like the lady I had met in the restaurant the other night when Matt and I were out for dinner.

She walked past me and I said to her, "Don't I know you?"

She looked at me and said, "Yes, we met at the restaurant the other night, didn't we?"

"Yes," I said. "I am Matt's wife."

"Really?" she said. "How long have you been married to Matt?"

"Twelve years," I replied.

"Really?" she said. "I didn't realize that Matt was married until the other night. It was a surprise to me to see him with you."

"Why is that?" I asked.

"Honey," she said, "you look like a really nice woman. Maybe I should just keep my big mouth shut."

"Look," I said, "please, if you know something about my husband, please tell me. I need to know, please," I pleaded with her.

"All right," she said. "I have seen Matt on several occasions, and the woman I saw him with hasn't been you."

"Mm," I said, "was it the same woman or a different one each time?"

"No, honey, it has been the same woman each time I saw him."

"Did you by any chance notice if this woman smoked?"

"Yes," she said, "she did, and I noticed that Matt would take his hand and wave it away. I am sorry, honey," she said. "There might be a good reason he was with her, maybe work."

"That night," I said, "when you came over to the table, you told Matt to get his life together. You know more, don't you?" I asked.

"Listen, honey," she said. "I have said too much as it is. I have got to run. Good seeing you. Take care," she said, and she ran out the door. She gave me just enough information to make me really worry and still have no answers. But now I knew Matt was seeing someone, but whom? When I returned home, I studied Matt's behavior and tried to think of the times he left and the strange phone calls he would receive at the house. I remembered that he said "I told you not to call here." It was beginning to make sense now. I was always in the hospital, and that gave him the playground to play in while I was gone away. I think back about Matt, the man I married, who stood by me through the hardest times any man could have stood. But now he was falling apart, and I guess this was the way he chose to deal with it. When Matt came home that night, I mentioned I had run into Lucy.

"Really?" he said. "How is she doing?"

"Fine, I guess," I said. "Funny thing: she mentioned she didn't know you were married."

"Um," he said, "I guess I never mentioned it to her."

"Matt, she told me she had seen you out several times with another woman, and guess what, Matt, it wasn't me."

"I know that, Isabella," he said getting mad. "It was my damn secretary. We had late dinners because of the workload. Now get off my back. I am tired, and I don't need your bullshit. God, Isabella," he yelled, "I think you are trying to drive me crazy."

"I will tell you what I told my mother years ago when she said the same thing to me: Don't forget, I am the crazy."

"You like to use that for your bad behavior, don't you?"

"Sure, I love hearing voices and seeing things that aren't there. It's fun, Matt. You know me, I love drama."

He slapped his briefcase down and said, "Don't you try to back me against the wall, Isabella. You will not win. I am better at this game than you are."

"I bet you are," I said, walking up the stairs thinking what an asshole I married. I heard Matt talking on the phone to someone. By this point, I didn't care anymore. I went to bed mad as hell. I had to come up with a plan to take my daughter and leave and get away from this asshole. I woke up about four in the morning, and I thought I heard someone talking. I listened and I could hear the sounds coming from Matt's bedroom. I walked quietly to his door and put my ear right up to the door. I heard Jill's voice. I heard her say, "I want to be with you," and I heard Matt say, "Not now, it's not a good time." I crept back into my room and studied this. Now I get it. All this time it's been Jill. Right in front of my eyes, and being my best friend. I was so mad, and I was going to confront Jill tomorrow. Jill and Matt, why didn't I figure that one out? The next day I called Jill.

She answered the phone, "Oh hey, Isabella," she said. "How are you?"

"Fine," I said. "How would you like to come over for coffee, and let's talk like we used to; girl talk, remember?"

"Yes," Jill said, "I would love that. Be right over." The doorbell rang, and I walked over and let Jill in.

"Come on in," I said. "Good to see you, Jill. Have you been OK?" I asked.

"Yes," she said, "I have been fine.

"I see you have changed the way you dress."

She laughed and said, "Yes, do you like it?"

"It's different," I said.

"Isabella," she said, "you need to dress a little more sexy and wear tight pants. It's the style nowadays."

"Really," I said. "I guess I am old-fashioned then. That kind of dressing makes a woman look cheap to me."

"Well, Isabella," Jill said angrily. "It's a good way to make sure your man doesn't stray."

"Really," I said, "keeps your man at home, does it?" I asked.

"Sure does. If you are sexy and hot in bed, you can't run him off with a stick."

"Isn't that funny that you would say that, Jill? My man has already been seeing someone else."

"Oh, get out of here," she said. "I don't believe that."

Finally I said, "Stop the bullshit. I know you are sleeping with Matt, so just come clean."

"Isabella, you are losing it, girlfriend," she said. "Not me, I have my own man. Don't want yours, don't need yours. I am leaving and don't call me after this," she said.

"Fine," I replied. "I am warning you, stay away from Summer. Do not take my daughter anywhere, do you understand me?" I asked.

"Isabella, you really need to chill. I only took her because Matt asked me, as a favor."

"Don't do us any more favors, do you get it?" I said and pushed her to the door.

"Fine," she said and slammed the door and got into her car and drove off. Damn bitch, I thought, I know she was lying. I will catch her and Matt yet. Well it wasn't long after she was gone that Matt called me.

"Isabella, what in the hell are you doing, accusing Jill of having an affair with me?"

"Listen, Matt, I heard her last night in your bedroom."

"Damn it, Isabella, I really can't take much more. Stop all your shit. I guess you need to go back into the hospital if you are hearing voices."

"Matt," I said, "it was the whispering. It was Jill's voice. Matt, I grew up with her, I know how she sounds."

"I got to get back to work," he said. "I will deal with you when I get home. Please leave poor Jill alone. She is beside herself with you treating her this way." He hung up and I stood there holding the phone thinking, I bet she is really beside herself. That damn slut. I decided I wanted to talk to Jack about Jill. He knew her better than anyone. I went to his shop.

"Hey, Isabella," he said, "what brings you here?"

"I just wanted to stop by and ask you a few questions," I said.

"What kind of questions?" he asked.

"I just wanted to hear your side of the story."

"What story is that?" Jack asked.

"About your divorce. What really happened? Jill told me you were cheating on her."

He laughed and rubbed his face. "Did she now? That is so funny. Did you believe her, Isabella?"

"I didn't think you were that kind of person, but Jill can be convincing."

"Yes," he said, "I know she can be. Listen here," he said, "I never cheated on Jill. I gave her my paycheck each week. She had credit cards. A brand-new car I bought her, but honestly the more I did for her, the more she wanted. Jill began to flirt right in front of me, and even with some of my friends, and I got tired of all of it and put my foot down, and that's when she said she wanted her freedom, so, Isabella, I gave it to her. And to tell you the truth, I have been the happiest I have been in years. I don't know why she lies about us. I guess it makes her feel better about herself. I really don't care anymore. But why are you asking about this after all this time?" he asked.

"I don't know," I said. "I just wanted to know if I could trust Jill or not."

"That's a good question. Good luck with that one," Jack said. "I tried to trust her, but she was always doing crazy shit that backfired into her face. For the last three years of our marriage, I know she was cheating with someone and then she tells everyone it was I. What the hell, I thought, let people make their own minds up, I will not argue the point. I know what I am about, and I certainly after all these years know what Jill is about. To tell you the truth, Isabella, it's a blessing she is gone. I feel as if I have recovered from cancer or something."

"Um," I replied, "I am beginning to see what you mean. I thought Jill was my best friend. We grew up together, and she was always there for me."

"I know," Jack said, "but people change, sometimes for good and sometimes for the worse. Isabella," he said, "don't think for one second she is the same person she was years ago. Jill has no friends; she thinks only of herself and her needs, so self-centered this woman has become over the years. I really feel deeply sad for whoever she trapped this time. I only know I am free, and I feel better and honestly say I wish her well, I really do. But keep your distance, Isabella, and be careful of her," Jack told me.

"I will, Jack," I said. "Thank you for telling the truth. It breaks my heart to think she has changed that much over the past few years." I left that day knowing I had lost the best friend in the world, and whom could I trust now? I drove home remembering the school days Jill and I had together and all the fun we had shared over the years. I got tears in my eyes and could hardly drive. I drove up in the driveway, and Matt was getting out of his car.

"What is wrong?" he asked. I smiled and said I was listening to a sad love song on the radio and it made me cry. He hugged me and said, "I just love that tender part of you, honey." I just walked back into the house. I just can't believe that Jill and Matt were having an affair, I thought. Maybe my mind was playing tricks on me that night. I didn't want to believe, so I tried not to think about it anymore that day. I asked Matt if I could go see Summer. It always made me feel better to see her. "Sure," he replied. "I will call Mom and tell her you are coming over."

"Thank you, Matt," I said and kissed him. I left and drove over to my mother-in-law's house. I got to the door and I rang the doorbell. She didn't answer. I got back into my car and looked through my purse and found my cell phone and called her. Finally she answered, and I told her I was outside.

"OK," she said, "but you must not stay long because we are making cookies for the church and have to take them there."

"Sure," I said and walked back to the door. Matt's mom hated me, I could tell, but I didn't care. I just wanted to see Summer. Finally Summer came into the room running as fast as she could to see me.

"Mommy," she said, "I miss you," and she jumped into my arms.

"I miss you too, my little darling," I told her.

"Mommy," she asked, "when could I come home with you?"

"Soon," I said.

"Mommy," she said holding her hand up across her mouth, "Grandma says I can never be with you because you are sick. Mommy," she asked again, "what are you sick from? Do you have a tummy ache that won't go away?"

I smiled and held her tight. "Honey, we will be together, no matter what anyone says." We visited and I asked Summer to go to her room so I could talk to her grandmother. I waited until I heard her shut her door, and then I walked into the kitchen where Matt's mother was. "Listen," I began, taking a deep breath, trying not to get as mad as I felt inside, "please don't tell Summer that I will never get well and that she will never come to live with me."

"Listen here, Isabella. Matt may overlook all you have done over the years, but my granddaughter will not live with you and all your so-called voices or whatever it is."

I looked her right in the eyes. "Don't you forget that I gave birth to that child, not you, and she is my flesh and blood, she is my daughter, whether you like it or not. And by the way, you old biddy, I will have her home again. Summer loves me, and you can never take that away from me or her."

She turned around and threw her dish towel down on the table. "You just wait until I tell Matt. He won't like the way you have spoken to me," she said.

"Really," I said. I was hot by now, and I knew my face was boiling red. "I really don't give a damn that you tell him." Then I turned around and walked out the door. Of course, she had called Matt the minute I walked out the door. Matt was standing in the living room when I walked in.

"Just can't leave it alone, can you, Isabella? Why on this good earth can't you let me take care of my mother? You know how much she loves Summer, and the thought of losing her upsets her."

"Upsets her?" I screamed. "What about me? I am the child's mother, not your mother, Matt."

"I know, honey," he said, "but there is no reason to keep everyone upset right now. If you love Summer as much as you say you do, then don't do things that will upset her. Think of Summer, honey," Matt said.

I thought for a minute and I said, "Sure, Matt, you are right. I don't want to upset Summer. She doesn't need that. I know she must feel sad being away from me and you." I went into my bedroom, my thinking place where I always go when I am upset. I wanted to be with my daughter so badly, but I knew I was still too sick to keep her.

That night at the dinner table Matt said, "Isabella, I want you to listen to me. I know you love Summer and want her home, but hear me out." I looked at him and saw seriousness in his face. "Isabella," he began, "I have seen you cut yourself and hurt yourself for so long. I know the things you thought you have seen are real to you, and knowing I was helpless in helping just killed me. The years of this have drained me, and I have tried to be strong, honey. I have seen you at your best, and I have seen you at your worst. But now we are talking about a little girl, honey. I know in my heart that you would never hurt Summer on purpose. The side of you that is a mother and a kind soul is very sweet and good. But, Isabella, there is a dark side of you also. What if that whispering sound that sends the voices started to tell you to hurt Summer. You never know, honey, are you willing to chance it with her? Right now, Isabella, if I tell you to go get Summer and bring her home, are you certain that in some way if this voice starts talking that Summer won't get hurt?

If you are certain, and you want to chance it, I am giving you my permission to go get her and bring her home." I stood up, and then I sat right back down in the chair. I thought about what Matt said. I love her with all my heart, but Matt was right; I wasn't being fair to Summer. I knew whether I liked his mother or not that she was good to Summer, and Summer loved her. Did I dare take a chance with my daughter' well-being?

I looked at Matt and said, "You know, you are right. I won't take a chance with her. Even seeing me acting out, it would frighten her and would affect her for the rest of her life. OK, I just want to see her twice a week at your mother's, and if we go out, you and I will take her out together."

He walked over, pulling me out of the chair, and said, "That's the Isabella I fell in love with. You may see her, honey, and we will take her out once a week together."

I told Matt, "Thank you for reminding me how very sick I used to be. I know it frightened me so as a little girl, and I know if Summer saw me at my worst, it would scare her to dead. I must do what is best for her." I told Matt I would like to go to Mass and maybe attend confession. He told me to go if it would make me feel better. When I got to the church, I went into the confession booth. I sat down, and the father slid his door open. "Father," I began, "I need to know what to do."

"What to do about what?" he asked.

"Father, I have been sick," and then I paused and took a short breath. "I mean mental sick, Father,"

"I see," said the father, "and how may I help you, my child."

"I have caused my parents and brother and especially my husband great pain. The problem is, Father, I get well and then I get sick again. I can't stand the pills and the shots I have to endure in order to maintain a normal life. I feel my family and husband would be better off without me. I have a daughter and I feel so lost at what to do. Father, if I took my own life in order for my family to finally have peace, would God forgive me?"

The priest paused and then said, "I don't think he would want you to take your life in your own hands and end it. God will help you, my child."

I started to cry. "I pray every day, and I don't get better," I said. "I have some good days, but the bad things happen again after a while."

"Dear child," the priest said, "have faith. Sometimes it is darkest before the dawn. Life is a trial on earth, and you must not give up. Keep the faith," he told me and then he closed the window. I went home that day thinking I was hurting my family so, not on purpose, but without me having control over what had happened or was going to happen. As I walked into the room, Matt was sitting reading the paper.

"Feel better, babe?" he asked.

"Yes, I do," I said. I didn't want to worry him anymore. I went into my room and lay down on my bed, thinking what I could do to make up the wrong I had done my family. The next day I called my doctor and made another appointment. I told Matt I wanted to go back and see if there was some new medicine to help me, so I wouldn't fall back. That's a good idea, he said.

"That is a good step forward, honey," he said, so at least that pleased him, and I wanted to try to put my life back together.

When I went to Dr. Orr, I walked in and he said, "Is there something wrong, Isabella?"

"Dr Orr," I said, "I am starting to hear that faint whisper again, and I see flashing lights at times. The images of other people in my room are reappearing, but please don't mention this to my husband. He has been through so much of this kind of thing; I really want to spare him."

"Sure," he said, "if that's what you want, but this sounds serious again."

"I know," I said, "and I am afraid and don't want this to begin again. Is there something new you can give me?"

"Well," he said, standing up. "Isabella, I was looking at your chart just the other day. Dear, you have been in and out of several hospitals over the years, and eventually we end up back here. There are a few new medicines out there, but they have a lot of side effects."

"I don't care," I said. "I am willing to try anything at this point."

"OK then," he said. "I will try you on a new medicine, and you keep me informed on how you are feeling. If there are problems, let me know right away."

"I will," I told him and thanked him and went home. The next day I had my medicine filled and started to take it. It started to make my heart beat very fast, and I thought I was going to have a heart attack. I didn't care; I had to try something. I hated that whispering and seeing shit. After a few days, the fast beating of my heart went away. But then something strange happened to me. I got worse; I began to get more paranoid and thought Matt was out to kill me. The whispering started at night and said to me, "Isabella, Matt wants to poison you." I thought at this time this was true. Every time Matt cooked or handled any food, I would throw it out. One night Matt made dinner for me, and the voice whispered to me, "Don't you dare eat that. It will kill you." I put the food in my mouth and ate it slowly, and then I told Matt I had to go to the bathroom, and I threw it up. I was beginning to lose weight again. The voice kept me up at night, laughing and talking to me. I would cover my head with a pillow. I would scream out, "Leave me alone, go away."

Then one night Matt heard me screaming. He knocked on the bedroom door. "What is the matter, Isabella?"

"Nothing," I answered.

"I thought I heard you screaming."

"Oh that," I said, "I just had a bad dream."

He opened the door and walked over to the bed. "Come, sweetie," he said, "come sleep with me tonight." I got up and walked into his bedroom. He laid me on the bed and covered me up and kissed me and said, "Go to sleep. I will be right here for you." I smiled and turned over, and he cut the lights out. I lay there trying to sleep. I thought I heard someone walking through the house. Matt didn't hear it. He could sleep through anything. I lay there shaking, and then I started to see images of faces in the dark. I fought this all night long, and I didn't dare tell Matt or wake him up. I knew he was trying really hard to help me. Every time I started a new medicine, I would start all this over again. I was so sad and tired of fighting a losing game of the mind. The next morning I was so tired. I had stayed up all night fighting off the whispers in my head. I went downstairs and got some coffee, and I was going to take my medicine when I noticed the bottle was almost empty. I asked Matt if he had done something with it. "Isabella," he said, "why would I of all people do anything with your medicine?"

"I just don't understand," I said, picking the bottle up and looking at it. "It was full yesterday. I have taken about five pills since I got it filled. What happened to the rest of the pills?" I asked.

"Honey, I don't know. Look in your purse; maybe the bottle came open, and some of them fell out into your purse."

I walked over and got my purse and looked into it. "No," I said, "I don't see any, but my things have been moved around inside my purse."

"What things?" Matt asked.

"My money is out of my billfold, and I always keep my money in there so I want lose any of it. Matt," I said, "someone has been going through my things."

"Now, Isabella," Matt said, "who would do that? No one has been here but you and I."

"Well," I replied, "I know when my things look different and know I won't have enough medicine for the month."

"Honey," Matt said, "call your doctor and tell him you lost them, and maybe he will call you in some more." Thinking of what had happened, I thought, maybe it's Matt. I thought he is trying to get me sick again so he can go on without me. I guess he just is tired of all my crazy things I do. Matt left for work, and I was sitting on the couch when the phone rang. I went to answer it and it was Sky. I was so happy to hear from him. He had been away with his wife on a trip. I missed my brother and wanted to see him. He asked if he should come by and see me.

"Of course you can," I replied. "I will see you in a few," and I hung up the phone and went to get dressed. Sky rang the doorbell, and I jumped with joy and hugged him. "I am so glad to see you," I said.

"I am happy to see you too, Sis," he said. "Come on, let's sit down and talk. First thing I want to know is why are you so thin. When I left, you were a little on the heavy side. What's going on, Sis?" Sky asked. I told him the medication I was on made me gain weight, and then the doctor put me on a different kind, and I started to lose weight again. "Isabella," he said, "you have that look again. I can see it in your eyes. You are sick again, aren't you?"

"Well I feel bad again, and I can't sleep, and I think Matt is trying to make me sick or even poison me."

Sky just put his hands over his face and said, "My beautiful sister, why you? Now, Isabella, Matt loves you, and this thing about him trying to poison you isn't real. That's in your head. Fight this, Isabella, you are strong. Please don't give in to it again. You were doing so well when I left. I just don't understand. Are you taking your medicine right?" he asked me.

"Of course I am. Do you think that I want to be the way I am? It's not like I asked God to make me crazy. I think I wanted more in my life than this."

"I know," he said, hugging me. "I am sorry, Sis. Is there anything I can do?"

"No, just pray for me. Sky, you just can't image how sick I am of being sick. Up and down, and I never seem to get well like I should be. I talk to the doctor, and he says I will have some quality of life, but this is a shitty quality of life."

"Well, Sis, I don't know what to tell you except please don't give up. Just remember, you have Summer to think about," Sky said.

"I know," I replied. "I guess that is the only real reason I keep trying to go on. If I didn't have her to think about, I would just end my life."

"Please, Isabella," Sky said, "don't talk like that. I love you. I can't imagine life without you."

"Oh," I said, "I wouldn't really act on that. I guess sometimes I feel sorry for myself."

"I understand," Sky said. "Come, let's go out for some pizza. What do you say?" he asked.

"Yes," I said, "that will be fun. I haven't had pizza in a long time." I left a note for Matt and told him I had left with Sky. We arrived at the pizza parlor and sat down. We were ordering, and guess who walks in? In all her glory. It was Jill and Judy, another girl we went to school with. They walked over, and Jill had jeans on that looked like she was melted and poured into them.

"Hey there," Jill said.

I smiled and said, "Good to see you, Jill. You're looking good these days."

"Oh, by the way," Jill said, "do you remember Judy?"

"Yes, I do," I replied. "How are you, Judy?" I asked.

"Just fine," she replied, and then Judy started looking at my brother. "Who is this good-looking fellow with you?" Judy asked.

"This is my brother, Sky," I said.

"Nice to meet you," Sky told her.

"By the way, Isabella," Judy said, "I heard that you have been sick. Are you better now?" she asked. I looked at Jill like I could run right through her. I knew she had been running her big mouth.

I answered Judy: "Yes, I am a lot better these days."

"That's good," Judy said and started to push me over. "Can we sit with you two?"

I sighed and said, "Well I guess, but we are just eating, and then we have to get going."

"That's fine," Judy said, and then she started to flirt with Sky.

He smiled and said, "I am honored that you are interested in me, but I am married."

"That's OK," she said. "I am too."

"Well," Sky said, "I don't cheat on my wife."

"Sorry," Judy said, "can't blame a girl for trying. You are certainly worth taking a chance on." Then I changed the subject and started asking Judy whom she married, and did she have children.

Jill said, "By the way, Isabella, where is Matt, and how is he these days?"

I replied, "He is at work, and he is doing fine. I will tell him you were asking about him."

"Please do," Jill said. "He is such a sweet guy."

"He certainly is," I said looking at her funny. We sat and ate pizza, and Sky and I both couldn't wait to get away from those two.

On the drive home, Sky asked, "What is up with Jill? I don't remember her dressing that way."

"I know," I said, "this is new for her, ever since Jack and her got a divorce, she has been dressing and acting different."

"That is odd," Sky said. "I liked her better the other way."

"Well," I said, "that old Jill is gone. Now it's the bitch from hell."

Sky just looked at me and laughed and said, "Isabella, you are so funny." Then he started to ask me about Summer, and I told him how sweet and pretty she was getting. "I would like to go see her soon. Would you ask Matt to arrange it for me?" he asked.

"I sure will," I told him. Then he walked me inside and told me good-bye and left. Matt still hadn't come home yet, so I walked into the kitchen and was going to throw away the note I left him. I looked on the table where I had left it, and it was gone. Maybe he came home and got it and went somewhere, I thought. I looked in the trash can, and I didn't see it. Now I know, I thought, I left a note for him. Oh well, this is strange, I thought, and I went into the living room to watch some TV. Finally Matt came in.

"Hey honey," he said. I walked over to him and hugged him.

"Guess what?" I said. "Sky came by and took me out for pizza."

"Really," he said sitting his briefcase down.

"Yes," I said, "we had a really good time. I left you a note on the table telling you that I had left with him. Did you get the note, Matt?"

"Honey, you saw me just walk in the door." I just didn't mention it again. We talked about how Sky was, and I told him that I saw Jill and Judy in the pizza parlor. "Really," Matt said, "and how was she doing?"

"Fine," I guess. "Same old Jill: loud mouth, tight pants."

"Well," Matt said, "I guess the way she dresses is her business. We have enough problems without worrying about how Jill looks." I just looked at him and thought, I bet you like the way she dresses, but I didn't tell him that. "By the way, honey, did you call the doctor about your medicine?"

"No," I replied. "I was going to, then Sky called and I went out with him."

"Don't you think getting your medicine is more important than going out with your brother?"

"Listen," I told Matt. "I haven't seen him in a long time. I will call the doctor tomorrow."

"OK then," he said, "don't you forget. It's important, honey," he said, and then he started to walk off making phone calls. I went upstairs and was running my bathwater, and I noticed that in the bathroom there were some things moved around differently. I walked down the stairs, and Matt was still on the phone. I waited until he hung up, and then I asked him if he had been in my bathroom. "Of course not," he replied. "What would I be doing in your bathroom?"

"Because," I said, "things have been moved around, you know, not where I left them."

"Really, Isabella," he said, getting mad. "It's the pills, and now it's your personal things. I guess a ghost came and moved everything around."

"You are making fun of me, aren't you?" I asked.

"No, Isabella, I was just trying to show you how stupid it is that you think someone is messing with your things."

"I just hate you," I screamed at him, "something is going on here. You are trying to make me think I am crazy again."

"No, I am not," Matt said. "I love you, but look, Isabella, this has to stop, even if you have to go back into the hospital."

"Sure," I said, "that's your answer to everything: back into the hospital if you don't agree with me."

Matt just shook his head and said, "I am really tired; I am going to bed. Call that doctor tomorrow. I mean it, Isabella," he said. Then he turned and walked up the stairs. I stood at the bottom of the stairs watching him go up. I was so mad at him. I heard him close the door, and I went into the kitchen to get a glass of water. As I was walking up the stairs, I could hear Matt talking to someone. I heard him say, "Have you been coming in the house when I have been out?" I leaned my head to his door to listen more; then right then, he opened the door. "What do you think you are doing?" he asked. I just looked stupid. I didn't know what to say. "Go back to bed and stop all this foolishness tonight, please, Isabella." Then he walked me into my room and pointed to the bed and said, "Go and rest and make sure you call that doctor tomorrow." He closed my door and walked out. I could hear him say, "Damn, will this shit ever stop?" I lay there in the bed really confused, but I didn't dare get back up for the rest of the night. The next morning he was so mad at me that he left without saying good-bye. I hated when he did that to me. It was like he was trying to punish me. I heard the door shut and his car drive off, so I decided to sleep in a little. I didn't really sleep too good, so I thought I could use the rest. I was sleeping when a bang woke me up. I sat up in the bed and listened. I could hear someone walking around. I walked slowly down the stairs and looked into every room. Then I went into the kitchen, and there was food all over the floor, and trash was thrown on the table. The coffee pot was broken.

I yelled out, "Who is here? Who did this?" I walked around the house, and I couldn't find anyone. I sat in the floor and cried. I called my mother and asked her to come over. I sat in the floor and cried until she came. I said, "Mom, just look at this mess. I woke up and I heard a noise, and when I came downstairs, this is what I found." Mom didn't say anything at first. She just walked around and looked at the house. Then she started to clean the mess up. I looked at her and said, "Mom, what do you think of this?"

She said, "I really don't know, honey. The doors were locked, and how would someone get in without you letting them in?"

"Damn," I yelled out. "I tell you someone was in the house." My mom just kept cleaning like she didn't hear what I was saying. "Oh, I get it," I said. "You think I did this, don't you?" She didn't answer me. "Mom," I screamed out, "I didn't do this," and I sat in the floor with my head between my legs, and I started to shake. "Oh, God," I said, "what is happening to me?"

My mother walked out of the room, and then she came back. "Where is your medicine, honey?" she asked.

"I don't want the damn medicine," I cried. "I didn't do this. Someone is trying to play tricks on my mind," I said. "Matt wants me back in the hospital, and he is trying to make me think I am losing my mind."

"Really, Isabella," my mother said. "Here they are, honey. Just take this for Mother."

"Damn," I said, "I am not a child, and medicine isn't what I need right now. I need to know the truth." I took the medicine and went back upstairs to lie down. I must have been sleeping for hours because the next thing I knew I could hear Matt talking to my mother. Then I heard them walking up the stairs, and then my bedroom door opened.

Matt walked in and said, "Honey, get dressed. We are going for a ride." When he said that, I knew what was about to happen, I knew this routine very well: it was hospital time. I got dressed and I didn't give them a fight, and then I went to the car and we were headed for the hospital. When we got there, the nurse at the desk started to ask all kinds of questions. My mother started telling her that I called her and what she had found then.

Matt told them about the medicine and the other good, old stuff I saw. Matt demanded they call Dr. Orr in to see me. The nurse explained to Matt that my doctor was out of town. "Well," Matt said sharply, "she will have to see whoever then, but she has to see someone, and tonight." I sat in the chair for hours before they called me back. Then I had to tell everything all over again I felt like I was getting undressed when I had to go into all this shit again.

The doctor listened and then looked at Matt and said, "I can certainly understand your concern, but really I can't put your wife into the hospital for making a mess in your kitchen. That really isn't a good enough reason to admit her at this time," he said.

"What about her medicine? It's gone. Just what are we supposed to do about that?" Matt asked.

"That's no problem," the doctor said. "I can get her some medicine. I really don't see any danger in Isabella. She seems fine to me."

"What about the mess she says she didn't make?" Matt asked.

"Young man," the doctor said, "I think you need to listen to your wife. I believe her. I don't think she did, but," he said, "even if she did, maybe she just got mad at you and was afraid to tell you the truth." Matt grabbed me by the arm, pulling me up out of the chair.

"Come on, Isabella," he said, "this was a total waste of time. We will just wait till your regular doctor comes back," he said.

"Sorry," the doctor said looking funny at and signing the papers to release me. "Take care, Isabella," the doctor said, handing me the papers.

"I will take those," Matt said, jerking them from me. This was a first for me, that someone actually believed me. I felt glad that he believed me; however, it didn't make things any easier for me. Matt cussed the doctor all the way home; he dropped my mother off and thanked her for coming and calling him.

"Sorry," Mother said, "if I had known he wasn't going to help Isabella, I wouldn't have called you."

"That's OK," Matt said, "we will take care of it later." Mom got out and said she loved me and would see me later. I was so tired from all the waiting, I could die. Matt instructed me to go straight to bed and no funny stuff. I hung my head down and walked into my room. I lay there on my bed, thinking of all the strange stuff that had been going on the past week. I know I was ill, but for once in my life, I wasn't doing this stuff. But who was and why? It was making no sense to me why someone would want to hurt me this way. I began to read a book and tried to get my mind off all my problems. I had to be careful because Matt was going to find a way to put me back into the hospital. So what should I do, just act like I don't see these things and fix them. Maybe if I did that, whoever it was doing this might stop. Um, I thought, now there is an idea. I just might try that next time something happens. The next morning I got up, and Matt was gone, and there sat my mother.

"Good morning, sleepyhead," she said. I could hardly open my eyes, and she was so cheerful first thing in the morning.

"Hey, Mom," I said, "what are you doing here?"

"I just wanted to come and see about you, so I thought I would come early and make us some breakfast."

"Mom," I said, "come on now, I know you better than that. What's up really?" I asked.

Mom walked over to the stove and poured me some coffee. "Come on, sweetie, I just worry about you, something I should have done years ago. Isabella," she said and then she started to cry, "I feel all this is my fault. You tried to tell me about all the whispers and things you saw years ago, and I just didn't want to believe it. This illness broke my heart years ago when it affected your aunt Jessie. She frightened me so as a child; I guess that is why I just didn't want to hear or believe anything you were telling me. Maybe if I had done more for you back then, you wouldn't be where you are now." She just cried and cried.

"Mom," I said, "don't beat yourself up like this. I understand better than anybody how this illness frightens you. I used to think I was possessed by demon for years, because I didn't understand this illness. Now I know it's in my mind, but Mom, the whisper soft voice that talks to you gets louder as the years go by. I used to blame you, Mom, but it's not anyone's fault. It's unfortunate for me that I got this from Aunt Jessie. But at least, Mom, you have one child that is normal."

She got up and hugged me and said, "Isabella, I love you no matter what. You are my daughter, and you are so beautiful, honey, and when you are acting normal, it makes up for all the other times."

"Mom, I love you," I said, and we hugged and cried and got close that day, and that is one of my best memories of my mother. She stayed for a while, and then she left for home. I had such a warm feeling of love that day, and I was at peace, but peace was there only just for a short time. I made sure I started to take my medicine again, and I started to carry it with me in my purse. Matt called to make sure I took it too. He was a little short with me on the phone, so I guess he was mad at me. He told me to make sure I made an appointment with my regular doctor, and I told him I would. Matt's mother called and asked me to have Matt call her when he got home, and then right before she hung up, she asked me, "By the way, are you all right?"

"Yes, I am fine," I said, knowing she was going to say something to upset me.

"I heard about you throwing food all over the kitchen. Really," she said, "Isabella, are you such an attention seeker for Matt to stay home with you that you are willing to try anything?"

"Listen," I said, "I don't want to argue with you, but what goes on in this house is really none of your damn business."

"That is my son, and I am afraid he is going to have a heart attack or something from all the bizarre things you keep doing."

Well by this time I was sick of hearing her bitch at me. "Take it up with your son, please," I told her, and then I hung up on her. Damn, I thought, I just couldn't win. Everyone thinks I am this awful person. I stood by the phone for a minute thinking, could I be doing these things like I used to cut myself when I blacked out? Could this be the case: I am passing out again, and instead of hurting myself, I am breaking things and moving stuff and not remembering? I started to remember back when I the cutting myself was going on maybe that is what it is I must ask Dr. Orr when I see him next week. I just wanted to have a normal life, and everyone in town knew my life history. I would ask Matt not to tell people about my business, and I am damned if the first thing I knew, he had told everyone he worked with.

He would tell me, "Well they asked about you, and I let it slip out." Sure, I thought, he just put my business on the street, and everyone in this town thinks I am really strange and crazy. Just the other day, I saw Jean and her little boy at the store. I walked over and said hello, and you would have thought I had the plague or something. I looked at her little boy, bending down talking to him.

He was so sweet and had the sweetest little smile, and then she grabbed him and put him in her arms and said, "Sorry, I can't stay to talk, Isabella. We have to run. See you," she said and hurried out the store. I knew she was getting away from me; I could sense the distrust in the air. So you see, I have no friends, and I thought maybe

I was going off the deep end again. I went upstairs and lay on the bed, and finally Matt returned home.

He walked in and said, "How is it going, honey?"

"Fine, I guess," I answered.

"Do you want to go out for dinner, honey?" he asked.

"I guess," I answered, "if you want to."

"Fine," he said. I told him I would just change clothes and be right down. I put a little makeup on and was looking in the mirror at myself. I had dark circles under my eyes. I tried to powder over them so they wouldn't look so bad. I was so skinny. My bones were showing. Yes, I thought as I looked at myself in the mirror, to eat is what I really needed to do. I was turning into a skinny, ugly woman right before my very eyes. "Honey," Matt yelled out, "are you ready?"

"Yes," I replied. "Be right down." So I grabbed a sweater, and down the stairs I went.

Matt said, "Honey, you look lovely."

"Thank you," I said. I knew he was just trying to make me feel better. I knew I looked like a pile of walking bones. We drove to the restaurant, and we got a table in the back. The restaurant was near the lake, and we could see the water from the table we were sitting at. A band was playing there, and they started to play a soft love song.

Matt said, "Isabella, dance with me."

I said, "I don't know if I remember even how to dance."

"Sure, you do," he said, pulling my chair out and taking my hand, leading me to the dance floor. He held me so tight I could hear his heart beating. At this time right then I knew somewhere in his heart he still loved me. I felt the love we had for each other that night. Out of the crazy stuff he and I had been through, we had these quiet few minutes together, and the world was right between us for just a few minutes. Then the music stopped, and we returned to our table. "Thank you for that lovely dance," Matt said. "You still have it, honey."

I smiled and said, "Yes, I guess I do." I hated that the dance had to end, for I felt so close to him on the dance floor, and I knew when it ended it was back to the real world. Finally our order came, and we sat and talked.

Matt said to me, "Honey, eat all of that. It looks so good." I put a bite into my mouth, and the whisper in my head started, "look at food before you eat it." I looked down and I saw worms on top wiggling around. I didn't want Matt to know that I saw this, so I took a small bite, and I started to really get sick. "What's wrong, honey?" he asked.

"I don't know," I said. "I'm going to the ladies room. Be right back." I got into the bathroom and started to throw up. I took a paper towel and wet it and started to wipe my face. "Stop it," I screamed, "leave me alone." Then a lady walked into the bathroom, and I shut up. I put myself back together and went back to the table.

"Are you OK, honey?" Matt asked.

"Yes, I just must have a flu bug or something," I said. "I am so sorry, Matt," I said, "I don't want to ruin our dinner out."

"That's OK, honey," Matt said. "We'll get your dinner to go. Maybe you will feel like eating later."

"That's fine," I said. "Do you mind if I go on out to the car?"

"No, honey," he said, "go ahead. I will take care of the bill, and I will be right out," and he handed me the car keys. Now I knew this awful thing was starting to happen to me again. What to do about it? Well, that was a different story. I just didn't know what to do. One thing was when I starting seeing things, I was getting sick again; the demon in me was rearing its ugly head again. Matt came out to the car and looked at me and said, "Honey, you don't look too good. Do you need to go to the hospital?"

"No," I said. "I think I will be OK if I lay down when I get home, and if I am still sick, I will go see a doctor tomorrow."

He smiled at me and grabbed my hand. "I am so sorry, honey, you aren't feeling well." I sat there the rest of the drive home, worrying about all this starting again with me.

We got home and I went straight up to my room and sat on the bed. Matt walked in and asked me, "Is there anything at all I can get you, honey?"

"Maybe some ginner ale," I said.

He kissed me and said, "I will be right back." I heard him talking to someone when he was walking back up the stairs. "I told you," he said, "stop calling me when I am at home."

"What?" I said as he walked into the room. "Were you talking to me?"

"No, honey," he replied, "it was a business call, and I have told them not to call me at home when I am with you." I looked at him. I wanted to believe what he was saying, but I felt deep inside he was lying.

I took the drink and told Matt, "Well, 'night," and I got ready for bed. I left the bathroom light on in case I thought I was seeing things again, but to my surprise I fell into a deep sleep and I was fine. The next morning I woke up and felt good for a change. Matt had left for work but left me a note saying he loved me, and he would see me tonight. I had a doctor's appointment at ten, so I hurried to go to that. On the way to the doctor's office, I thought I saw someone sitting in the back seat, just laughing; I looked again, and it was gone. I want to go into the hospital, I thought. I want to go for a change. Isn't that a hoot? When I got to the office, I was sitting in the waiting room, looking around, and the people sitting there all acted so nervous and on edge. Some of them were so sad looking, but I guess everyone thinks that I do too. I certainly don't have all my eggs in one basket. Finally they called me back.

Dr Orr said, "Isabella, I got the report you were in the emergency room the other night. What was all that about?" he asked. "Did you do all those things and just don't remember, or you remember and you don't want to admit doing it?"

I told him I really don't know if I did it or not. I only know I don't remember doing it. "It seems the whisper has come back, with the seeing things again," I told him.

"Tell me about it, Isabella," he said.

"Well last night my husband took me out for dinner, and I was eating, or trying to eat, when the whisper told me to look close at my food, and then when I did I saw worms in my food. I didn't want my husband to know, so I went to the bathroom and threw up. Doctor," I asked, "what is happening to me?"

He looked over his glasses and said, "Well for one thing, Isabella, you don't look healthy, and you are way under the weight you should be. I am really concerned about that," he said. "What has been going on with you losing all this weight, Isabella?"

"I can't eat," I said. "I get sick when I try and it looks like it has things in it."

"Really," the doctor said, "what kinds of things?"

"Well," I said, "it looks like it has worms or bugs caging around in my food."

"Delusions again," he said and looked me straight into the eyes.

"Yes," I said. "I have had a lot of them lately. Please," I said, "just put me back into the hospital."

"Are you thinking of hurting yourself again?" he asked.

"No," I replied, "it's just things keep happening, and I don't know how, and everyone in my family thinks I am losing it again."

The doctor kept looking at his paper; then he took a book out of his desk drawer and read in it. "Isabella," he said, "I really wish I could put you in the hospital, but right now I can't on just these delusions. But if you continue to lose weight, that is a different story. I am going to increase your medicine and see if this helps with these delusions you are having."

I said, "OK, whatever you think."

"I want to see you back here in two weeks, but if you have any other problems, let me know." I got the scripts from him and left to go home. On the way home, I was really concerned that no matter what the doctor did for me, I wasn't going to get any better. I was so tired of living this way. My life had passed right by me, and I couldn't catch up with it. I felt so hopeless that afternoon, and I prayed for the strength to carry on. When I got home, I called my mother and told her what the doctor said.

"Well, dear, I hope you get better. Do you need me to come and stay with you a while?"

"No mother," I replied. "I will be all right." Truth was I would never be all right. I got really depressed after that. I stayed in bed a lot, and I had just given up hope.

Matt would come in and say, "Get out of the bed. You have to move around, Isabella."

"Move around for what?" I asked.

"For us," he would say. Then finally one day he convinced the doctor that I wasn't eating and staying in bed all the time, and he wanted me in the hospital because of my not eating. Matt took me to the hospital and checked me in, and I was to the point I just didn't care anymore. Matt left and told me he would be back tomorrow, and I told him that would be fine. The nurse came in and put an IV in my hand, and I asked her what was that for.

"It's to help you gain your strength until you can eat again."

I looked at it and told her, "I don't want this in my hand for long."

"Sure," she said and wrote notes in her chart and walked off. They gave me pills, and I know I slept for a very long time. When I opened my eyes, there stood Jill. I looked at her, rubbing my eyes.

"What are you doing here?" I asked.

"I came to see you. I bumped into Matt at the store, and he told me that you had to go back into the hospital. I was worried about you, so I brought you some flowers to cheer you up."

"You really shouldn't have," I said. She acted as if she didn't hear me and started to run water in them.

"Your favorite kind, red roses," she said.

"Yes," I said, "they are lovely."

She sat down on the end of the bed and asked me, "Isabella, what are you going to do?"

I looked at her puzzled. "Do about what?" I asked.

"Well, girlfriend," she said, "about being sick all the time. Aren't you afraid that Matt will get tired of all this and leave you for someone else?"

I sat up and looked at her and said, "First of all, I am not your girlfriend, and what happens in my life is certainly none of your business. I don't understand why you take it upon yourself to pry into my life's affairs."

"Isabella," she said, "I have been your best friend for years. I just worry about you, and I just want to help you if I can."

"There you go," I said, "used to be my best friend; not anymore."

Jill just stood up and said, "I don't know why you try me this way. You know I love you, Isabella," she said.

About that time Matt came in, and he walked over to the bed and leaned down and kissed me and asked, "How is my beautiful wife?"

I smiled and replied, "I am fine but just weak, honey. Look who has come to see me," I said.

Matt looked at Jill and said, "Hello, it was nice of you to come and see Isabella. I know she appreciates you coming."

"Really now," Jill spoke up. "That isn't what she was telling me right before you came in."

"Jill," I said real fast, "let's not get Matt involved in our little talk."

Matt smiled and said, "Well I don't want to even hear about it."

Jill grabbed her purse and said, "Fine then, you two have a nice day," and walked out.

Matt said, "Honey, what is it with you and Jill? You two used to be like sisters."

"I know," I replied, "but have you noticed how Jill has changed, Matt?"

"Not really," he replied.

"Well, for instance," I said, "just look at the way she dresses now. you know honey with it all hanging out and then some more."

"Honey," he said and laughed, "she doesn't even come close to you, even in your phi."

"Ha," I said, "you are really funny."

He smiled and said, "Anything to make you smile, honey." Then he began to ask was I eating, taking medicine, the old drill that he always gives me.

"Honey," I said, "I couldn't eat right now. That is way I have these IVs in my arms."

"I will be glad to see you get better," he said.

"Speaking of getting better, Matt, have you ever thought about what if I just never get better? What then, honey?" I asked.

"You will get better. I don't want you to even talk like that." Matt got tears in his eyes, and his voice was sad. I had never seen this side of my husband before.

It broke my heart to see him this way, so I told him, "You're right, honey. I will get better. I am afraid us southern peaches you can't keep us down for long."

Then he smiled and said, "Thank you, honey. I need you to fight for us and for Summer. She loves her mother so." The nurse came in with my pills, and I swallowed them like a trooper and smiled and said thank you.

The nurse looked at me and said, "You have the most beautiful eyes I have ever seen."

"She sure does," Matt said. "I told you, honey, you are beautiful. You just won't believe it." We talked about Summer for a while, and he showed me some drawings she made for me. Matt posted them above my bed. Finally he told me he had to go and would be back tomorrow. Then as he was walking out the door, he noticed the red roses. "Have you got a secret admirer that I don't know about?" he asked smiling.

"No, you won't believe who got me those roses."

"Who?" Matt asked.

"Jill did," I said. "Isn't that strange that she would bring me those flowers?"

"It's strange," he said, "but a nice thing to do. But, honey, you know Jill loves you."

"I guess," I said as I waved good-bye to him. I lay there thinking about Jill. Maybe she was trying to be nice, but just something about the way she got into my business and always knew when I was in the hospital, something just didn't click right. Well, I just don't need anything else to worry about right now, I thought. For days I tried to eat small amounts, and my poor stomach just couldn't handle it. The doctor told me if I didn't start being able to keep something down soon, he was going to order a feeding tube. "No," I said, "I don't want that."

"I am sorry, Isabella," he told me. "I have already spoken with your husband, and he has signed all the insecurity papers." I just sat there helpless again. So that night I tried to eat dinner. I looked at it and it looked green and the smell made me sick. I would put the spoon near my mouth, and I would start to throw up.

The nurse came in and asked, "What is wrong, honey, can't you eat?"

"No," I said, "I just can't. I am sorry. I just can't do it."

"It's OK, sweetie," she said, rubbing my hand, and she took the food away. The next morning the doctor came back in and pulled up a chair near my bed.

"Well, Isabella, today we must insert the feeding tube."

"I know," I replied sadly.

"It won't be that bad," the doctor said.

"How long will I have to be fed this way?" I asked.

"Well," the doctor replied, "at least until you have gained a little weight and have some strength back."

"Mm," I said, "guess I have no choice in the matter. My life is in your hands."

"Yes," he said smiling, "and I promise I will get you well soon, and the tube will come right out. OK?" he asked.

"Sure," I said smiling and forcing myself to seem OK with all this. I lay there in the hospital bed, just waiting to get the tube. My mother and father came by to see me. My father assured me that the doctor was doing what was best for me. My parents stayed for a while, and then they left. The nurse came in finally with that feeding tube. I just hated this. I wished I could just eat on my own, but everything I tried I just couldn't keep it down. Days went on for me, which seemed like months. Matt was very attentive and visited me every day, and he looked so sad to see me in this shape. One night I was resting really well when I awakened for some reason, and then I heard that whisper. I couldn't make out what it said. I shook my head, and then the whisper turned into a loud laugh. I turned, and it just got louder. I started to scream, and I yelled out, "Leave me alone." And then I tried to get out of bed. I rang for the nurse. "Come help me," I screamed.

She came running in. "What is wrong?" she asked, turning the light on.

"Make it stop," I screamed holding my head.

"Make what stop?" she asked.

"That laughing," I said.

"I don't hear anything," she said.

I just started to scream and tried to get out of bed. The nurse was trying hard to hold me down. "Stop it," she said. "You are going to pull your tube out." She rang the buzzer and told the desk, "Send help now." Two other nurses came running in. One of them ran out and came back with a needle with something in it.

"Leave me alone," I yelled.

"Calm down," the nurse told me. By this time they were holding me down and gave me the shot. I don't know what was in that shot, but it knocked me out. In the morning, the doctor was in to see me.

I rubbed my eyes and said, "I didn't hear you come in."

"That's OK," he said. "I heard that you had a really bad night last night."

"Yes, I did," I said.

"Hearing those voices again?" he asked.

"I am afraid so," I replied. "What am I do now?" I asked.

"Well," the doctor said, "I just don't understand why you aren't responding to this new medicine. I will have to try something else."

"Doctor," I said, "I am so tired of shots and pills."

"I know," he said looking at me strangely, "but, Isabella, we have to find a way to give you some kind of quality of life."

"Life? What is that? All I know is hell on earth."

"Seems that way for you, I know," the doctor said.

"No, doctor, you really don't know until you hear the things that I do and see the things I do."

"I am sorry, Isabella," the doctor said. "You are right. That is why I won't give up on you." He wrote down some notes and told me good-bye, and then he left the room. I just started to cry and think of my family and of Summer. The doctor started me on the new medicine, and I started to feel better. The whispering went away, and I hadn't seen anything strange in a week. I had gained weight, and the doctor said the tube could come out next week. I was so happy. I finally was getting better for the first time since Dr. Belmont had moved away. Matt came to see me, and he was so happy for me and said it was the best news he could ever want to hear. My parents just thought the world of my doctor and were pleased at how he stayed right on top of my problems.

Finally Monday came, and the nurse came in and said, "Good news, we are going to take the tube out today."

"Thanks heavens," I said. "I just hate this thing."

"I know," the nurse said. She came over and took it out. "Now, Isabella," the nurse said, "you have to eat or the doctor will order this to go right back in."

"I know that," I said. Finally she had it removed.

"It's almost dinnertime, and we have to mark down what you eat," she said.

"I will eat everything if it will keep the tube out."

"OK," she said, smiling at me as she walked out the door. Her name was Linda. She was one of the nicest nurses on the floor. She was very understanding. She had mentioned that her son was slow and people would make fun of him and that made her so mad. That night's dinner came, and I had to eat. I ate slow and was able to keep it down. I didn't eat it all, but I gave it all I had. The next morning, I was able to eat even better. I was gaining strength each day. My doctor told me if I kept this up, I could go home next week. I was happy. The next day the doctor asked me to call Matt to come in and talk with him.

"Why?" I asked.

"Isabella," he said, "we have, and I mean we because you have worked as hard as I have to get you well. I want you to go to your mother's for a while, just until you are eating real good and all your voices and delusions are completely gone."

"They are gone," I said.

"Dear," he said, "you know as well as I do how quickly they can come back, and I don't want you alone until I know for sure you will be OK on your own."

"Matt will never go for that," I said.

"Then I won't release you until I know, which will make you have to stay in the hospital longer."

"Talk to Matt then," I said, "and tell him this, and maybe he will let me stay with my mother."

"What would be the big deal anyway?" the doctor asked.

"Nothing," I said. "I don't mind staying with my parents. Lord knows they know better than anyone about how quickly I can get sick again."

"Fine, then. Call Matt and tell him to come by my office between 11 and 12 tomorrow. See you later, kid," the doctor said proud of you Isabella than you I said and then the doctor walked out. Later that afternoon I called Matt and told him that the doctor wanted to see him.

"What does he want?" Matt asked.

"I think he wants to talk to you about my condition."

"I will go by there tomorrow," he said, and then he asked me how I was doing, and I told him I was fine, and then we hung up. The next day Matt came in to see me and walked over and sat down on the bed beside me. "Honey," he said, "do you want to stay with your parents for a while?"

"Matt," I said, "you know I would rather be home with you, but the doctor knows best. Look at how he has got me well again for the first time in a very long time."

"Yes," he said nodding his head, "you are right. He has helped you, and I thank him for that. So let's do what the doctor wants you to do for right now."

"Fine," I said, "then it's settled," and I smiled and hugged him tight.

"Honey," he said, "this is so great. I just can't wait to tell Summer that you will be home soon." We talked for a while and then he left. The next day my parents came to take me home.

"You are early," I said. "I thought I was going home next week."

"I know," my father said, "but the doctor called this morning and said that it was OK to come to get you this morning."

My mother walked over and hugged me and said, "Isabella, I am so happy for you. Finally, my sweet daughter is better."

"Yes, how about that," I said, smiling and feeling happy inside. My mother packed all my clothes and I got dressed. My father signed the discharge papers, and the nurse came and wheeled me out to the car. We drove home laughing and happy together as a family. We got to my parents' house, and my father helped me to the guest room. Matt came by to see my parents and me. I told him he was welcome to spend the night and stay with me.

My father laughed and said, "Well, you are married, so I think it would be OK."

"I really would like to," Matt said, "but I have some unfinished business to take care of."

"Really," I said, "and what is that, honey?"

"Work-related, last-minute things that have to be taken care of tonight."

"You aren't going out of town again, are you, honey?"

"Oh, no, just have to go back to the office and finish up."

"Well call me later, will you, honey?" I asked.

"You know I will. If it's too late, I will call you first thing in the morning." We kissed good-bye and he left. I watched him from the window as he drove off and wished he could have stayed with me.

Mom said, "Come, Isabella, let's make those cookies we made when you were thirteen."

"Sure," I said, going into the kitchen with her. "Mom," I said, "do you think it is wrong of me to stay with Matt as sick as I get at times?"

"Oh, Isabella," she said looking at me and pulling my hair back. "Sweetheart, Matt loves you for better or worse. He would never want to be without you. Why do you doubt yourself so, honey?"

"Mom," I said, "look at my illness, in and out of the hospital. What kind of life is this for Matt and especially for Summer."

"What do you want, honey, to give up your daughter? She will think you don't love her."

"Mom," I said, grabbing her and hugging her. "Why me of all people? All I ever wanted was to marry, have children, and live happily ever after."

"Isabella," Mom said, "even if you didn't have this illness, there is no happily ever after. We have to make our own happiness, honey. Don't start that worrying. Just enjoy life and try to stay focused."

"Mom, I hate to bring this up, but what about Aunt Jessie? Was she as bad as Dad told me?"

"Yes, honey, she was not like you at all. Jessie got joy out of frightening me. She loved to hurt people; she never would hurt herself. She hated me because I didn't have this illness and she did, and she blamed me for that. I loved Jessie; she was my sister. But she made it to where I couldn't stand to be near her. Come on now," Mom said, "let's make these cookies and talk about something else."

"OK, Mom," I said. "I understand." We made the cookies and had hot cookies and milk. It made me feel like a child again. I told my parents good night and went into the guest room. I called the office, and Matt never answered. Um, I thought, that's odd. Then I called his cell phone, and I got his answering service. So I left him a message to call me. I lay in bed waiting for him to call. I read a book, and now it was three in the morning. I finally called his cell again. No answer. Then I called the house; still no answer. Oh well, I thought, he must have just gone to bed. By this time I was very tired, so l lay down and fell asleep. The next morning I still hadn't heard from Matt, so I called the home phone. The phone rang and rang, and finally someone picked up, and I said, "Hello, Matt, are you there?" and no one said anything, and then they hung up. I called again, and the phone rang and rang and no one answered. "Mom," I said, "would you do me a favor?"

"What's that, dear?" she asked.

"Would you call my house and see if Matt is home?"

"Why don't you call him, honey?"

"I am a little dizzy. Please, Mom," I pleaded.

"OK, honey," she said. I heard her dialing the numbers, and finally she called out, "Honey, there is no answer right now."

I said, "Thank you, Mom. I will call him later.

"Come on, honey," she said. "I have breakfast ready."

"Be right there," I said. So I went to the kitchen and tried to eat. The food still had a funny smell to it. The only thing that helped me eat was thinking of the feeding tube. I know how bad that thing was, and I didn't want to go through that again.

Mom and I ate, and she looked at me and asked, "Does it taste OK, Isabella?"

"Yes, Mom, it's really good, but it's hard to start eating again after you haven't eaten in a while."

She smiled at me and said, "I know, dear, you have been through so much in your life."

"Mom?" I asked. "Do you think life is fair?"

"Sometimes, honey, but not all the time, and certainly not in your case. Isabella," my mother said, "when you were born, I prayed that this illness would miss you. It skipped Sky, and instead you got it. That's why when you starting telling me about the whispering and the loud voices, I didn't want to admit this was happening. I thought if I just didn't admit it, just maybe the voices would go away. Isabella," my mother said, "I am so sorry that I didn't get you help when I should have."

"Mother," I told her, "it's OK. I still would have had this, no matter what."

My mother got up and hugged me and said, "It just isn't fair for this to happen to a beautiful, young woman like you."

"Mother," I told her, "I suppose there are a lot of other families that are saying the same thing to their son or daughter."

"Yes," she said, "you are right, honey. I feel so sorry for anyone who has to go through what you have over the years."

"Mother," I said, "let's quit talking about all this. It makes me sad. But, Mother, I will tell you this. I do feel ugly and like I don't measure up to others around me."

"Isabella," she said, "if only you saw what others do when they look at you, honey. Long blonde hair, green eyes that could melt any cold heart. Why you just can't see it, honey, how very beautiful and sweet you are."

"Thank you, Mother," I said. "Let's go out shopping," I told her. "I really would like some new clothes.

"That is a great idea," my mother said. So we got dressed and drove to the mall. We were walking around the mall when we saw Jill.

She walked over and said, "How are you doing, Isabella?"

"Fine," I replied.

"I was going to come back and see you, but Matt said I better not."

"Really?" I said, "When have you talked to Matt?"

"Oh last night. I gave him a buzz to see how you were doing. He informed me that you were staying at your mother's to recover."

"Listen," I said to Jill. "I really don't want you to be calling my husband. If you want to know about me, you have my cell number."

"Well," Jill said, "I don't see the harm in calling him. He is my friend too." I was getting really mad by this time.

My mother said, "Come on, honey, let's get our shopping done. See you later, Jill," my mother said, "but we really needed to get going. Isabella," my mother said as we walked away, "don't let her get to you, honey. Matt wouldn't take her on a silver platter."

"I don't know, Mother. I haven't been a wife to him in a long time." We shopped and found some good buys, and then we went home. "Mother," I said on the drive home, "only one thing bothers me about what Jill said. She made the statement that she had called Matt last night. I called Matt last night and didn't get an answer. That is strange that she could get a hold of him, but I couldn't."

"I wouldn't worry about it, honey," Mom said. "She made that up just to make you mad."

"Maybe so," I said, "but she really knows how to get to me."

"I don't understand. You two you were so close years ago," Mom said.

"I know, Mom," I replied, "but Jill has changed in every way, her dress, her attitude, and all. I just don't know, Mother. Something is wrong with the way she knows everything about me. It's like she is staying in contact with Matt."

"Honey, come on now, don't spoil our day. We have had just a wonderful day."

"You're right, Mother, just look at all the nice buys we found today. Nothing makes a girl feel better than a lot of shopping and good buys." We laughed and drove home. When I got out of the car, Ronnie came running; she was so happy to see me. I had this dog for years, and I loved her so, but sometimes when I was sick, she wouldn't come to me. Today she came running; that was a good sign. I got into the house and put my new clothes away. I called Matt again and he answered this time. "Where were you at last night?" I inquired.

"I was home," he said.

"Why didn't you answer the phone?" I asked.

"Isabella, I was asleep. I guess I woke up at the desk about three in the morning."

"I tried to call you all night. I called on your cell."

"Honey," he said, "calm down. I had been working on the Allen's case and I fell asleep. I was going to call you in a little while."

"Mother and I went shopping today and ran into Jill, and she said she had called you last night."

"I think Jill has her days mixed up. That was night before last."

"Matt," I said, "I don't like Jill calling you. And must you tell her all my business?"

"Listen, honey, please don't try to argue. I told her because she asked. I really didn't see any harm in telling her that you were OK."

"Please, Matt, don't tell her anything else about me."

"OK," he said, "you tell her your damn self. I am really getting tired of being thrown in the middle of you two." And then he hung up on me. I stood there holding the phone in my hand like a fool and feeling like a fool.

My mother walked past me and asked, "What's wrong, dear?"

"Oh nothing," I replied, and then I walked outside to sit on the porch. I sat there for about thirty minutes or more when Matt called me back.

"Forgive me?" he asked. I sat there with the phone up to my ear hearing him breathe.

"Yes," I said. "I love you, Matt," I said.

"I love you too, honey. I am just tired and it seems you question all I do anymore."

"I know," I said. "Sorry. It's just I feel like I am losing my life. It is walking right past me, and I can't catch up with it. I feel sometimes that I am losing you and Summer."

"No, honey," he said, "you are not losing us. Our lives just have been put on hold for now."

"Matt," I said, "I want to come home soon. I miss being with you."

"I know, honey. Just as soon as the doctor OKs it, I will come and get you." Matt didn't come and stay the nights with me, and he wasn't attentive to me. I always talked to my mother about this, and she would always reassure me that Matt loved me. Finally the day came that the doctor said I should return home.

"Just keep eating and taking your medicine," he said. I called Matt to come and get me.

"Good," he said. "I will come and get you after work." It was getting later and later, and he still hadn't come to get me. I called and called, and there was no answer. I was sitting watching TV, and it was almost ten o'clock, and the doorbell rang. It was Matt.

My father looked at him very mean and asked, "You are a little late, aren't you, Matt?"

"I had to work over. I got here just as soon as possible."

My father looked at Matt and said, "It seems you are always working over these days. I bet you are bringing home the big bucks, aren't you?"

"Listen," Matt said to my father, "I don't need this."

"Well," my father said back, "neither does my daughter."

I said quickly, "Come on, it's OK. Let's go, honey. I have my bags packed." Matt took my bags out to the car, and I looked at my dad and said, "Please don't do this."

"OK," he said and kissed me and said, "Call us tomorrow," and I said good-bye to them and left.

On the way home Matt asked, "What's up with your father? What have you been telling him?"

"Nothing," I said.

Matt said, "He acted as if I were up to something."

"My dad is just dad. He has always been that way. He thinks I shouldn't stay up past nine o clock. He treats me like a kid, that's all," I said. We didn't talk the rest of the way home, and I felt tense inside. I thought just maybe I should have stayed longer at my parents. When we got home, Matt took my bags into his room. I looked at him funny.

"Yes," he said, "I want you to sleep with me tonight."

"OK," I said feeling strange. It had been along time since he wanted to be with me. He ran my bathwater and lit the candles.

"Come, honey, let's take a bath together," he said.

I said, "OK," I started taking off my clothes. I noticed all the scars that were all over my poor body. My wrists had cuts on them, and my legs, and I was so embarrassed, even though Matt was my husband. We played around a little in the tub and kissed, and then we got out and went to the bed, and that is when he really started to act strange. He kissed me funny and looked at me with tears in eyes. I moved on top of him, and he pushed me off.

"I just can't," he said.

"Why?" I asked.

"I just can't, just not right now. This was a bad idea," he said. "Honey, just go back into the guest room for now."

I grabbed a towel and wrapped it around me and said, "What is wrong? Am I that ugly to you?" and started to cry.

"No, honey," he said, trying to pull me close to him again.

"No," I yelled at him, "leave me the hell alone." I went back into the guest room and plopped on the bed and began to cry.

Matt came to the bedroom door and said, "I am so sorry. I didn't mean to hurt you, honey."

"Just leave me alone for now," I cried.

"OK," he said, and I could hear him leaning at the doorway. Finally I heard him walk away, and I just lay on the bed. In a few minutes, I heard his cell phone ring. I heard him say, "Stop calling me. I need time to think." I sat there wondering if there was another woman with the way he was acting. The next morning I woke up to the smell of fresh coffee, and I walked down into the kitchen, and there sat Jill of all people. She and Matt looked like they were talking about something, and they both shut up when I walked into the room.

"Well," I said, "isn't this a surprise first thing in the morning."

"Jill came by to see if you wanted to go see Summer, and she offered to drive you there."

By this time I was really hot. "Um," I said, "I don't need her to drive me over to see my daughter."

"Honey, she is just trying to be nice, that's all," he said.

"Matt, I don't want Jill here or calling or ever getting into my business."

"See, Matt," she said, "how she treats me after I was the only one in high school that stayed a friend to her after everyone found out," and then she stopped.

"Found out what?" I said, "That I am crazy, is that what you mean, Jill?" I asked.

She just told Matt, "See you later. I am not going to stand here and take this kind of talk from her."

"Good," I said, "please let me show you to the door. Oh, that's right, you know where the door is and where everything else is in this house." Then I shut the door behind her. Turning around to Matt, I said, "I mean it. Don't let that woman back in this house."

"OK," Matt said. "I get the point, just don't keep going on about it." He straightened up his tie and kissed me and said, "Got to run. I am going to be late for work."

"Wait a minute," I said. "Are you really going to let me visit Summer?"

He stopped and looked real hard at me and said, "Don't fight with Mom."

"I won't," I said. "I promise."

"You better not, Isabella," he said, and then he left for work. I drank some coffee and thought about Jill being here this morning. Well, I thought, I better call Matt's mother and ask her if I can visit Summer this morning. I called her, and of course she was her sweet self.

"I guess," she said, "but don't say or do anything to upset her."

"I wouldn't do anything like that," I said.

"Fine, then," she said. "Come on over because we have an appointment later on today." I got there and knocked on the door, and Summer came to the door.

"Mommy," she cried as she hugged real close to me, "I have missed you."

" I missed you too, honey. I got you some candy."

"Good, Mommy," and then Matt's mother came over and jerked it right out of my hand.

"Not this early in the morning. We will save this for later."

"Fine," I said, remembering what Matt said about me getting along with her.

"Come sit down, Mommy," Summer said, so I walked over and sat with her. Then Matt's mother sat down in the other chair. I was talking to my daughter, and every time I said something, Matt's mother put her two cents in.

"Come on, now," I said. "I see my daughter once a week. Can't I please have some time alone with her."

"OK," she said, "but I will be right in the kitchen."

"Mommy," Summer whispered, "I don't think Grandma likes you."

I laughed and said, "You know what? I think you are right," and then we just laughed. Soon my time was over, and I had to leave. I told Summer that I loved her and would see her soon and told Matt's mother good-bye.

She looked at me and said, "See you later, Isabella," and I got into my car and drove back home. As I opened the door, there was dirt on the carpet, and some pots were broken on the rug. I looked and they were from the garden out back, and again the doors were not broken into. I didn't even bother to tell anyone because they would say I did it. This time I knew I hadn't done this because I was with my daughter. I got it up the best I could, but of course Matt noticed the stains in the rug when he came home.

"What happened to the carpet?" he asked.

"I don't know," I said.

"They look dirty to me, and I know they didn't look that way this morning."

"I don't know," I said again, and he just shook his head and walked off into the other room.

"Call someone tomorrow to come and clean these carpets. You think you can remember to do that?"

"Of course I can," I said, looking puzzled at him being so smart with me. Something sure put him in a bad mood, I thought. "Come on down, Matt," I said. "I have made dinner for us." He came in and sat down like he was mad at the world. I sat there looking at my food.

"Seeing worms again?" he asked.

I threw my folk down and said, "That was really uncalled for. You know my stomach is adjusting to eating."

"I'm sorry, honey," he said. "That was really wrong of me. Please forgive me. You just don't know what I am going through."

"Tell me then," I said, "maybe I can help in some way."

"No, honey, you really wouldn't understand this problem, but thank you anyway. I love you, Isabella."

"I know," I said and kissed him and started to do the dishes.

Matt said, "Let me help you with those dishes."

"No, honey," I said. "Go get your shower and relax."

"OK then," he said walking upstairs, and I heard the shower running. About that time the phone rang. I answered, and they hung up. I looked at the caller ID, and it was a blocked number. When Matt got out of the shower, he asked me who it was. I told him that it was blocked, and they hung up when I answered.

"That's odd," he said. "They have been doing me the same way lately."

"Really," I said and just sat down and started to read. He must think that I am stupid, I thought. He won't sleep with me, strange calls; maybe he is having an affair with one of the women at the office. That night I never said any more. I really didn't want to accuse him until I knew for sure. I asked him, "Do you want me to sleep with you tonight?"

"Not tonight, honey. I am bushed," he said.

"OK," I replied and told him that I was going to bed. I could hear him talking to someone on the phone, but by this time I just didn't care. Sometimes I loved Matt with all my heart. He could be so warm and kind, and then he had a flip side and he could be the biggest ass that anyone could be, like making fun of me at times because I used to see things. Thank God I haven't done that in a long time. But we had our problems, and I just wanted to gain Matt's trust so that Summer could come home. So I just went to bed and tried not to think about him or anything and rest my mind. The next morning I got up and was going to take my medicine, and I noticed two pills were missing. I ran down the stairs, and I told Matt, "Look at my bottle of pills. Two are gone."

He counted them and yelled at me, "Damn, Isabella, you are taking too many of them. You are going to run short."

"Matt," I said, looking at him like I could run right through him, "I have been taking my pills the way the doctor told me. Someone is messing with my medicine."

"Good God, Isabella," Matt said, "who in the world would want to take your medicine?"

"I don't know," I screamed, "but I know I didn't take them."

"Call your doctor again," Matt yelled at me. "I am going to be late for work again for the second day in a row. Go see that head doctor today," he yelled at me as he closed the front door. I sat down on the couch and began to think. I just can't bear to go through all this again. No one believes anything I say anymore, I thought. I guess once you are labeled crazy, that's the way it will continue for the rest of your life. I called the drugstore. I thought maybe they had made a mistake, but they said they gave me the right amount. I know I was taking my pills right. Then the other day there was dirt on the floor. What was up with that, I thought. I would pinch myself to make sure I was awake and not in one of those old stupid trances I get into sometimes. I called my doctor and had him paged, and finally after a couple of hours he returned by call.

"What's wrong, Isabella?" he asked.

"I don't really know," I replied.

"What?" he said. "How can I help you if you don't know what is wrong?"

"This morning," I began, "I went to take my medicine, and some pills were missing, and I know I didn't take too many."

"Are you hearing whispering or low voices again?" he asked.

"No," I said sharply, "I am telling the truth."

"Well," he said. "I would make you an appointment for you to come back in to see me."

"Sure," I replied. I could tell that he didn't believe me either. That day I walked the floor and cussed like a man. "Woman, what the hell is going on here? I am better, then I am worse, is it black or is it white?" The more I worried, the more paranoid I got. My poor mother called me, and I snapped at her. "Sorry," I said after seeing what I had done.

"Having a bad day?" she asked.

"You could say that every day is a bad one for me lately."

"Come on now, honey," she said, "get into a better mood."

"Why?" I asked.

"For yourself, Isabella. I can't bear to see you like this."

"Well," I replied, "get used to it because I am tired of trying."

"What about Summer?" she asked.

"For heavens sake's, Mother, you know, and so does everyone else know, that little girl would be better off without her crazy mother."

Mom said, "Well I am not going to talk with you if you are going to talk that way."

"That's fine," I said and slammed the phone down. I was walking around in circles like a madwoman, wondering if I was going crazy. I was getting worse by the moment, and I thought for sure now that Matt was having an affair and trying to drive me crazy so he could go on with his life. That night I was making spaghetti and meatballs, and I heard the voice whisper to me, "Put dog food in his food. He treats you like a dog, make him eat like a dog." I caught myself just laughing, and before I knew it, I had opened a can of dog food, mixing it in with the beef. I will teach him, I thought.

That night when he came home, he opened the door and said, "Something smells good, honey."

"I made your favorite, spaghetti and meatballs," I said. That night we sat at the table, and he began to eat. I watched every bite he put in his mouth; then finally, I just couldn't help myself. I started to laugh.

"What are you laughing about?" he asked. I got out of breath just from laughing so hard.

Then finally I asked him, "Do you like your dinner, honey?"

"It's very good," he answered.

"It's good for dog food, isn't it?" I said laughing.

"Dog food," he yelled, spitting out the food in his mouth. He stood up and wiped his mouth off and said, "You crazy bitch, I will never eat another thing you cook." I started to clean the kitchen up, still laughing. Matt walked back into the kitchen and said, "You are losing it again, aren't you?"

"Losing it?" I replied. "I never had it together, or haven't you noticed?" I heard him call someone, and then he went upstairs. I knew I was getting worse. It didn't take a lot to throw me over the edge.

The next day Matt said, "Honey, you need to make yourself something to eat. I will eat out this morning and tonight."

"Afraid of my cooking?" I asked.

"Really, Isabella, what made you do such a thing to me?"

"To you? It's always about you. What do you do to me? Take my pills, throw dirt in the house, try to make me feel like I am losing my mind."

"I will not argue with you like a child," he said. "It's got to stop. I can't take too much more."

"Me either," I told him as he walked out the door. My mother called me back and asked if I wanted to get out for a while. "No," I said, "I am tired. I am just going to sleep in today." She hung up and I went back upstairs, and the voice whispered to me again. "Don't take that medicine. Matt put something in it," so I throw it down the sink. As I watched it go down, the whisper kept talking to me and I lay on the bed; I locked myself in my room. I didn't eat or drink all day. Finally Matt came home and made me come out of the room.

"What is wrong with you?" he asked.

Whisper

"I don't know," I said, "feeling tired." Matt sat on the coach and held my hand.

"Why, Isabella, just can't we have a normal relationship?"

I looked up and him and answered, "Because, honey, have you forgotten that I am not normal? You don't need me," I screamed. "No one needs someone like me that is possessed by the very devil himself."

"Stop it," he screamed at me. "Sit down and calm down right now."

I sat back down on the couch and began to cry. "What are we going to do?" I asked.

"I don't know, but we will get you some help," he said.

"Face it," I screamed at him. "I will never get any better," then I ran up to my room and closed the door. Days and days went by. I never told Matt that I threw my pills away, and when he asked me if I went to the doctor, I told him I did. I was really getting out there. I didn't know what was real or unreal anymore. By this time my mother had started to come and help keep the house clean and cook for Matt and me. I would look at her at times with hate in my eyes.

She would ask me, "Why are you looking at me like that?" And I would just act as though I didn't hear her.

One day I smarted off at her, and Matt said, "That's enough. You shouldn't talk to your mother that way."

"That's not my mother," I would say, "that woman just has a mask on trying to act like her." Believe me, I was getting spaced out. Even when my period would start, I would think someone had cut me. Matt didn't want to put me in the hospital. He tried everything to help me. He called the doctor and asked what was wrong with me, and the doctor told him I had canceled the last three appointments. Matt was really hot by now.

"Where is your medicine, Isabella?" he yelled out.

"Don't know where I put them," I said. "I guess I lost them."

He screamed at me, "Do you enjoy being sick, or is this all a big game to you?" You have to know without my pills and with the voices, I was long gone to any kind of reasoning. Matt asked me,

"Don't you want to get better for Summer? I know how you adore her."

"I don't want to see her anymore," I said. "You and your mother take care of her. I am dating the devil right now, if you know what I mean."

"God," he screamed, "your ass is going back to the hospital tomorrow, and might be tonight if you don't behave." I just laughed because the voice was laughing and skipping around the house like a small child. I think Matt was frightened of me that night because when he went into his room, I heard him put the lock on. I just sat in the floor drawing pictures of strange things and singing until I feel asleep. The next morning I heard my father and Matt talking, and I walked down the stairs singing.

"Good morning, Isabella," my father said. I just walked past him, not paying any attention to him.

Matt said, "The hospital is ready for you, honey. Let's get dressed so we can go." I was just singing and in a state where all I heard was the whispering in my ears.

My father spoke up and said, "Isabella, get dressed now." I went upstairs and threw on some clothes and slowly walked back down to where my father and Matt were. I slumped and fell to my feet. My dad said, "What is wrong with her? Why is she falling down?"

"I don't know," Matt said. "Let's us get her to the car." I could hear them talking, but I couldn't understand what they were saying because now I heard lots of voices. They were arguing with each other in my head. I screamed out once "stop it" and banged my head against the seat. My poor father was terrified at the sight of me acting this way. Poor Matt, he was used to all my strange behavior. Finally we got to the hospital, and Matt ran in and brought out a wheelchair. He rolled me up to the front desk and demanded a doctor be called right away. My father stayed with me, and to this day I will never forget the sad look upon his face. Matt came back and sat down and told my father it would be a while. He went to get coffee, and I sat in that chair waiting to be put back into the hospital. I lost count how many times it made.

My mother came running in and said, "What happened?"

My father said, "I will tell you later. Let Isabella rest right now," and Mother sat down and rubbed my hand and got tears in her eyes. Finally the nurse called me back, and Matt came with me. He told my parents he would come for them later. The nurse took my blood pressure and told Matt my pressure was a little high. She said they wanted some blood work.

We stayed at that hospital for four hours, and finally Matt said, "When is my wife going to get to see the doctor?" The nurse told Matt that the doctor had been called and would be here soon. Matt walked the floor up and down, and he was a nervous wreck. The nurse walked in with the needle to take my blood. She walked over to me and started to take the blood, and the whisper said to me, "She is trying to hurt you. Don't let her do it. Don't," it said over and over.

I started to scream and yell out, "Leave me alone," and I pulled the needle out of my arm. I threw her tray across the room.

Matt yelled out, "Stop that, Isabella, right now."

"Get out," I screamed, "get out. Leave me the hell alone," and the nurse ran out of the room frightened to death.

Matt walked over to me and said, "Cut the bullshit out right now. You need help, and that is all anyone is trying to do."

"No," I said yelling at him. I hated his very soul at that time. "You want me gone, don't you?" I yelled out.

"No, I love you. I only want you to get help and feel better."

"I will never feel well," I screamed, and I got off the table and started to run out the door.

"Isabella," Matt screamed, "come back here." And then he yelled, "Help me, Someone help me get my wife. She isn't well." The orderly came and got me and held me down, and someone gave me a shot, and I was out like a light. The next thing I knew I woke up in the mental unit again with a lot of crazy people worse off than me, or I thought so. I guess I really didn't understand how I acted when the whispers started to take over me. I was to have no visitors or no phone calls until the doctor OK'd it. I was very sick and weak and confused. I just didn't remember all the things that my parents told me I did. The doctor came in that morning and talked to me.

"Isabella," he said, "do you know why you are here?"

"No, I don't," I said.

"Well," he said, "I guess you took it upon yourself to decide you didn't need your medicine, and you got delusional again."

"I guess I did," I said. He left the room, and I lay in the bed thinking of what had happened. That night I woke up to thunder and lightning outside. It was real dark, and then it would light up, and just once in the dark, it got light and I saw Jill standing there. I jumped straight out of my bed and turned the light on, and she was gone. It must have been a dream, I thought, and then I starting thinking I remember one morning when I was so sick right before I had to come here, I remember seeing Jill in my house. I recall I yelled out and said, "Jill, is that you?" and she put her finger up to her mouth and said "Shh, you are seeing things, Isabella. Go back to sleep." My God, I thought, is it Jill doing all this to me and making me think I am going crazy? She is after Matt, that's it. She has been the one coming in my house, but how can I prove it? Lord knows, no one believes anything I have to say. The next day I asked the nurse to contact Dr. Orr, that I need to talk with him.

"I will see what I can do," she told me. A day went by, and finally the doctor came to see me.

He walked in and smiled and said, "How are you today, Isabella?"

"Fine," I said. "I need to ask you some questions."

"OK," he said smiling. "You got questions. I got answers," he said laughing.

"If a person like me that has a mental illness such as mine, can she or he ever have a normal life?"

"Of course they can, if they take their medicine and follow all their appointments with the doctor and making sure the blood work is done on time."

"Then, Dr. Orr, what has happened to me?"

"Um," he said, "I guess, Isabella, you would get well, and then you didn't want to take your medicine, and when you quit, you got sick again."

"Listen," I said. "I am about to confide in you, and please don't tell anyone."

"No," the doctor said, "I won't."

"I think my friend Jill has been coming into my house and taking my medicine and doing things in my house and making me think that I was the one doing it."

He listened and rubbed his head. "Now, Isabella," he asked, "why would this Jill want to do such a thing to you?"

"Because of my husband, she wants my life and my husband."

"Well," he said, "you would need proof of such a thing."

"I know," I said, "one night during the storm I saw her just as plain as day, like a sign from God that she was doing this to me."

"Isabella," the doctor said, "I just don't know. That's quite a story."

"I know," I said, "but it is true every time I get sick, she is around my house. She always has some excuse to come over, and I know she has mentioned that she would like to find a man like Matt."

"Isabella," the doctor said, "that still isn't a good enough reason to make her to do that to you. Isabella," the doctor said, "the mind is a very strong thing and can play tricks on you, and you have been sick for so long."

"Yes, but when I get well, look how good I do."

"Yes," he said nodding his head, "this is true. But I just can't believe that someone would be that mean to try and do such a thing."

"You just don't know Jill," I said.

"Well," he said, "let's just get you well again, and then we will deal with this Jill." He patted me on the head as if he believed me in a way and felt sorry for me in another. In about a week I could have visitors again, so I thought I am going to act nice to Jill, and just maybe she will trip herself up in her lies. So that afternoon I called her.

"Hey there," I said and there was silence. I said, "Hello, are you there?"

"What do you want?" she asked.

"Listen, Jill," I said, "I am sorry for the way I have been treating you, and I would like us to be friends again."

"I don't know," she said.

"Come on down," I laughed. "You know how crazy I can be. This is one of my sane days. Please come see me. I would like to talk to you, I am so lonely."

She paused and then said, "OK, only if you don't fuss at me."

"You got it," I said, and then we hung up. I walked and looked out the window. I have to be careful how I handle this, I thought. I need to prove that she has been doing this to me, so I have to trick her into telling me. I sat in the chair and waited for her to come, and finally she came. I could smell her a mile away. She had on leather pants and a low-cut top with it hanging out again. I think she dressed like this just for the attention of all the men up here. If there was one thing she loved, it was the attention from men, and it thrilled her for them to look at her, and she didn't mind telling you that. Very open in that matter; now if I can only get her to open up that she was after Matt.

She walked in and said, "Hey, girl, I am so glad that you and I can be friends again. I have missed you, Isabella," she said.

I had to make myself say, "I have missed you too, Jill. Come on, sit down and tell me what you have been up to."

"Not a whole lot," she said. "I went to a new club the other night, and I saw some guys we went to school with. Do you remember Tony?" she asked. "You know, Tony the football star, the one that loved you. I wanted him to like me, but instead he wanted you, Isabella. Even when the kids would say you had some kind of problem, he said he didn't care, he wanted to go out with you. I think you broke his heart, Isabella."

"Really, I never knew he felt that way," I said.

"See, Isabella, all the good guys always wanted you, and I got your leftovers."

"Jill," I said, "you had plenty of guys."

"Yes," she said, "but not the good ones. I always felt I didn't measure up to you."

"Jill," I said, "you were my best friend. I told you things I never told anyone. I trusted you with my life, my secrets, and you had my love as a true blue friend. Have you always thought of me the same way?" I asked her.

"Sure I have," she said, and then she changed the subject. "What do you think of my new pants?" she asked.

"Yes," I said, "they are you, and if you like the way you look, that's all that counts."

"Well, Isabella," she asked, "are you better now?"

"Yes, I feel much better."

"I hear that you made quite the scene up here when Matt brought you up here."

"I guess I did," I said, "but how did you know about that?"

"I saw Matt at Ingles, and he told me how worried he was and how you acted, and he said he was afraid you would someday kill yourself."

"What?" I yelled out. "Matt said that?"

"Listen," she said talking softly. "Please don't mention to Matt that I told you that. He will really be mad at me; he said for me not to tell anyone."

I got my thoughts together and said to myself, be careful, don't blow this. "Well," I said, "I would never kill myself."

"I hope not," she said. "You do have some battle scars though, don't you?" and then she laughed.

"Yes, I said, "I do," thinking about what a bitch she was. She really is a bitch in every way, I thought, and I have to eat crow right now, but whatever it took, I was going to get the truth out of her. I was going to beat her at her own game, or at least I thought I could at this time.

"Oh," she said, "I have to go," and she walked over and gave me a little hug.

I thought I would throw up, but I smiled and said, "I have enjoyed this visit. Please come back to see me."

"OK," she said, and she left. I sat there thinking about all this.

When my father walked in, he asked, "Was that Jill?"

"Yes," I said.

"What in heaven's name is she doing here?"

"Oh, daddy," I said kissing him. "Be nice."

"I'll be nice, but don't let that snake too near you. How are you feeling, honey?" he asked.

"Better," I said, "much better."

"Well," my father said, "you seem like you are in a good mood."

"Yes, I am, daddy," I said. "You know, I think I can get well if I can get certain people out of my life and out of my house."

He looked at me so puzzled. "What does that mean?" he asked.

"Just something only I can take care of," I said. We started to talk about him seeing Summer at the mall and her asking about me. She was so sweet; she loved me no matter what anyone said about me. I was her mommy, and that was that. It was late, and I was getting ready for bed when Matt called.

"How are you?" he asked.

"I feel good today," I said.

"That's great," he said.

"What have you been doing?" I asked.

"Oh just working, the usual stuff I have to do."

"I see," I said. I wanted to mention about Jill, but I was going to play this out without getting Matt mad at me for asking a lot of questions.

The next day Matt came by to see me and said to me, "Funny thing, I ran into Jill this morning at the coffee shop, and she said she had been to see you last night. I thought you hated her."

"Well," I said, "I decided to bury the hatchet and live a better life."

"That was very nice of you, honey," he said. "You need to try to get along with her because at one time you were best friends."

"Yes," I replied, "you are right," and then I started to tell him the goals I had set for myself.

"That's great, honey, but are you going to stick to it this time?" he asked.

"I am really going to try," I said, "but, honey, when I do get home, at least for a month, I would rather no one come over to the house. I don't trust anyone to come for a while."

"What do you mean you don't trust anyone?" he asked.

"I meant to say I would rather try to do things myself to prove I can make it alone."

"Not even your mother?"

"That's right," I said, "not even my mother."

"We will see when you get closer to going home," he said. I asked about my little girl, and he said she was doing so well. Out of this bizarre life I lived I felt so guilty that I wasn't a good mother to Summer. My heart was so heavy with sadness because I couldn't watch her grow up. I bet when she gets older, she will hate me for all this. I wish I could change things for us, but I am who I am, and God knows, I didn't ask for this illness. I finally got to sleep after the nurse brought my pills to me. Isn't that sad, I thought, a pill to get me going and a pill to put me to sleep. The next morning I called Jill again.

"Hello," I said. "Would you bring me a hamburger?" I asked her. "I am so sick of this hospital food."

"Sure," she said. "I will be over in an hour."

"OK," I said. "Thank you." I hung up the phone and walked over to the window, looking out, thinking what is next, I have to think of something.

Finally Jill came. "Hey, girl," she said, "got your burger."

"Thank you," I said, and then I asked her to sit for a while.

"Aren't you going to eat?" she asked.

"Sure," I said. "I am saving this for dinner. No telling what they will send me."

"Yeah," Jill said, "I guess it's hard being in these places all the time."

"It's not easy," I replied. "Well," I said, "what's new with you? What have you been doing since last time we talked.

"Oh, not much, just working and dating this cute guy."

"Oh yes," I said, "I remember that. Isn't he married?"

"Yes for now, but someday he will be mine."

"What about his wife?" I asked.

"He doesn't really love her; he just feels sorry for her."

"Um," I said, "why does he feel sorry for her?"

Jill paused for a minute and then said, "because she is overweight, and they have four children together."

"Four children?" I said. "He must be older than you."

"Yes," she said, "he is older, but that doesn't matter."

"But still," I said, "Jill, do you think that is right, dating a married man?"

"Oh hell," she said, "all is fair in love and war."

"Really?" I said and then I asked her, "Do you think maybe when I come home you could come over and help me some in the daytime when Matt is at work?"

"Really?" she said. "If you want me to, I would be glad to help you."

"Fine," I said. "I will let you know when I am getting out."

"That's great," she said. We talked about small things, and she would always talk a lot about herself. Jill was a very self-centered person, and that would be her downfall. I talked to my mother on the phone, and she said when I got home, she wanted to have a special dinner for me. Sky and his wife would be there, and Matt was going to let Summer attend.

"That's great," I said. "I am looking forward to it, Mother." I said good night and went to bed thinking of my little girl. I was going to get well this time and stay that way for my daughter and myself. The next morning I was talking to another woman that had the same thing I did, and she told me that when she didn't take her medication that she went off the deep end and sometimes had to be in the hospital for a month at a time. That was so sad, but I had been in and out, so I knew how she felt. The doctor came in and told me that I was improving, but he wanted to make sure I wasn't hearing or seeing anything before he let me go home. I got a phone call, and Matt was on the phone.

"What in the hell are you doing?" he asked.

"What do you mean?" I asked.

"Asking Jill to come and help you when you get home? Isabella, what kind of game are you playing? Someone is going to get hurt."

"I don't know what you mean," I said. "I am just trying to give Jill another chance, but by the way, she didn't waste any time telling you. Where did you run into her at this time?" I asked.

"Isabella," he said, "I will not play these childish games with you. I love you. Talk to you later," and then he hung up. The doctor finally gave me a discharge date, but he said he wanted me to stay with my parents until he knew I wasn't going to hear voices or see things again. I told Matt what the doctor said and he said, "Well, that might be good. I have to be out of town for the next few weeks anyway, and that will give me time to hire a nurse."

"I don't want a nurse," I said.

"Well just for a little while," he said.

"OK," I said, "but just for a little while." We said good-bye, and then I started to read a good love story. Finally my doctor gave me a discharge date. I was so happy, but it wasn't till next week. And of course it seemed to take forever, but finally the day came when I got to go home. My parents came to get me, and my father checked me out, and out of that hospital I went. I was so glad to get to go home, and when I got to my parents house. I put my clothes away.

I was coming into the living room when my mother said, "Would you like to watch some old films with dad and I."

"Sure," I said. "What kind of films?"

"They are of you and Sky when you guys were young."

"OK," I said, "that sounds like fun," so I sat down beside my parents and began to watch. There I was at three years old. I looked a lot like Summer. My parents got so quiet as they watched me and Sky playing as children. My mother got tears in her eyes, and I could see the pain in her. I sat close to her and hugged her. "Mom," I said, "it's OK."

She looked up with tears in her eyes and said, "I love you, honey."

"Mom," I said, "look at me. You wouldn't have ever known I was sick; I looked so happy."

"You were happy, honey," she said, but I could see for the first time in years the pain my parents were in. I had been selfish. I always thought my mother hated me for being sick and thought she was ashamed of me. Instead she was blamed herself for me being sick because it ran in her side of the family. That night my parents and I bonded in a way that we never had before. We laughed at the movies and had so much fun that night. I told them that I was going on to bed and my mother said, "Honey ..."

"Don't forget to take my medicine," I said.

She laughed and said, "I love you," and I told them I loved them too. I tried to call Matt that night, and he wouldn't answer the phone. I just went on to bed. The next morning I woke up to the smell of coffee and pancakes. I walked into the kitchen. I saw my mother with her hair up in a bun and her apron on. How cute she looked, and there sat my father reading his paper, and they were picking at each other. What a cute pair they made. I was lucky at least to have wonderful parents. I told my mother it smelled like heaven in there.

"Heaven?" my father said.

"Yes," I told him, "you eat that hospital food, and you will know what I mean."

"I guess so," he replied.

"I tried to call Matt last night, and he would not answer his phone," I said.

"Oh really," my mother said. "That's odd."

"What's odd about that?" my dad said. "He is working."

"Dad," I said, "you always take up for him."

"That's my job, to take up for mankind," he said. I sat down to eat and enjoyed my food for the first time in a while.

Finally Matt called. "Hey, honey," he said.

"Hey," I said.

"How are you?"

"I am fine," I answered.

"Isabella," he said, "I just called to tell you I love you and miss you, and I want things to be like they used to when I get home."

"I would love that," I said.

"I will be home later on in the week, and I want you to come home. I have arranged a nurse for you, and I think you will like her, honey."

"Just for a while, Matt. I don't want to be treated like a child."

"OK, honey, fine," he said. "We will work together so you will stay well. I want my wife back."

"I love you, Matt," I said, and then he hung up. I thought to myself, if he is having an affair with Jill, he certainly doesn't love her. I had a good time with my parents that week. Sky and his wife came for dinner one night. We all were getting closer, and I thought I was really going to make it, and I almost did. The end of the week came, and Matt came to get me. My mother told me if I needed to come back for any reason, she would love to have me. I thanked my mother and father and said good-bye, and Matt thanked them also. When we got home, I had a nurse named Mary. She seemed real sweet and told me whatever I needed, to let her know. I told Matt he did well, and he just smiled, and then we both sat down on the couch and talked. The next day Matt went to work, and I heard arguing, and I walked downstairs to see what was going on. There was Jill, screaming at Mary. "What is going on?" I asked.

Mary spoke up and said, "This woman opened up the front door and just walked in. She said Mr. Matt gave her a key."

"Matt gave you a key?" I asked.

"Well not exactly," she said. "He gave me a key one day and told me to get you some clothes. I had a copy made so I could come help out if I was needed."

"Give me the key," I said holding my hand out.

"Fine," she said and dropped it into my hand.

"Leave," I said, "and don't come back." Jill turned around and gave Mary a dirty look and walked out.

"Who was that woman?" Mary asked.

"Used to be a friend of mine years ago."

"That frightened me," Mary said.

"Me too," I replied and walked off to call Matt. I finally got a hold of him, and I told him about Jill.

"Oh that," he said. "I did give her the key one day when I was going out of town, just to make sure the house was cleaned up good for you."

"Matt," I said, "we really need to talk about Jill when you come home. There is something strange going on here, and I need to know the truth."

Matt said, "Honey, I can't talk about this right now. I will be home around five. I love you," and then he hung up. I paced the floor all afternoon and was hot about Jill having a key made to our house. How dare Matt give a key to her and let her go through my things. Finally Matt got home, and I was waiting at the door. "Let me please pour myself a drink before we start this conversation," he said. He walked over to the bar and poured himself a drink. He sat down beside me, drinking from his glass and said, "OK, now I am ready to talk to you."

"I just want to know why on earth would you give a key to Jill?"

"Well, at the time I was working, and she called and offered to help. I told her I would leave the key under the door," Matt said. "She was supposed to have put in back."

"She did," I said. "I found a key there after she told me she had a key made from yours."

"Isabella," he said, "how was I to know that she was going to make a copy of the key? Did you get the key back from her?"

"Yes," I said. "I only hope she had only one key."

"Me too," Matt said.

"Listen," I said, "why is it that she is talking to you so much?"

"Honey," he said, "please don't start on me. You know I love you. Jill isn't anything to me except she has tried to be a friend. How do you like Mary?" he asked.

"I just love her," I said. "She is the one who caught Jill opening the door and walking right in."

"Good for her," Matt said. We talked a little longer, and then Mary came out and said dinner was ready. She was a wonderful cook, and the food looked so good. For the first time in months, I was relaxed and was able to eat without seeing things in my food. No voices, no whispering, and I loved it. I felt like a real human being for a change. I asked Mary to sit down and eat with us. She look so surprised.

"Are you sure?" she asked.

"Yes," I replied. "I insist."

"Thank you," Mary said, and she sat down with us. I said the blessing for the first time in a long while, and life was really good at this time in my life. If only things could have kept going on this way, Matt and I would have been back the way we used to be when the whispering was gone for a while. That night ended too soon. I offered to help Mary clean up the kitchen, and she told me no, that was her job. I told a long hot bath and relaxed and was happy inside, but little did I know my world was coming to an end very soon. The next day I got up, and Matt had already left. I asked Mary why he left so early.

"I don't know," she replied. "He did get a phone call, and I overheard him say, 'I will be there to talk to you but stop calling here.' I thought that was a little strange," she said. "But that's none my business, if you know what I mean."

"Yes," I said, "I understand." I walked around in a circle trying to put this puzzle together. Who could have that been? I need to talk to Jill again and try to trick her and see if she is calling Matt and find out if she is chasing him. That afternoon I called her cell phone, and she answered. "Hey there, Jill," I said, "what are you doing?"

"Oh nothing right now," she said. "What do you want, Isabella?"

"I just want to talk."

"Right," she said. "One day you are my friend, and the next day you hate me. Please make up your mind."

I laughed and said, "You know me, Jill, I am crazy."

"Yes, you are," she said. I took that comment, but it hurt and I wasn't going to let her know that I cared what she thought. "Seriously, what did you call me for?"

"I was lonely, that's all, and needed someone to talk to."

"Well I am busy today. I have an appointment at four o'clock this afternoon."

"Can't we go to something before then?" I asked.

"No," she said sharply, "I have other things to do. Really, Isabella I have to run."

"OK," I said, "where is your meeting?"

"That's none of your business," she said angrily.

"Fine," I said, "just asking," and then she hung up on me. Um, I thought, where did I see Matt last time with a woman, and I was sick back then and couldn't make out who it was? I thought for a while, and then I remembered it was the Bay Coffee Shoppe downtown.

Four o'clock, just maybe I should drive by there at four, and just see if they are meeting there. I paced around until three thirty, and I told Mary I was going for a little drive to get out for a while.

"Be careful, Miss Isabella," she said. I grabbed my keys and drove downtown, and I drove around the block looking for Matt's car. I drove in circles until four fifteen and was about to leave when I spotted it pulling in across the street. I got down in the seat to where he didn't see me. Matt didn't look very happy at this time. He was walking very fast. I waited for a while, and then I walked up to the coffee shop. I looked in the front, and I didn't see anything, and then I glanced at the back, and there they were sitting at a booth. Matt looked like he was angry, and Jill was trying to hold his hand. He would slap it off each time she laid it on his. I slowly backed out of the coffee shop and left, and I started to cry.

"Damn it," I thought. "He has had an affair with her for real, I can tell. Why else would they be meeting? He is just afraid he is going to get caught because of the key thing." I drove home crying, and I could barely see to drive. Cars beeped at me, and I almost had a wreck; I finally made it to the driveway. I was shaking so badly I couldn't even get my key into the door. I finally rang the doorbell. Mary came to the door.

"Oh my goodness," she said, "what is wrong?"

" I can't talk right now," I said. "I am going to my room. Please don't let anyone disturb me for a while."

"OK," Mary said, and I walked to my room. I sat on the bed and cried for hours it seemed.

Mary called out, "Dinner is ready." I was really sick to my stomach just thinking of that bitch sleeping with my husband. No matter what happened, I was going to stand my ground and talk to him. It was about six o'clock when he finally got home, and he walked in all bent out of shape.

"Hey, honey," he said, "how was your day?"

"Not good," I said.

"Mine either," he replied.

"Matt," I said, "I was downtown at the coffee shop and guess who I saw there?"

"I don't know, honey. Who did you see?"

"Matt," I yelled out, "don't play dumb with me."

"Just what are you saying then, Isabella?" he asked.

"I am saying I saw you with Jill, and she was trying to hold your hand."

"Oh that," he said. "That was nothing, honey."

"Nothing," I yelled out. "You were with Jill, and she was trying to hold your hand, and that was nothing you said." I threw my hands up and said, "What the hell."

"Calm down, Isabella," Matt said. "Look, I am going to tell you the truth. You were in and out of the hospital so much, and I watched you suffer from all the self-mutilation and the mental breakdowns. Well, honey, I am human too. I got depressed, and Jill would call and ask about you. One night she brought over dinner and had a glass of wine with me. She started to come and visit and talk on the phone. She was just company. We went out for dinner and dancing and just as friends, that's all. When I met with her today, I told her that you were my wife, and I loved you and no one else. She was trying to hold my hand for comfort, that's all. Isabella, you left me so many times to go to that damn hospital, I was just lonely."

"Why Jill?" I asked. "Why her of all people?"

"It just happened. I can't explain it," he said. "Honey," he said, "I did not sleep with her, kiss her, anything like that."

"You really expect me to believe that?" I asked.

"Well that is the truth," he said. "You can believe what you want, I guess. Listen," he said, raising his voice, "I don't want to talk about this anymore." Then he yelled out for Mary: "Please get my dinner ready," and he walked into the kitchen. I stood there just hanging on like a fool. What should I do, I wondered. Even if he thinks of her as a friend, I know Jill, and I know that she won't settle for friendship from a man. I asked Matt that night why he wouldn't sleep with me. He said he was just stressed out and didn't feel like it right now. "And no," he said, "it's not because of Jill."

"Are you going to be talking to her anymore?" I asked.

"No, honey, I am not going to talk with her or see her again. It was just a thing I did out of loneliness, and it is over. I made a mistake, but I am human and I was lonely," he said.

"OK," I said, "just don't get mad at me. I just can't stand her going out with my husband."

"Isabella," he yelled at me, "you were always gone to the hospital."

"God, Matt," I yelled back, "do you think I wanted this illness, that I just looked up in heaven and said 'God, please made me crazy'?"

"I know you didn't want this illness, and I know you didn't deserve this to happen to you. We didn't deserve this. Come on now, let's get past this and live our lives and try to be happy."

I smiled at him and said, "Of course, you are right." I couldn't sleep that night thinking about all that had gone on in my life. I was only thirty-one, and I felt like I was a hundred. I asked myself could I get through this, could I forgive Matt? Will I ever be able to trust him again? I guess time will tell, I told myself. That was a long night for me. I was in and out of sleep, and I was so sad. I know my illness was a burden to Matt, and if I could take anything back, I certainly would. The next morning Matt came into my room and told me he was leaving for work and he loved me. He told me that he wouldn't ever hurt me again. "Matt," I asked, "what if I get sick and have to go back into the hospital again? Then what?"

"Honey," he replied, "we aren't going to let you get sick enough to go back into the hospital."

"Don't say that," I said. "You never know with me."

"Please stop this, and let's live what is left of our lives in love with each other."

"Really?" I said, "Then just when would I get to come back into the bedroom with you?"

"Soon," he replied; then kissing me softly and smiling at me, he walked out of the room. Um, I thought, it better be soon, and then I went downstairs to get some coffee.

Mary was cooking me something to eat, and she said, "Oh, honey, do you remember that old crazy woman who walked into the house the other day?"

I said, "Yes? You mean Jill?"

"Would you believe I caught her looking into Matt's car this morning?"

"Really?" I said. "Did you happen to mention this to Matt?" I asked.

"Yes, honey, I did, and he said that he would take care of it, and then he left." She just won't give up, I thought, so I grabbed the phone and called her.

She answered and I said, "Jill, were you at my house looking into Matt's car this morning?"

"I don't know what you are talking about," she said.

"You better leave my husband alone," I told her.

"Whatever," she said and hung up on me.

"Damn," I said.

"What was that?" Mary asked.

"She told me it wasn't her."

"Oh, honey," she said, "I know that woman when I see her."

"I know you do. I believe you, Mary," I said. I tried to forget about it for a while. I needed to stay calm for my own good. So I decided later that day I would go for a walk at the park. I was walking alone and suddenly I saw Summer playing at the swings; I walked over and said, "Hey, honey," and she came running to me.

"Mommy," she cried out. She jumped right into my arms. How wonderful this little girl could make me feel. Then Matt's mother came over.

"Summer, go back to the swings," she said.

"I want to see my mommy," she said.

"No," she said, grabbing her arm and pushing her away from me.

"Wait just one minute," I said. "She wants to visit with her mother. What is wrong with that?"

"Really, Isabella," Matt's mother said, "you know exactly what is wrong with that. It's not your visiting day."

"You are being silly," I said. "She just wanted to see me."

"I don't care. We have to go," she said, and then she pulled Summer away from me.

Summer cried out, "Mommy, please," and then I got mad and pulled her close to me. "I am going to visit with my daughter, so you take your fat ass over and sit down on the bench quietly or I will take it there. Your choice—you know how crazy I am." She looked like a scared rabbit and went and sat down. I pushed Summer in the swings and played for about thirty minutes with her. Then I walked her back to her grandmother and said, "Now that didn't hurt too bad, did it?" She started to say something, and I said it first. "I know, just wait until Matt hears about this. I just can't wait," I said waving good-bye to Summer.

Summer was waving back, saying, "I love you, Mommy." That was the funniest thing that happened with Matt's mother. I loved it. That was so much fun, putting that fat bitch into her place. I went back home, and I had to call my mother right away to tell her what happened. She laughed and said she would have liked to see that.

That night when Matt got home, I heard his mother call him, and he said, "What is the big deal? You were there," and then he told her to just forget about it. For the first time he took my side over his mother's. That was odd for him to do that; maybe he was feeling bad about what he had done to me. I began to watch Matt a lot and see what he did and whom he called. I wanted to make sure Jill wasn't coming around him.

That night I walked into the bedroom and asked him, "Matt, let's make love tonight, and see if we can put our marriage back together."

He said, "I wish I could, but I can't right now."

"Why?" I asked. "If you didn't sleep with her, then why won't you sleep with your own wife?"

"Please," he said, pushing me out the door. "Go to bed, honey. Just know I love you." What kind of bullshit is this, I thought. He has slept with Jill, or he would be able to sleep with me. He feels ashamed, that is what it is.

Well I got so upset I ran down the stairs and was screaming. "I can't take this," I yelled out.

Mary came out of the bedroom and said, "What is wrong?"

And then it started, the whisper, "I told you he doesn't love you. He loves Jill. You are too crazy for him, and you need to just make the pain go away." I ran into the kitchen and I grabbed an ice pick, and the whisper said, "put in your leg, and you won't care what Matt does. Make the pain go away," it said. I took the ice pick and stabbed it into my leg.

Blood flew all over the floor, and Mary came in and said, "Mother of God, what are you doing?" She tried to get it away from me, but she couldn't. "Matt," she screamed, "help me. Come help. It's Isabella."

Matt came running down the stairs. "What is it?" he asked.

"Come into the kitchen. Hurry, she is bleeding badly."

Matt said, "My god, Isabella, what are you doing?" He grabbed the ice pick away from me, and I started to hear the whisper turn into the laughing sound. I grabbed my head with my hands covered with blood, getting blood all over me. "Get some towels," Matt said. "Let's try to stop the bleeding." Mary stayed with me until Matt brought the car around to the front of the house. He hurried in and put me into the car, and back to the hospital again I went. The laughing just got louder.

"God," I cried, "make it stop. It makes my head hurt."

"Please, honey," Matt said, "take it easy. We will be at the hospital soon." Finally we got there and Matt picked me up and carried me in, blood running down my legs onto the floor.

The nurse saw him carrying me and told him, "Bring her right in here." Matt laid me on the table and pushed the towels hard, trying to stop the bleeding. He was breathing really hard from carrying me. The doctor came in and looked at my leg.

"That's a naughty stab. What happened?"

Matt said, "She did it to herself with an ice pick."

The doctor looked and him and said, "Why did she do this?"

"She heard that voice again, and she started acting out on what it told her to do,". Matt said, breathing hard. "Just read her charts, and you will see she has a history of this type of abuse to herself."

He glanced down at my chart and said, "Yes, I see." He said, "This is going to numb the pain," and he gave me a shot and sewed up my leg. "Come out here," the doctor told Matt, "and let's talk," so Matt walked outside with him. "We will have to admit her, you know, or you can take her back home and just watch her."

"Do you think you can just keep her here overnight until she can see her doctor and see what he has to say?" Matt asked.

"I think I can arrange that," the doctor said. So Matt came back in and told me that I would have to stay in the hospital overnight. I didn't care right then because the voice wouldn't leave me alone; they took me into a room, and I finally fell asleep. The next morning Dr. Orr came in to talk to me. He looked at me angrily.

"Isabella," he said, "I am surprised at you. You were doing so well, and then you just stop taking your medicine, and then here we go again. Don't you get tired of this place and me?"

I looked at him with pain. "My leg is killing me," I said.

"Yes, I guess it is," he replied. "You cut yourself really badly."

"I don't remember doing that, doctor," I told him.

"Well, little lady," he said, "on your blood work that was done last night when you were brought in, there isn't a single drop of your medicine in there. Can you explain that to me?"

I looked at him and said, "I did take my pills."

"Then why aren't your pills in your bloodstream?" he asked.

"I don't know," I said crying.

"Isabella," the doctor said softly. "One of these days you may cut yourself enough to bleed to death before someone can get to you."

"I know," I said. "I don't like doing this, I really don't."

"Well your husband wants you to come home, so I will have to let you leave. I think you should have to stay for a while, but he wants you home. I am going to increase your medicine and give you a sleeping pill and some painkillers, and I want to see you in a week. Do you understand me?" he asked.

"Yes, I do," I replied. Matt came in to get me right after the doctor left.

"Honey," he said, "I called your mother to come and help me with you. I hope that's OK."

"Sure," I said, trying to sit up in the bed.

"Take it easy, honey, she should be here soon."

Matt sat on the foot of my bed and cried. "This is my fault."

"No, honey," I said, "the doctor told me my medicine wasn't in my bloodstream."

"I thought you were taking your medicine," he said.

"I was. I just don't understand any of this."

Then my mother came in and walked over to the bed. "Isabella," she said, "honey."

"Mom," I said, "please don't say anything. I feel bad enough." Mother helped me put a robe on and rolled me out in a wheelchair, and then Matt picked me up and sat me in the car. We got home and I couldn't go upstairs, so Matt and Mother made me a bed on the couch.

Mother sat down and said, "Honey, when is this going to stop? Why can't that doctor help you? Over and over you keep cutting yourself. Your poor body is running out of places to cut."

"Mother," I said, "stop it. I can't bear to hear this any longer."

"OK, honey," she said. "Can I get you something?"

"Some water is all," I said. I was in a great deal of pain, and the pain pills made me fall asleep. I fell into a deep sleep. I was dreaming of being a little girl again and playing out in the water with my brother. I dreamed my life was so good. I dreamed of my wedding day, and I was so happy and I was kissing Matt.

Then all of a sudden I saw the devil's face and it said, "Isabella, you belong to me." I woke up in a cold sweat. Maybe the doctors had it wrong. Maybe I am possessed by the devil, and that is why I can't get any better.

"Oh God," I cried out, "save my soul."

My mother came back into the room and said, "Honey, did you have a bad dream?"

"Yes, I did," I said and drank some water.

"Matt has gone to work and will be back around five, and I am going to the store to pick up some things we need. Here is the phone, and if you need anything, your father can be here in five seconds."

"I'll be all right," I told her, and then I fell back into a deep sleep.

I thought I was dreaming when I heard a voice say, "Wake up, sleeping beauty," and I looked up half asleep, and it was Jill standing over me.

"What are you doing here and how did you get in?" I asked.

"Oh, Isabella," she said, "you know me better than that. I had two keys."

"You need to leave now," I said.

"Not right now," she said. "I came to visit an old friend of mine. Now just what have you done to yourself this time?" she asked. She pulled back the blanket and said, "I bet that hurt, didn't it? But then again I give it to you, Isabella, you can stand pain. You look like a cut-up piece of meat, you poor thing, you."

"Please leave," I said, trying to sit up.

"Don't hurt yourself, honey," she said.

"What do you want, Jill?" I asked.

"No what do I want?" she said. "What is mine."

"And what is that?" I asked.

"You know, Matt," she said. "You know, Isabella," she said, "all through school I watched you and walked in your shadow, and no matter how crazy you acted, the guys still liked you. You were beautiful and smart and everything I wanted to be—except being crazy, you could keep that one. I was your friend, but I got tired of getting your leftover boyfriends. When Matt came to our school, I liked him, but no, he went for you. High school sweethearts in love, oh how sweet," she said.

"OK, Jill," I said, "that is enough. Leave me alone."

"You are so stupid, Isabella," she said. "I have been sleeping with Matt since day one of your hospital visits."

"Leave, I mean it," I screamed.

"OK," she said, "but I will be back. We need to have this girl talk again. Oh, by the way, if you tell anyone that, they will think you are delusional again. Don't get up, honey, I will let myself out." Then she left. I was just shocked at her coming in, and one thing she was right about, no one would believe me. Jill would lie and I would look like I lost it again. But she was right: Matt had been sleeping with her, and he had opened up a can of worms that he won't be able to put the lid back on. I lay there on the coach, sweating and shaking.

My mother came back and yelled out, "Honey, it's me. Did your father call?"

"No, Mom, no one called."

"Good heavens," she said, "he should have called. Sometimes that man drives me nuts. I told him to let me know when Sky called and tell him I won't be home this afternoon." She walked into the kitchen, putting things away. "How is your leg, dear?" she said.

"It's still here. I haven't cut it off yet," I said.

"That's not funny, Isabella," Mom said.

"Oh come on, Mother, it hurts. That's all I can say."

"I need to change those bandages soon," she said.

"Not now, Mother, I can't stand the pain."

"Soon," she said. "You know what the doctor said."

"Yes, I do, Mother," I said. "By the way, Mom when are you going home and get on with your own life?" I asked.

"Soon, honey," she said, "when I think you are well enough to get around some."

"Mother, where is Mary?" I asked.

"Well, Isabella," Mom said, "the night you stabbed yourself in the leg so many times and you were laughing, it frightened her and she quit."

"That doesn't surprise me," I said. "That's too bad. I really liked her, and she was really a good cook. I will miss her," I said, "but I don't blame her at all."

Mother said, "Oh well, Matt will find someone else good, I am sure."

"Mother," I said, "come sit in this chair, and let's talk."

She said "OK" and sat down. "What do you want to talk about?" she asked.

"Me," I said. "I want to talk about me when I am well. Do you think that I am a good mother and a good person?"

"Isabella," my mom said, "you are a lovely woman and lovely mother."

"Mom," I said, "I feel so bad for Summer. Here she is with a mother that can't take care of her."

"Isabella, you are the most giving person I know of, and most unselfish person there is. You dislike Matt's mother so much, but yet you put your own feelings aside and do what is best for your daughter and you spare her from all the times that you aren't at your best. That is love, and that is a good person, honey."

"Mom, why do I feel like my life is going to end badly?"

"I don't know, honey. It's that your sick and feel bad, and things are getting to you."

"Mom, come feel my head," I said. She walked over and felt the top of my head.

"What is it I am looking for, honey?" she asked.

"This is where the voice hurts my head so bad that it sounds like bees are whispering in my head and in my ears. It drives me crazy. Mother, please pray for me to get well. I am so tired of this. One month I am fine, and then I get sick again. I don't know how much more I can stand, Mom," and then I started to cry.

Mom put her arms around me and cried with me. "It's going to be OK, honey, I promise you. Have faith."

"I am trying, Mother, I am trying." Then the phone rang, and Mom went to get the phone.

It was my father calling. I heard her say, "It's about time you called me. Did you tell Sky that I won't be home? OK," she said, "tell him to come over here, and I will sign the papers here. I can't leave Isabella alone right now."

"Mom," I said. "I wish you wouldn't have told Sky to come here. I hate it when he see me like this. He goes all to pieces."

"He will be fine. Come now, we've got to get that leg cleaned out," and she started to work on my leg.

"That hurts," I said. The cuts in my leg were going to give me another pretty scar for my collection. I just hated that I put my poor

Whisper

body through this. The doorbell rang, and Mother got up to let Sky in. He walked over to me and looked at my leg.

He shook his head and said, "I just can't believe those doctors keep letting her do this."

"Don't blame the doctors," I said, "they do the best they can."

"Where was Matt when she was cutting the hell out of her leg?" Sky asked.

"Upstairs, I think," Mom said.

"Why didn't he know you were doing this? Doesn't he care about his wife?"

"Now calm down, Sky, here he comes."

Matt came into the room, and he knew right away that something was wrong. "Hello there," he said.

Sky walked right over to him and looked him in the eyes. "How did you not know she was cutting the hell out of her leg? Look how deep. What is going on here?" he yelled.

"Listen," Matt said, "I was upstairs, and Isabella came downstairs. Mary found her, and she had already cut herself. Do you think I would watch her cut herself without stopping her?"

Sky said, "Mom, I love you," and he walked over to me and said, "Sis, stop all this before you do something to yourself that can't be sewed up." And then he walked out the door. My mother told Matt she was sorry for the way Sky acted.

"Don't worry about it," he said. "I know how close they are, and I understand." Mom fixed dinner for us, and they came out into the living room with me. I was feeling some better, and the doctor had ordered walking the next day to get the leg going again.

The next morning my mother got me up with a walker and said, "You have to stand up."

"Oh no," I said.

"Come on now, honey, you can do it," so I pulled up, and I tell you I felt like a truck had run over my leg. I cried out in pain, but my mother insisted that I not give up and made me keep walking. I was still hearing that little soft whisper in my ear, and it would try to tell me I had no reason to get better. I just tried to think of something else instead of listening to it. I hated that whisper, so one day I asked my mother if she would get me some headphones with a little radio. She got me one, and I used it to drown out the little whispers. I still wasn't right and didn't feel well. The medicine seemed to help some days, and then other days I had to hold everything I felt inside. I wanted to tell someone about Jill coming over, but I knew that no one would believe me. I was starting to walk a little better on my leg. My leg was scarred for life. It really looked bad, but I had to live with what I had done. I called Matt's mother to talk to Summer since I hurt my leg and couldn't go see her. The phone rang, and Matt's mother answered.

"May I speak with Summer?" I asked.

"No, you may not," she said.

"Come on now, please," I said. "I miss her."

"Listen, Isabella, if Matt keeps letting you see Summer with the crazy things you are doing, his father and I are going to take him to court. You are dangerous to yourself, and Lord knows what you might do to Summer if you heard those damn voices, so don't call back," she screamed. I stood there with my mouth open, and I didn't know what to say or do at this point; the only good thing in my life was going to be taken away from me. I knew I wasn't going to be able to take this.

I talked with Matt about it, and he said, "She can't do anything, don't worry."

"Why do you have to tell her everything that happens to me? The whole world know. Poor Isabella, I'm crazy."

"Who cares?" Matt said.

"You would care if you were going through this," I said.

"Isabella," he said, "I am going through it with you, so I feel what you feel."

"Oh really," I said, "well I wish you understood scizophrenic." I was getting stronger each day and walking a little better. I still had to use a walker when I was going out. I was going to get better somehow, some way, but I knew it would be a hard road to go down. I was really trying hard to take my medicine and get better. For some reason, I just got worse.

Whisper

Matt questioned me. "Are you sure you are taking it the way the doctor said to?"

"Of course I am," I replied. Then one afternoon I was asleep on the couch, I heard the door open. I raised up and the door was crashed. I walked over to it and looked out. "Is there anybody there?" I called out. No one answered, and I walked slowly down the hall. When I got back in the living room, I walked to the door and shut it. That was odd, I thought, but I took a pain pill and lay back down and fell back asleep. My mother woke me up asking me if I wanted something to eat. I rubbed my eyes and asked her what time it was.

"It's five thirty, honey," she said.

"I have been asleep for a long time," I told her. Matt came home soon after that. Mom got him some food, and then she said she had to get back home. She came over and kissed me good-bye and told me she would see me later. Matt helped me get ready for bed and sat in the chair next to me until I fell back asleep. That night it began to rain really hard. The wind was blowing loudly, and it kept waking me up. I would fall back asleep, and I would think Jill was standing over me. I would shiver at the thought. Why was I dreaming of her all the time? I was trying to get past the thing with Matt and Jill, but it was truly hard. I prayed each night, please let me get well so I can be a good mother and a good wife; I am so sick of this illness. Finally, after hours, I fell into a deep sleep. The next morning I had a doctor's appointment to have the doctor take a look at my leg. My mother—she was so faithful, bless her soul—was right there on time.

"Ready to go?" she asked.

"As ready as I will ever be," I replied. "Come now, let's get going, so we won't be late." So off to the doctor we went. Finally we were there, and I hobbled into the office. We walked in and everyone was staring at me. I sat down and Mother went to the window to sign me in.

I sat there waiting to be called back, and I heard a lady next to me say, "I heard about her. That is Isabella, Jill's friend." They were talking low, and I heard one of them say, "She had that illness."

"What illness?" the other one asked.

Right then I stopped them. "You know if the law made everyone wear a tag around their neck saying you have an illness and you are stupid and you are a gossiper, I wonder which would outweigh the other," I said. They just looked and then turned around and shut their mouths. My mother smiled at me and patted me on the knee.

"I liked the way you handled that, honey. Good for you," she said laughing. Finally they called me back, and the doctor looked at my leg and said it looked good and I was doing well; there was no infection. We went back home, and Mom made me something to eat. I told her that I was still hearing that soft whisper in my ears, and it sounded like bees humming in my head. "Please call that doctor back tomorrow, or do you want me to?" she asked.

"No, mom," I replied. I told her I would call him tomorrow.

"Do you promise me?" she asked.

"Yes, I do. Go home, take care of Dad," I told her.

"If you need anything, call me, honey."

"I will," I told her. "Go on and get out of here."

She came walking over and gave me a big hug and cried, "I love you, baby, you will always be my special little angel."

I smiled and said, "Well how about telling that to these voices and maybe they will go away." She looked at me that day so strange, as if she knew something was going to happen. The sadness in her eyes I can still see in my mind to this day. It was around six o'clock when Matt called and said that he would be a little later tonight, but he would be home as soon as he could. I hung up with him, and my first thought was I hope he isn't messing around with Jill. Then I told myself, I have to try to trust him again, and I started to watch TV. I heard the doorknob turn, and in walked Jill. I sat up on the couch and said, "What are you doing here?"

"I came to tell you something I think you need to know."

"And what is that?" I asked, really mad.

"Well," Jill said, "I am going to marry Matt, and you are going to go back to the hospital."

I looked at her and said, "Now who is crazy?"

"Isabella, poor sweet Isabella, what are the voices saying now, honey?"

"Cut it out, Jill," I yelled.

"Calm down, Isabella. We need to talk, and you need to free Matt. He doesn't want a sick wife that cuts herself and looks like hell."

"Get out of here," I yelled, trying to reach for the phone. She grabbed it away from me and threw it across the room. She opened her purse and pulled out a gun. "God, Jill," I said, frightened this time for my life. Then I looked at it, and it was Matt's gun that he kept in his bedroom drawer for safety. "Where did you get Matt's gun?" I asked.

"I can get to anything I want," she said.

"Put that thing away now," I told her.

"Well, Isabella," she said, "you are always trying to hurt yourself. I thought I would just help you end your pain a little sooner."

"Are you planning on shooting me?" I asked.

She laughed and walked around the couch. "No, honey," she said, "I wouldn't have to. You are going to shot yourself."

"Jill," I said, "you have really lost it. I will not shoot myself."

"Oh yes you will, if you love Matt and especially that sweet little girl of yours."

"Leave Summer out of this," I cried.

"Isabella," she said, "since you are about to end your life, I am going to tell you the truth. I have been coming into this house for months now," and she started to laugh. "And you and Matt, your sweet mother, no one has caught me."

"Why would you want to come in the house without anyone knowing it?" I asked.

"Because, honey, I had to make you stay crazy so I could have Matt."

"Just how were you planning on making me stay crazy?" I asked.

"Isabella, sweetie, I already made you that way. I took all your medicine. Each time the good old doctor tried to make you better, I switched it with sugar pills. That's why you kept hearing those voices; I even moved things around in the house, made big messes so everyone would think you were mad. I was pretty smart, wasn't I, Isabelle?"

"Yes, you were. So I wasn't getting the right medicine all this time?" I asked. "And you were coming in and destroying things to make me think I was doing it, not remembering?"

"That's right, honey. You see Matt wanted to break it off with me every time you came home. His heart is with you, and I just couldn't have that. You were just a sick bitch in my way," she said.

"Jill," I said crying, "we were best friends all our lives. How could you do this to me?"

"Isabella, I worked hard all my life. You know the kind of parents I had. My father was a drunk, and my mother didn't give a damn about me. You had everything going for you: good parents, a loving brother. The only thing wrong was you got sick. And yes, for years I pitied you and thought it was sad. But then one day I looked around and I saw Jack for what he really was and I saw you doing crazy shit the entire time cutting, slicing, dicing yourself, and I thought Matt doesn't need that, and I don't need Jack. So one day I put my plan into action, and I got rid of Jack and I had Matt. Only thing, every time you got your medicine, you got better and Matt would say, 'I can't do this to Isabella. Don't call me anymore,' so back to the drawing board again I had to go. So this time I want it to stop here. No more hospitals for you, honey."

"Wait just one minute. Answer one question for me. So I would have gotten well, no whispering and no voices or even seeing things if you hadn't bothered my medicine and did things to make me look like I did them?"

"That's right," Jill said, "you would be pretty normal, and I would have never gotten Matt back."

"Listen," I told her, "Matt was never yours. He is my husband," I said.

"Not for long, honey, because you will be out of the way. Isabella, now you know everyone in town knows you are crazy, so if you shoot yourself, shit, no one will be surprised."

About that time Matt walked in and said, "Honey, you left the door open," and he walked into the living room. He saw Jill there and asked, "What is going on here?"

Jill laid the gun down on the couch when she heard Matt's voice. Jill spoke up and said, "Please don't be mad at me, but Isabella called me and asked me to come over because she had your gun and was thinking about killing herself, so I drove straight over. Look," she said, "there is the gun."

I sat there so confused and shocked and said, "Wait a minute, that's not true; Matt she brought the gun over and was trying to talk me into killing myself."

"Really, Isabella," she said, "why on earth would I do that? See Matt," she said, "Isabella is delusional again."

"No, I am not," I screamed. "Matt listen me. She told me that she had switched my pills for sugar pills. Honey, she is the one who has been coming in here and doing all these strange things to make me think I was losing my mind."

"Come on now. Do you believe this shit, Matt?"

"I tell you, Matt, it's true. She has a key, look in her purse. Please," I said. Matt looked at me and then at Jill, really confused.

Then Jill started saying, "Matt, remember when you told me how good it felt to hold a warm body again."

"Shut up, Jill," he yelled, getting mad. I started to cry.

"And remember how you talked about if Isabella didn't get well, you might have to put her away for good?"

"Damn, Jill," he screamed, "shut the hell up. Stop it now."

"No," she said. "Isabella needs to know that she made you sick at times."

By this time I was stressed out, crying so hard I could barely see them in the room, and the voice started to whisper, "Jill is right; you are in the way. You are ugly and cut up and sick all the time. Take the gun— it won't hurt long—and get yourself out of this pain." I pulled the gun up and put it to my head and crying said, "God, forgive me."

Matt rushed over and grabbed the gun, trying to take it away from me. "Listen," he said, "wait just one minute. I love you with all my heart. If you shoot yourself, you will have shot my soul. I will never be able to make it without you."

Crying hard I said, "Why did you tell her all those things?"

"I was drunk and mad and afraid of losing you forever. She is lying about the rest of what was said. You are my heart, honey. I love you no matter what."

"What about me being so mentally ill?"

"I don't care about that. I hated to see you hurt yourself, but I have loved you from the day I first saw you. You were beautiful then, and you are beautiful now. I don't care if you have a hundred cuts to your body. Isabella, please live for me and Summer. Don't listen to the voices or Jill."

Then Jill laughed out and said, "He is just saying that because he doesn't want you to shoot yourself. As soon as you put that gun down, he will call 911 and put you right back into that damn hospital like he always does. He loves me; he just doesn't want to hurt you, Isabella."

Matt was mad and yelled out, "Shut the hell up," and Jill just kept talking about sleeping with him. He shoved her across the room and said, "Damn, shut up now," he demanded. By that time I was shaking and was really getting ready to shoot myself, and Matt ran as fast as he could and grabbed the gun, and it went off. Matt fell to the floor. He was bleeding badly.

"Oh God," I said, "call 911 and get him help." Jill called 911 and the ambulance came, and so did the police. When they got there, I was lying beside Matt, holding his hand and saying, "Please, honey, don't die, please," and the police pulled me up and sat me down on the couch. They took Matt to the hospital, and Jill, the good friend she was, told the story that I had called her over because I found out she was having affair with my husband. We got into a heated argument, and I was going to shoot her when my husband came in and tried to stop me, and I shot him instead. I tried to tell the police the truth, but they believed Jill instead of me. They handcuffed me and took me to jail. Matt lived, but he was in a coma and still is. The doctors don't know if he will come out of it or not. I stayed in jail until the hearing. My lawyer tried to say if the gun was in her husband's bedroom drawer, how did I get to it with a bad leg? But the other lawyer argued it was predated, but because of my mental illness history, I got lucky and I got the grand hotel. If Matt ever comes out of the coma, he will be able to tell what really happened. But until then if that ever does happen, I will spend my life here. They granted me the right to see Summer but only one time a month. But as I think back on those days, if there had never been a Jill, I would be home with my husband and my daughter. I would have finally been as close to normal as I was going to get. Jill, well, she met someone else right after Matt got shot. All the trouble she put me and my husband through; I don't see her crying over Matt or waiting for him to get better, so you tell me who is the crazy one here. To plan all this out and to play it out and destroy three lives and for what? I just don't understand any of this. You would think since she has gone on with her life that she would come forward and tell someone the truth. I would never have shot Matt on purpose. I loved him. There were times when I played tricks on him and hated him at that time. But I would have never shot him. I wish that gun had gone off on me instead of him. Matt's only mistake was getting involved with a deadly snake. I might have had my illness and was crazy at time, but I wasn't evil enough to try to break up a couple who really loved each other. Poor Jill, someday all this will come back to haunt her, because I believe you reap what you sow. Someday Jill's turn will come, and she will hurt really badly. Life isn't fair, but you take it and try to do what you can. Me, I sit here day after day and cry and think of what I have done; I used to not want to take pills and shots. I just wanted to have a normal life. I have finally accepted that without pills and shots, I can't make it through the day. I have to keep pills in me to sleep and to walk around and then pills to make me lie down. My poor mother comes to see me, and she cries and she blames herself. I don't blame anyone. I don't know what to do or say. I just wait for the sun to come up and then go down. I watch people in here eat dirt and eat their shit, and God, it's pitiful to see all this. One lady every day at the same time pulls her clothes off, and the men in here are so sick, they just sit and stare into space. This place is worse than hell, and I can't get out. But Father is sick, and I can't even be there for him. My story is sad, I know, but be careful who you choose for a friend. Once my mother told me there are friends in world that the only friend you ever have is your mother. I never understood what she meant by that, but I do now—a little too late, but it's a good lesson to learn.

"Oh, Isabella," the newspaperman said, "that is so sad. Oh you were actually getting better each time you went into the hospital. Then when you came home, this Jill switched your medicine with sugar pills. That's why the whispering started back each time. Then she planted all the messes so they would think you were delusional again. If she hadn't done all this, you would have had a better chance of living a normal life with your husband and daughter. Then you got sick and they sent you back to the hospital, thinking you weren't taking your medicine, but you were. But no one knew they were sugar pills. God," the newspaperman said, "that Jill woman was evil to do that. And no one believed you?" he asked.

"No," I said, "there was no one at my house except Matt and me and Jill. Matt was out of the way, and I had been already labeled crazy by everyone who knew me except my parents; Matt's mother even got on the stand and said bad things about me, so I just really didn't have a chance. Sometimes I think of Jill and think how I hate her and wish bad things on her, and then I change my mind. If I do that, then I am no better person than she is, and I don't want to be like Jill."

"That breaks my heart," the newspaperman said. "That just isn't fair. If only your husband would get well and come forward and tell what really happened."

"Yes," I said, "but I don't think Matt will ever come out of that coma. I just hope in his heart he knows somehow that I am so sorry and I am paying every day of my life for shooting him. God, just to know if he forgives me would give me peace. I hate to think of him lying there with all those tubes running in him. I asked if I could go see him, but his mother has forbidden me to come near him. I picture him lying there sometimes, and I think he gets up and says to me, 'Isabella, have you taken you medicine?' I wish I could hear him say that one more time. I miss him so; it's strange that you don't miss someone until they are gone. We as human beings aren't thankful enough for each other. The world looks down on each other instead of trying to help each other. If you think about it, does it make a person no good if they have a mental illness? When you tell someone you have a mental illness, they will look at you strange, and then will back away from you. I never wanted to hurt anyone. I never really wanted to hurt myself; it was just those voices that kept telling me things and making me see things that weren't there, until I got so delusional, I ended up hurting myself. If I had gotten my real medicine, I know I would have been OK. But without it, I didn't have a chance because my poor brain had a chemical imbalance that without the right medicine, as you see, a bad ending."

"This is just awful," the newspaperman said. "I want to write this up, with your permission, Isabella. I want the community to know the truth about you, and I will write about Jill."

"Listen," I told him, "no one will believe this story, but I think it's worth a try. Maybe someone will reopen my case and look into this more."

"Yes," the newspaperman said, "I think they will. Something needs to be done to protect people like yourself against anyone just blaming anything on you because you had a prior mental illness."

"I am so sorry this happened to you," he said. "It's so sad.

"Yes," I said, "it is, but that isn't where the story ends. I am afraid there is more."

"More?" he said.

"Yes, remember I told you I get one visit a month with my daughter, Summer? Well I get a visit, but it's with an orderly standing with her. Last month Summer came to see me. I was so happy to see her; she keeps me in the best of moods when she is with me. She came in the room in her cute, little dress and long, blonde hair. Her eyes bright and shining with the excitement of seeing me.

"Mommy," she said running and jumping into my lap.

"Honey," I told her, "slow down, honey, Mommy is getting too old for all this."

"You're not old, Mommy," she said, playing with my hair. "I miss you, Mommy," she said, looking up at me with tears in her eyes.

"Honey, don't cry," I said. "It will be OK."

"Mommy," she said, "Grandma told me you hurt my daddy. Is that so, Mommy?"

"Yes, I did, Summer, but Mommy didn't mean to. I would never hurt your daddy on purpose. Please believe me, Summer, no matter what Grandma says, OK?" I said, moving her hair out of her eyes.

"I believe you, Mommy. You loved my daddy, didn't you, Mommy?"

"I sure did, honey," I told her.

"What's been happening," I asked her.

"Oh, just playing with my dolls and going to play school. Grandpa takes me to the park sometimes," she said. "I wish you could take me to the park, Mommy," she said.

"Me too, honey," I answered her.

"Mommy, when are you going to get to come home?" she asked.

I said, "I really don't know right now, honey. Someday. We will see," I told her.

"Mommy," she said, "Grandma says you are here because you have been very bad."

"No, honey, I am here because I am sick right now."

"Grandma tells me that you are a very bad person. Why does she say that, Mommy?"

"Well, Summer, to her I am a bad person, and I guess I have been bad lately."

"Mommy," she said, crying.

"What is wrong, Summer?" I asked, holding her tightly.

"Mommy, am I going to be in one of these places too?"

"Summer," I said, pulling her little face up, looking at her with tears running down her face, "baby, why in the world would you think you would be in a place like this, honey?"

Whisper

"Mommy," she said, "sometimes late at night I get real scared and Grandma makes me sleep in the dark, and then this whispering voice says to me real quiet, 'Summer you are a bad little girl.'"

THE END